In Two Minds

K.T. Findlay

Copyright © 2019 K.T. Findlay

All rights reserved.

ISBN: 9781086902037

This is a work of fiction.
King Offa, Queen Cynethryth, Ecgfrith, Eadburgh, Ealfflaed, Alfthrytha and Archbishop Jaenberht were real people, but their words and deeds in this book are imagined.
All other characters and events are fictitious products of the author's imagination.
Any resemblance to actual events or locales or other persons, living or dead, is entirely coincidental.

DEDICATION

This book is dedicated to Deborah whose incredible support made it possible, and to Hazel and Colin for forging the tools I needed to write it.

CONTENTS

	Acknowledgments	i
1	The strands of life	1
2	Coming to terms	12
3	Testing the waters	18
4	Dinner and destiny	27
5	First steps	44
6	Manor from heaven	56
7	Foundations established	66
8	A matter of choice	80
9	New ways and means	91
10	A natural fit	103
11	When all at once	115
12	Double digits	128
13	Steeling themselves	137
14	The game's afoot	153
15	A visitation	165
16	Marwig's education	182
17	Making good	194
18	A last meal	207
19	A clash or arms	224
20	The aftermath	237

ACKNOWLEDGMENTS

I would like to thank James Burke for his incredible Connections, and The Day the Universe Changed television series which sparked off the whole idea in the first place.
I'd also like to thank Lewis Dartnell for his superb book, The Knowledge, which provided an excellent framework on which to build the technical aspects of the story.
Finally, I'd like to thank the wonderful people who played such important roles in bringing this book to fruition. They include Brett who got me started down the author's path, Deborah and Hazel for their incredible support and quality control, and my team of wonderful beta-readers who always told me the truth, especially when something wasn't right.

1 THE STRANDS OF LIFE

Fresh bread, now leather, then cheese, next cattle, every breath filled his lungs with a different smell as Wulfstan raced through the palace market place at top speed. He threw out his arms to counterbalance a jink around a large lady carrying a basket of wood, and slightly increased his lead. As long as there were people and things to run around, he could stay ahead. He'd always been the nimbler of the two.

The pair raced on, jumping over a pig here, twisting around a stack of spears there, flashing through the blast of heat from the smith's forge, until they hit the wall of the market street warehouse. Wulfstan turned sharply to the left, again stretching his lead a fraction. He was running as fast as he could go, but he knew he was in trouble now. Ethelwulf was faster in a straight line and he was sure to close the gap. Wulfstan couldn't go right because of the wall, and the stalls, animals and produce to his left didn't have a gap where even a ten year old boy could fit.

Above his own ragged breathing he could hear Ethelwulf's pounding feet getting closer and closer. Surely he must be almost able to touch him, and then the game would be over! If he could just reach the corner, he might be able to lose his pursuer.

Twenty feet, ten, five, made it! Wulfstan's shoes scrabbled for grip in the gravel as he turned hard right. Half way round the bend he risked a look back, Ethelwulf was indeed almost upon him, fingers stretched out towards Wulfstan's back, but he was already running wide and losing ground.

'Yes!' Wulfstan exulted, planning to do a spin turn and head back into the market.

He heard the noise of the impact, and a brilliant flash of light filled his brain. There was no pain, just a sense of floating.

Standing above Wulfstan's body, Hengist looked down in horror. He'd had time to twist his sword before it hit the boy's head, but couldn't stop the swing. The flat of the blade had hit hard on the left side of the skull, and Wulfstan's body simply crumpled at his feet. The young face gazed sightlessly up at him, blood oozing through the hair, falling each side of the ear, staining his cheek and neck before pooling in the grass.

Hengist's sparring partner gasped 'You've killed the King's son!'

A crowd was already beginning to form, and the clamour, yammer and uproar of dismay began to rise.

A world away, an old man was working on a life sized diorama in the Dark Ages section of the Rumstratten museum. He adjusted the dummy Anglo Saxon warrior until its spear was held vertically, and bent to pick up a cloak from the floor. He groaned inwardly as his sciatica stabbed ruthlessly down into his legs.

Henry, fifteen years old with an enquiring mind, had a burning question. 'Thomas, why were people back then so dumb?'

Thomas Woodcock, the museum's curator smiled gently. 'Any specific examples you have in mind Henry?' He carefully set the cloak around the warrior's shoulders, making sure the chest armour was still partly visible.

Henry frowned. 'Well what about thinking the sun goes around the earth, instead of the way it really goes? I mean that's obvious!' He flicked his head to clear the fringe out of his eyes so he could see to put on the dummy's sandals.

There was a short pause, 'Mmmmmmm. But I wonder what it would look like to us down here if the sun really did move around the earth?'

There was a longer pause while Henry digested this and thought about the answer. Finally he sighed and said 'You mean it would look exactly the same unless you knew what to look for?'

Thomas smiled, eyes sparkling behind his bifocals, 'Exactly! Next example?' He dropped down on his knees with a quiet groan, moved a knotted rope aside and began to make chalk marks on the floor.

Henry was ready, keen to level the score. 'Okay, how about choosing base twelve instead of the decimal system for numbering things? All that twelve inches to a foot rubbish! The decimal system is so much easier to use!'

Again, there was a smile on the face of the old man. 'Up to a point. Divide ten by three for me.'

'Three and a third.'

'Ten by four?'

'Two and a half.'

'Ten by six?'

'Uummmmm . . . . . one and two thirds.'

'Did you find that easy?' asked Thomas, his smile widening just a little.

'No of course not.' snapped Henry. 'I had to really think.'

'Okay then, let's try this. Divide twelve by three.'

"Four."

'Twelve by four.'

'Three.'

'Twelve by six.'

'Two!'

Thomas nodded happily. 'So if you didn't have a calculator, and were measuring stuff to make a castle, or weighing out equal portions of bread for your villagers, which would be easier, dividing into ten or dividing into twelve?'

'Oh…' said Henry thoughtfully. 'You mean twelve can be divided by more numbers, so it's easier to use?'

'Yep. And we can use it to make stuff too. Look at this.' Thomas said, picking up the knotted strand of rope off the floor. 'At every foot along this cord we've tied a knot, and it's twelve feet long.'

'So?' asked Henry.

Thomas stood up, wincing as his knees creaked and cracked. 'Here, you take one end and I'll take the other. Now, we can use it like a tape measure by counting the knots, but that's just beginner's stuff.'

'What else can it do?' asked Henry.

'Pull it out straight, away from me until the third knot and put it on the floor. That makes a three foot length.'

Thomas carefully knelt down and put his left hand on the knot. 'Now, I'll hold this in position while you pull the rope off to the right and count out another four knots.'

Henry did as he was asked.

'Okay,' said Thomas, 'you hold that knot up there and throw me the other end of the rope. Now keep the four foot line straight and taut, but allow the rope to move left or right as I pull the end you just gave me.'

Thomas held down the knot in his left hand, and moved the free end of the rope back down to touch the original end to make a triangle. Henry allowed his knot to move, and kept the rope tight on both the lines that now came from it.

'Now my friend,' said Thomas, 'if the sides of a triangle are three, four and five units long like this one, you get a right angle triangle. Every single time. We can use rope, string, cloth, wire, anything at all to make it, and it will always be a right angled triangle. Once you're certain you've got ninety degrees, you can then divide that up so you can measure any angle you want to. And that means you can make pretty much anything, and it'll all fit together properly. Watch.'

Thomas picked up a yardstick and marked out the right angle's two lines with chalk. Then holding the right angle knot, he grabbed the next knot along with the chalk and pulled it down to the other line, marking a perfect quarter circle.

He rubbed his hands together to get rid of the chalk dust. 'Now, that curve is ninety degrees, so if we break it into ten equal parts, we'll have ten wedges of nine degrees each. Divide each of them into three, we'll have three smaller ones, and divide each of those by three again and we have a protractor with one degree marks. We've just made a protractor with nothing more than a piece of rope, and can now measure any angle we want! This isn't just a knotted bit of rope, it's a computer and a drawing tool!'

Henry shook his head in wonder. 'I had no idea.'

Thomas nodded, his slightly too long hair flicking into his eyes. He brushed it away. 'All technology is like that. You need to know how to use it before it makes sense. Your mobile phone is the most useful thing you own, but give it to an Anglo Saxon and it's just a pretty box you can't even put things in. Useless in fact.'

Henry mulled it over for a moment or two. 'So is it always like that? Is it always that there's a reason for something, but it looks stupid to us because we've forgotten the thinking behind it?'

The old man laughed. 'Not always. Sometimes they had it completely wrong, but culture, religion, or politics locked their heads into a box and they couldn't get out of it. They needed a rebel, like Galileo, to break the mould and move on.'

'Or you!' said Henry, and they both burst into laughter.

The pair worked in silence for the next few minutes, until Thomas offered a contrasting thought.

'Funny folk the Saxons.' he murmured while twisting the warrior's spear. 'You couldn't find a braver people anywhere, but too wedded to their own macho sense of honour to ever be truly great in my opinion. That's a good example of a cultural belief getting in the way.'

Henry, examining the warrior's pattern welded sword, was a little taken aback. He was proud of his Anglo-Saxon origins. 'What do you mean? They did all right until the Normans came along, didn't they?'

Thomas was fiddling again with the spear and did not look up. 'You know these violent criminal gangs we have these days, like the Mafia? Well I reckon the Saxons weren't that different from them, especially in times of war. Might is right, and personal honour were their catch cries. Oh sure, they had the odd gifted king like Alfred the Great, who did tremendous things, but you have only to look at King Harold's family to see what it was usually like…'

The old man stepped back for a last look, and walked off to the next job. Henry picked up the toolbox and followed him down the hall. A five minute walk found the pair of them on the mezzanine floor above the Anglo-Saxon display. They spent the next hour attending to the steam engine to be used in the following day's demonstration, and then went home.

Morning found Thomas and Henry back at said engine, surrounded by a group of young schoolchildren from the local high school's junior science class.

'The thing about steam,' Thomas was saying, 'is that the engine often seems like a living thing.' He looked carefully over his young audience, and then gestured at the inert machine. 'It doesn't seem like it at the moment I'll admit, but we can soon change that!'

Animatedly he reached up and pulled the whistle cord. 'The whistle is meant to tell people to stand clear, but it also tells us that we have pressure in the boiler. Blowing the whistle releases a tiny amount of that pressure. Can anyone tell us how else we might release it?'

He looked around the sea of faces. Between the spots and freckles, Thomas could see the typical reluctance of the teenager to draw attention to itself. He sighed inwardly and continued. 'The most obvious way is to allow it to operate the machine.' and stepping to the rear of the steam engine he pulled a lever that set the pistons into motion. 'You can hear it breathing now as the pistons move in and out. It's that breathing sound that captures the imagination, and makes it seem as if it's alive.'

The children stepped back slightly in alarm as the piston began to gather speed, and the huffing and chuffing drifted up from gentle wheeze, to frenetic and athletic gasps.

Henry, enjoying the show, knew another way to release pressure. Sensing that Thomas was having trouble grabbing the kids' attention, he was contemplating a joke.

Thomas moved back down the side of the engine and gestured out over the balcony of the mezzanine floor to the exhibits below. 'Half the stuff you can see down there would never have existed if it had not been for engines like these.' He turned back to his audience, resting his backside on the railing. 'In fact...'

His sentence was abruptly cut off by a huge cloud of shrieking steam that enveloped him as Henry hit the release valve. Childish screams almost drowned out the blast, and tapered off only as the laughing teen released the valve and bounded around the machine to see the state of his victim.

Thomas was no longer there.

Henry stared blankly, puzzlement creasing his young brow. A young girl, horror written deep in her face, pointed to the balustrade and gasped 'He fell over the rail!'

Appalled, Henry rushed to the edge and looked down. Below lay Thomas, now a key fixture in the diorama, with the spear that he himself had placed with such care, thrusting out through his chest.

'Thomas!!!' screamed Henry, and then spinning on his heels, he made a mad panicked dash for the stairs.

Thomas watched him go.

From his viewpoint, about six feet above the mezzanine floor, he could see all that was going on. He was puzzled by the fact that one of the things he could clearly see was apparently himself. The more he looked at it, the more glad he was that it definitely wasn't him, because it didn't look too comfortable.

As Henry reached the body and started searching desperately for signs of life, Thomas, now floating about the level of the mezzanine floor, became aware of something above him. Looking up he saw what looked like the entrance to a brilliant, white tunnel.

He flew away from it, down towards the floor, following a thin gleaming white strand that connected him to his body, and he could clearly see now that it really was his own body. Equally clear was the fact that the wound was fatal, and he was going to die very, very soon. Strangely, this didn't disturb him much. He was more concerned about Henry, and the amount of anguished guilt etched onto his young face.

He laid his hand gently on the boy's shoulder, but Henry didn't seem to notice, and was now commanding one of the children to call the ambulance, while he tried to support the body. Some of the children were in tears, others sobbing in fright, but about half simply stared at the sight of Henry cradling the body in his arms, watching the growing blood stain that steadily covered more and more of his clothes.

Then Thomas felt himself being gently lifted up from the floor. He looked up, to see the tunnel had followed him down. Before he could even try to resist, it softly and silently sucked him in, and up he went. He twisted to look back down, and was astonished at how far away he was already. Very quickly, the only thing visible was the thin strand that connected him to his body. It was getting thinner by the second.

'Oh well.' he thought. 'It's an adventure. There's nothing I seem to be able to do about it. Let's see where things lead! At least the arthritis doesn't seem to hurt anymore.'

Suddenly, about ten feet away to his right, another tunnel flashed into life, visible through the walls of his own. As he watched, the young boy in it seemed to drift upwards with him, keeping pace.

The boy had spotted him too, and was smiling and waving. Thomas reciprocated. Each curious about the other, the two moved to the walls of their respective tunnels to see more clearly. Thomas put his hand up against the wall of his tunnel. The boy did likewise. Suddenly, and without warning, the two tunnels swung rapidly towards each other, and the two hands were placed palm to palm.

Thomas tried to pull his away, but it was glued in place. The boy's face registered real fear, and he too struggled to wrench himself free.

He screamed, but Thomas could hear nothing. The wall of the tunnel slowly changed colour, and began to become more translucent than transparent. Then abruptly it split, like water when a diver plunges into a pool, and the two hands properly met. A heartbeat later, Thomas was sucked from his own tunnel into the boy's. The hole slammed shut behind him, and even before Thomas could turn around to look, his own tunnel winked out of existence. His silvery cord, severed now, lashed around wildly, both man and boy ducking their heads instinctively to avoid it as it flashed past their faces. Hands stuck together, they were like German duellists in a mensur, unable to pull apart, waiting to see who would be struck first. In the end it was the boy, who took the blow full in the forehead.

The cord welded itself firmly into place. The child recoiled in horror, his screams now horribly audible, and tried to jink sideways away from Thomas. The cord stretched easily, but their hands remained welded together, resisting the boy's efforts to free himself.

'Calm down lad!' yelled Thomas, himself on the edge of panic, but it was no use. The boy was lost to his fear. And then they were tumbling, end over end back down the boy's tunnel.

For just a second they fell free of it, before smashing into what Thomas assumed was a body. The boy shot straight through it, which convulsed with the impact. When Thomas hit, a fleeting sheet of pain shot across his head which vanished as he too carried on out the other side and into another tunnel, this one dark as night.

It wasn't completely black though. He could actually see. But the walls of this new tunnel were a very dark grey, almost completely lacking in sparkle or lustre, lifeless except for the odd strangely black glints that sparkled as they fell. But there was an upside. The trip through the body had stripped his cord from the boy's face, and also freed their hands. They fell separately now, each trailing their own silvery strand back to the body, the boy accelerating away from him.

A red glow began to appear in the distance. Rapidly, it grew both larger and brighter, silhouetting the boy's spinning form. The child's screams seemed to echo off the tunnel walls, and then abruptly the volume dropped as he fell clear of the tunnel into open space. For another five seconds the pair tumbled down into a huge cavern.

A second is a precise measurement of time. All well adjusted clocks will count one off, regularly, and in harmony with their colleagues. But there can be a huge difference in how long a second feels.

A child reading a favourite book in the few minutes left before lights out, thinks a second is cruelly short, and stolen away before proper use could be got out of it.

A man tumbling vertically into a lake of boiling lava thinks a second lasts for a very long time indeed. He thinks he has never held his breath for so long. He thinks longingly of cool refreshing water. He thinks of things he has done, both treasured and regretted acts of childhood. Only one of those seconds has gone.

In the next he thinks longingly of his first real love, and the pain of discovering he was only her infatuation for the day. He thinks of the girl he married, their wedding day, her smiles and laughter. He thinks of his daughter, her birth, her first steps, her first book, her kiss goodnight on her seventh birthday in her new pyjamas. And there are still three seconds to go.

He thinks of his work. Was it worth while? Was it a waste? Should he have taken that promotion? Why didn't he see that opportunity? Ah, but that was good, that idea really worked! It pleased many people. He smiles at the thought. There are two seconds yet to go.

Is there any way out of this? The heat is fierce on his face, his hands, and it's getting stronger all the time. Will he feel the burn at the finish, or will it all be over in an instant? Will he drown? Will he be burned alive? Will he be crushed by the weight of the molten rock? Will he simply smash onto the surface, as if it's ice, and then sink beneath it, flames flickering over his body as it goes down?

And now there's just one second left. What's going to happen? Is there an after life? Is there a soul? Who got it right? All those religions, each purporting to be the right and only one, each demanding they be taken on faith, without questioning. Humph! That's all very well, but how would you know? In the quiet of the pub, enjoying a pint and a chat, you could be academic about it all. After all, there was so much life left to live, there was time for debate. Now, one second from incineration, the debate seemed much more real somehow! Had he made the right choice? What if it was wrong? Was it too late to change? If he was given some new information, could he reconsider?

And then it was over. Time's up.

Thomas closed his eyes. And kept them closed. For a long time. The heat still baked his face, but it hadn't got worse. Cautiously he opened his eyes again. He hung about ten feet above the lake surface, from the slenderest of threads. He twisted his head. Twenty feet to his left he could see the boy, likewise suspended, mouth frozen open in terror. Another twenty feet beyond that, lay what he thought was the edge of the lake, but swirling clouds of sulphurous gas made it impossible to be sure. Were those vague shapes amongst the clouds people of some kind?

He tried to move, and discovered that he could fly quite easily. He slid over to the boy, then reached up and carefully grabbed his own cord. He pulled gently, and was pleased to note that the lava was a little further away! On the other hand, the extra height allowed him to see more clearly through the billowing clouds and there seemed to be a lot more of the strange shapes. They appeared to be moving, and somehow they alarmed him even more than the lava did. 'Time to leave.' he thought.

Thomas gazed into the boy's eyes, gently put out both his hands and said. 'I'm just as lost as you, but,' he nodded towards the shapes, 'I don't think this is the right place for us. Wouldn't you rather go home?'

'Yes please!' sobbed the boy, his eyes pleading.

'Then give me a hug, and hold on tight.'

The two clasped their arms around each other, and Thomas slowly spun on the spot, spinning the two strands into a single cord. He pulled gently, and slowly they started to ascend back towards the roof of the cavern, slipping into the welcome, cooling embrace of the tunnel. Initially they were travelling slowly enough for Thomas to notice that the light on the walls came from small pieces of jet, set in what was otherwise a granite like surface. The boy's fingers gripped hard, nails stabbing into his shoulder, and even harder when they began to accelerate. The boy buried his face ever deeper into Thomas's neck, shutting out the view of the walls flashing past.

The pieces of jet were moving past so quickly now that Thomas could no longer see them individually, and the walls once more became the shimmering grey he had seen on the way down. For an instant they fell free of the tunnel before slamming hard into Wulfstan's body.

Hengist gasped, as without warning the corpse jerked itself three feet off the ground, tumbling and summersaulting before crashing back to earth.

Thomas heard screams erupting all around him, and the thunder of many feet running away. His head shrilled in a pain such as he'd never felt before. He held it in his hands, and rolled around on the ground moaning.

'Your Highness!! You're alive!!' gasped Hengist.

A world away, Henry felt Thomas's body go completely limp, becoming quite literally a dead weight in his hands. Tears streaming down her face, a little girl reached out, and gently closed his eyes. It seemed the right thing to do.

2 COMING TO TERMS

The pain wasn't going away.

Forcing open his eyes, Thomas looked around him. There were two men dressed like Anglo Saxon warriors above him. One was looking agonised, the other just shy of panic. He could see the jumbling, rumbling backs of around a hundred more people as they ran away in all directions. Between them he could see what looked like a wonderful model of an ancient marketplace.

Then the smell hit him. It was an ancient marketplace!! 'Dear God, what's happening to me?' he groaned. As if in answer, the pain washed over him once more, making him close his eyes again and writhe. When he could bring himself to open them again he fixated on some willow trees.

'Willow?' he thought. 'They can help somehow, can't they?' And then he remembered. 'Salicylic acid...' Well, aspirin was better than nothing!

'You there.' He croaked to the panicky warrior.

'Yes Your Highness?' the startled man replied.

'Go to those willow trees and bring me back some fresh bark. Two handfuls, and make sure they are clean as possible.' Then he closed his eyes again, listening to the shimmying clanks of the chain mail bouncing off the man's legs as he ran to the river.

Three minutes of eternity later, the man was back, followed by a number of the peasants as they realised there didn't seem to be anything to fear after all. Wordlessly he handed the bark to Thomas.

Thomas looked it over carefully. Why could he see it so clearly without his glasses? Come to that, how come he could see the willows themselves so clearly? Oh well, never mind. He put the bark in his mouth and began to chew. He knew the bark contained the pain killer. What he didn't know was how much he needed to have any effect.

Slowly, carefully, gently, he chewed the bark. Heavens it tasted foul! But he took care to allow the juice to sit under his tongue for as long as possible before swallowing, giving the drug the best chance of entering his bloodstream before having to swallow it.

Chewing willow bark isn't quite the same as taking aspirin, but the effect still came quite quickly, and he was able to think a bit more clearly. He opened his eyes again, and this time looked more at himself than at anything else. He carefully let his hands explore his body. Well, no wonder he wasn't feeling himself! He was feeling someone else!

And oh dear heavens, what was that smell?!?!?? Clouds of effluvium pushed ahead of the people as they warily got closer and closer, hopeful now, that the supernatural jumping and twisting of his body didn't presage a dragon or evil spirit coming for their immortal souls. Thomas's eyes watered. The combination of the willow bark and the stench of BO was taking the edge off his headache.

Then he remembered. 'Boy?' he thought quietly, 'Are you there?'

A very faint 'Yes.' echoed in his mind.

'Where are you? Is this your body I'm in?'

There was a frightened sob at the back of Thomas's mind, and then 'Yes.' followed by a pause, then 'Can I have it back please?'

'Ah.' thought Thomas. 'I don't know how. Do you?'

Again there was the distant sob.

'I'll assume that means no. Perhaps it will sort itself out?'

Another sob, but this time one that went on, and gave no signs of stopping any time soon.

Thomas closed his eyes again and concentrated. 'Now look, just calm down. We'll sort this out somehow. It's your body not mine. I promise I'll give it back to you as soon as one of us figures out how to do it. Agreed? Given I just saved you from hell itself, maybe you could trust me a bit longer?'

The sobbing sounding a little closer in his mind, broke up, and slowly quieted. There was a soft 'All right.'

Thomas tried to ease the stress, took a long slow breath, held it, and then slowly released it. The butterflies in his stomach calmed a little. He repeated the action, ignoring the increasing hubbub around him, and with slightly less success, trying to ignore the overwhelming BO.

'Right,' he thought, 'we need to figure a few things out. First off, can you see, hear, feel?'

The child's voice spoke right in his ear. 'Yes I can. I can see when you open my eyes. I can hear you. I can hear the people. I can feel the breeze on my skin. I can hear Hengist's breathing –'

'Hengist? Who's Hengist?' asked Thomas.

'He's the really worried one with the sword. I think he must have hit me with it. But he'd never have hurt me on purpose. He's looked after me, and played with me, forever!'

'Looking at his face, I believe you!' thought Thomas. 'Right, question two, can you control the body in any way at the moment?'

'No!' came the sulky reply.

'Ah.' thought Thomas. 'Well, no wonder you're cross. But for now, can we make a deal that you can be cross with the world, but you won't be cross with me? This isn't my doing. So for now, I'll control the body until we figure out how you can have it back. But this is your world, your people, your place, so you'll need to tell me what's what and who is who. We need everyone to think this body is still…'

'Wulfstan. Prince Wulfstan, son of King Offa of Mercia.'

'Oh good…' thought Thomas. 'That will make things easier, and also very, very hard.'

At that moment the crowd's mumbling became suddenly louder, then equally quickly died to silence. They parted to allow a strongly built man, richly dressed, bearded and fierce looking, to stride quickly towards him. He looked at the two soldiers.

'Who did this to my son?' he demanded, eyes flashing fury.

'It was I, Your Majesty.' bowed Hengist. 'It was an accident, truly. We were sparring when the two boys came running suddenly around the corner. I couldn't stop the blade in time, only turn it so the flat hit and not the edge.'

King Offa stared at him for a moment. 'Your life is forfeit. Immediately.' So saying he drew his own sword. The six men behind him drew their weapons as well, to make sure there was no resistance.

Thomas gasped in horror, and then suddenly was no longer in control but he could hear "his" body speaking.

'Father, no!!!! Hengist is right. It was all my fault. He had no chance to miss me! I shouldn't have been playing tag near them!'

Wulfstan struggled to rise to his feet. The willow bark had done good work, but the blood still trickled down his face, and he was uncoordinated. He failed to make it and collapsed back to the ground.

Offa looked at him. 'There is never an excuse to strike a prince, especially one of mine!' He looked at Hengist, 'Prepare yourself for death.'

Wulfstan heaved himself back up on his elbows and bellowed 'No! That isn't fair! I died and went to hell just now! Devils tried to capture me, but I was saved by an angel who saw me back safe to my body. Hengist is a good man, a friend who would never do me harm! If I have come back at all, it must be to save him from your wrath!' He locked eyes with his father, his face firm, pleading but not meek.

Offa wavered. Slowly he lowered his sword. Hengist hadn't moved at all, but stayed where he was, head bowed, awaiting the King's judgement. Offa thought for a full two minutes.

Thomas could hardly bear the stress. All his senses seemed to sharpen. He could hear the insects hum and buzz, the feeling of a single ant that was exploring his left ankle, the songs of the birds, and the rustle of the willow leaves. He desperately wanted to get up and stand between Offa and Hengist to continue Wulfstan's argument, but he was no longer in control.

Finally Offa came to his conclusion. 'He can live, because you have asked for his life. But it is now your life. He is no longer a thegn. He is now a slave, your slave, and you will run his property. It will do you good to learn some responsibility. Then perhaps you won't have so much time to run around playing like a child. And speaking of being a child, I'll thank you not to make up any more fairy stories like the one you just told me!'

He turned on his heel and walked back towards the Palace.

Hengist knelt down, holding his sword flat in both hands, proffering it to Wulfstan. 'My lord, as a slave I can no longer carry a weapon. I offer it to you to do with what you will.'

Wulfstan twisted around to face him, groaning a little as his wound sent its signals again. 'Don't be silly Hengist! Everything will stay exactly as it always was between us. You will keep your arms and armour as my body guard. I will run your manor in my name, but you'll run it in reality. We'll do it that way until my father has calmed down and pardons you.'

The other soldier hesitantly broke in. 'Your Highness, I feel I must remind you that the laws on slaves handling weapons are very clear. Your father will be angry if Hengist continues to carry arms.'

Wulfstan smiled grimly. 'Then he's going to be cross for a long time! Now, help me up and get me to my bed so I can rest properly.'

Thomas dropped a little thought into the mix. 'Who were you playing tag with? And where is he?'

Wulfstan faced the soldier again. 'Can you please arrange for someone to find Ethelwulf? Make sure he knows he's not in any trouble. He'll be very frightened, especially if he saw what my father did just now.'

'You'll need that head wound cleaned too.' said Thomas. 'It must be safe, so call ahead for water to be boiled for 20 minutes, including a clean cloth in the water, to be brought to your room for your wound to be cleansed.'

'Why such a lot of trouble?' asked Wulfstan.

'You know how many people die after getting an open wound? Horribly, in great pain, with green coloured limbs, and suppurating puss oozing onto everything?'

Wulfstan shuddered at the thought.

'Well then. Water from a stream or a well can do that to you, but water newly boiled will not. And don't let anyone put any ointment in the wound. Oh, and assuming you have them, make sure the bed has new clean sheets on it! I know you'll make them dirty, but it's important you keep this wound clean!! Understand?'

Thomas was almost strident in these demands, and Wulfstan winced under the onslaught. He nodded, too sore to argue, and then passed on the request to Hengist, who passed it onto another soldier, who ran ahead to the Palace.

As Hengist and his sparring partner carried Wulfstan away, Thomas decided to try a few things. He discovered that he was able to pop outside "his" head, and when he did so he could see, hear and smell as if he was a real body again. He could even feel the breeze on his face. The now familiar white strand kept him attached to Wulfstan's body, like a lifeline from an astronaut to a space ship

What really delighted him though, was that his ghostly form was as he had been in his prime. From what he could see of his hands and the rest of his body, he seemed to be about twenty years old again. A cautious exploration of his face with his fingertips seemed to confirm this.

Of course it was all completely academic, as nobody else could see him. Not even he could see his face. And of course it made no difference at all to how he felt. Or did it? Certainly all the arthritis aches and pains stayed away, just as they had when he was inside Wulfstan's body.

Well, that alone was worth having, and looking young again gave him a completely unjustified feeling of smugness. However, this was no time to dwell on such fripperies as a regenerated appearance, especially one that nobody else could see. There was work to be done, and to be done right now.

He soared high above Wulfstan and had a really good look around. He could see the town spread out on either side of a river, a hodgepodge jumble of houses, cum manufactories, cum shops. A water mill was working away on this side of the stream, with a small boat loading sacks of something from its door. Immediately below him he could see the crowd of people parting as Wulfstan was carried through the marketplace towards the palace. Happily, at this height the stench of body odour was a lot less!

This was all rather terrifying really, if you thought about things too seriously. But after escaping hell itself, what could possibly be thought of as serious? Both of them had been on the way to heaven before the fall, so they must have been doing something right! And if that was the case, all he needed to do was to keep on being himself, and everything would turn out fine. It was a comfortable thought, which left him free to explore his new world.

And seeing as he was avoiding the headache by all this flying around, he just bobbed happily along, taking everything in. Below him, Wulfstan was trying to be stoic through the jostles and jolts of being carried to his room in the Palace.

3 TESTING THE WATERS

Wulfstan was carried carefully through the Palace to where the royal family's private apartments were located. He groaned quietly as his head rocked to and fro with the movement of his bearers, occasionally more loudly when his head smacked against the wooden rods that made up the sides of the stretcher.

Thomas had discovered that for all his new found ability to fly, and go pretty much anywhere he pleased, the one thing he could not do was fly through solid objects. Being able to feel, also it seemed, required the world to be solid. So when Wulfstan was carried through the main door of the Palace, Thomas found that he too had to drop down the wall and follow through the same door.

He floated ahead, just below ceiling height, enjoying looking at the adzed oak beams and the plastered walls in between, comparing what he saw with what the archaeologists had believed in his own time.

The main door into the Palace opened directly into a great hall. In the centre of the room there was a huge pile of wood set up in a hearth for an open fire. People were walking in and out, groaning under the weight of enormous tapestries that were being put up on the walls.

Great tables were being scrubbed clean by the servants. They were using sand to rub firmly and evenly across the table tops, gently smoothing the surface and removing any dirt, before sweeping sand, sawdust and dirt straight onto the rushes on the floor. New rushes were being carried in and stacked in the corners ready to be strewn once the rest of the work was done.

One table was set on a raised platform above the rest, furthest from the outside door, its back protected by a solid wall, and its front set to enjoy the warmth from the huge fire. This table had already been scrubbed clean, and the maids were down on their hands and knees doing the same thing to the wooden floor boards. No rushes here. Another difference was it had individual chairs around three sides, instead of the long benches of all the other tables. Right in the middle, protected from the rear by the wall, and able to see the entire room, was the biggest chair of all. It wasn't hard to imagine whose that was!

Going past the wall he could see the entrance to the kitchens off to the left. The Wulfstan party however was going to the right instead, down a corridor with beautiful tapestries on the walls, and into a bedroom.

Thomas scooted ahead into the room. A beautiful lady was waiting, shoulders hunched inside a stunning blue dress trimmed with garnets, concern on her face, and hands clasped in front of her. To her right was a small fire, a small cauldron above it, the water roiling away. He was pleased to see that there were some cloths inside it, twisting and turning in the convection currents. Smiling to himself, he turned and looked past the lady to the bed.

Horror filled him as he looked at the filth and squalor on the sheets. Bloodstains, to the extent of actual clots of dried blood, were spattered across it, especially in the middle. Dirt adhered to the edges in places. And oh dear heaven, it actually smelled as bad as it looked. His mind recoiled with revulsion.

Without warning he was back in the body, the pain almost blinding him once more. He writhed in desperation as the men carried him towards the filthy bed.

'No complaints young man!' exclaimed the woman. 'Unbelievable, you demanding clean sheets when all you're going to do is make them filthy!' She leaned over him, and smiling, kissed his forehead. 'You lie down, we'll clean you up, and once you've stopped bleeding, you can have a clean bed.'

Thomas struggled to raise his head from the stretcher. He looked her straight in the face and snapped 'I am not lying in a bucket of blood and dirt with an open wound! I have no wish to die of gangrene, or some other baleful scourge!!' He had completely forgotten to speak as a 10 year old boy.

The woman stepped back in shock. 'What did you say my son? When did you learn to speak so?'

Thomas, aghast at his mistake, hesitated before answering 'The bed is filthy. I will die if I lie in it, and I do not want to die! Again!' He winced as another wave of pain washed over him.

'Well!' she said. 'I've never heard the like. Your aunt Mathilda gave birth on those sheets only yesterday, with no complaints!' She placed her hands on her hips, the bright dark blue of her dress highlighting her face, white with annoyance, framed by ash blonde hair.

Doing his best to manage the pain in his head, Thomas struggled out of the cloth of the stretcher, smacking away Hengist's gently restraining hand and staggered towards a stool close to the fire. He collapsed onto it, holding his head.

The Queen came to him, knelt down, and took him in her arms. 'My son, you've had a bad knock on the head, and don't know what you're saying. There's no harm in good blood, especially royal blood. Come, lie down, and I'll clean your wound.'

Thomas looked up at her through his tears. 'Thank you for the hot water and cloths. If it's all right by you mother, I'd rather you cleaned me up right here, after the cloths have boiled for another ten minutes. And when you think I'm clean enough, please have the sheets changed and I'll go to sleep in the bed.'

'That's my mother you're being rude to!!!' Wulfstan's outraged boyish voice echoed loudly in his skull. Thomas flicked his head up in surprise. 'Don't you dare tell her what to do! She'll give us a thrashing!' continued Wulfstan.

'Okay. Okay.' thought Thomas back at him. 'I'll be more polite.'

He turned his face once more to "his" mother, who was looking very worried and confused. 'I'm sorry mother. I've just been to hell itself and back. I mean I really have!'

He looked deep into her eyes. 'And now I seem to know many strange new things, one of which is that when you have an open wound, it is very important for things to be clean.'

His mother continued to stare.

'Please believe me mother. Just humour me. Please.' he pleaded. 'You're boiling the cloths as I asked, which you would never normally do. This is just one more step. And it won't dirty the sheets if you clean me and bind me before I lie down.'

The two looked into each other's eyes, his desperate, hers confused, frightened, and just a little cross. Finally she nodded, rose, and turned to the bearers. 'Please find Ravena, and tell her to bring the best and cleanest sheets we have. We'll change the bed.' She turned back to Thomas. 'I'll go and get some tongs so I can get the cloths out of the water. I don't know what's come over me, giving in to such silly demands from a child, even if you are a prince!'

Then she smiled, and went to call some servants to change the bed.

'You were still very rude!' Wulfstan hissed, still clearly aggrieved.

'Sorry,' grimaced Thomas, 'The pain isn't making me very tolerant. By the way, can you feel the pain too?'

'Of course!'

'Want to make it stop?'

'Of course twice over!' Thomas could feel the boy's anger.

'Try and leave the body. You'll be attached by the thread. All your senses will still work, and you'll be able to come back when you want to. That's what I did on the way here, and the pain stopped as soon as I was out of the body.'

'Then why did you come back and steal it again if it was so great out there?!?!' snarled the boy.

'Good question.' replied Thomas. 'When I saw the sheets, I was back in control. I didn't do anything. It just happened!'

'A likely story!'

Thomas sighed, 'Why don't you just try for a few seconds and see what happens?'

'And what if you won't let me back in again? Eh?!?'

Thomas sighed even deeper, enough to alarm Hengist such that Thomas had to hold up a hand to indicate he was okay. 'Look, neither you nor I seem to be able to control who has the body from moment to moment. Maybe we can learn in time, but right now it's all chance. But I'll tell you this, we need to make sure the sheets are properly clean, so it would be really good if you could go and check on this Ravena lady to make sure she's giving us what we need. Otherwise we'll neither of us have a body to live in, and you can have it while it dies writhing in agony covered in its own pus!'

There was a shocked silence while Wulfstan digested this idea. 'Alright then,' he said sullenly, 'but if you don't let me back in I'll haunt you forever!'

Cautiously, Wulfstan imagined one arm going outside the body. That seemed to work okay. He could feel the warmth of the fire on his fingers as he rotated the arm. A little more confident now, he thought the rest of himself out. Immediately the pain in his head stopped, and his focus was entirely on the delicious warming sensations from the flames. A moment of alarm caused him to spin his head, and to look down. Relief washed the panic away as he saw the silver strand tethering him to safety.

Emboldened, he took a few steps away from his real body, and felt the fire's effect reduce as he did so. He began to relax, and sensed his face begin to smile, truly smile, for the first time since the sword had hit him. Suddenly a huge metallic clash and clatter echoed from the kitchen where someone had dropped an armful of iron spits.

Unable to help himself, he jumped a little in alarm. And stayed there, a few inches off the ground. Entranced he moved his arms and legs slowly, amazed at the feeling of weightlessness as he moved gently in space. 'I wonder if I can get to the ceiling?' he thought to himself. To his delight, that thought was all that was required to cause him to rise gently up until he bumped softly against it.

He rotated carefully, so he was looking down into the room. Two men walked in below him, and lifting the entire palliasse as well as the sheets, stripped the bed down to its frame. A flaxen haired woman set to with scrubbing brush and a stout cloth to remove the congealed blood that had trickled through the straw from yesterday's birth. She finished just in time for the two men to return with a fresh palliasse of clean sacking stuffed with new straw which they placed on the wooden bed. Two minutes later they were back with another, this one stuffed with feathers, which they put on top.

Then he remembered that he too had a job to do, and he set off out of the room, turned left and floated three rooms down. Inside he could see Ravena sorting through the sheets in the best linen trunk, muttering to herself.

'... spoilt brat... don't know what they're thinking of! ... blood over these beautiful things...'

She turned her head to her right and looked at a second trunk, slightly less opulent. Opening it, she took out a table cloth, badly stained, but clean. She nodded her head, closed the two trunks, and with some nice flax linen sheets over her left arm, and the table cloth in her right hand, walked out.

Wulfstan shot ahead, and had just enough time to tell Thomas what she was bringing.

The Queen turned to greet her. 'Ah, thank you Ravena.' she smiled.

'Your Majesty, I thought perhaps we could put this table cloth folded over a few times, between the Prince's head and the sheets? The table cloth is already badly stained and you were thinking of giving it away. So it won't matter if the Prince's wound drips a few marks onto it.' Ravena's face managed to mix helpfulness, deference, and a wall of stiff disapproval all at the same time.

Thomas managed a smile despite the pain. 'That's a great idea Ravena. I don't care if the cloth is stained as long as it's clean.'

She shot him a look, a micro expression of contempt flicking through the deference. Thomas caught it, and laughed, his head flicking slightly with the effort. Immediately he regretted it, unable to suppress another groan.

The Queen knelt down by his side, 'It's time we cleaned that head of yours. Ravena,' she turned towards the door, 'that's an excellent idea. Please make the bed, with the table cloth as you suggested.'

Taking the tongs, she took out the first cloth from the cauldron, letting the steaming drips fall back into the bubbles. Once it was cool enough for her to touch, she gently sponged away the blood and dirt from his wound.

It had been fifty years since Thomas had last felt the incomparable feeling of love a child gets when being nursed by a doting mother. The gentle but firm touch of her hands, her face anxious yet strong, broadcasting confidence and certainty whatever she felt inside herself, the soft enveloping scent of her hair, and the velvety brushings of the fabrics of her dress. He relaxed, deeply relaxed, the smile on his face a mirror of the smile in his soul, and drifted happily into a world he had almost forgotten.

Wulfstan on the other hand, was exploring again. He sidled up against the window frame, peered out, and launched himself into space. He soared higher and higher above the ground. At around 100 feet he levelled out and looked at the world in wonder. It took him a while to identify the various landmarks, so different was the view to what he knew, but eventually he got his bearings. About two miles away he could see a party of riders, coming into town on the road from the east. He went to investigate, just for the fun of being able to do it.

There was a goodly wind at that height, but it was no problem to hold whatever course he wanted. He dropped lower as he approached the riders, feeling the wind drop to a breeze, and much to his puzzlement, changing direction. 'Why is the wind a different direction up there from down here?' he wondered.

The breeze was still enough to ruffle the horses' manes as they trotted down the road. Four men, each armed with sword, shield and spear were at the head. One of the four wore a helmet, conical in design, a nose guard, a band of etched designs that went around the helmet at forehead level, and a stylised wolf head above that. He was strongly built, and his eyebrows reflected that. Underneath them, his grey eyes darted keenly ahead, looking both sides of the road for potential trouble. There was a swagger about him, a sense of playful mischief, but those eyes showed steel behind it all. Here was a man used to getting what he wanted.

Behind him came three young women, and behind them another ten armed men. The girl in front was finely dressed, with long flowing auburn hair that cascaded over her shoulders, while her fringe danced across her brow. A lightly made braid from woven strands of copper wire strung with small jewels, sat above the fringe. Wulfstan would have said she sparkled, had it not been for the slight air of resigned melancholy that suffused her face.

The lady behind her had almost luminescent blue eyes, set in a creamy skin lightly dusted with freckles. It was an exquisite face, but it was her hair that truly dazzled. The brightest of reds, her hair sparkled with gold and copper highlights. She needed no braided wire and jewels. Indeed, even the finest of crowns would have seemed dull if placed on her head. Yet that hair was cut short, telling everyone that here was a low woman, a slave despite her mount.

But Wulfstan sensed that had not always been the case. Her bearing was proud, confident, and almost totally lacking in deference. The man in the helmet twisted in his saddle and looked back. The girl with the long hair gave him a weak smile. The redhead simply locked eyes with him, her expression passive aggressive in its neutrality. He shook his head, smirked, and once more faced the front.

In her mind, the redhead replayed the events of two days ago.

'Where's my food Rowena?!!!'

The roar echoed off the walls to the far end of the hall, where she had been wiping down a table. She turned slowly and stared at him, her face set hard and defiant. The silence was chilling, such that the only thing to be heard was the scampering and rustling of the mice fossicking through the rushes on the floor.

Grimketil smiled. 'You'd best learn and accept that you're no longer a thegn's daughter. You're just a slave now.' The smile broadened into a grin, the ends of his moustache highlighting his amusement 'Specifically, you're my slave, and you'll learn to do what I tell you to do!'

Rowena simply stood there, and continued to stare into his eyes.

Grimketil's smile faded into a frown, but he couldn't match her gaze and was the first to turn away. He shook his head as if in sadness, 'You can learn, or you can be taught. The choice is yours, but you will serve me, and you will serve me with due respect.' Recovering himself, he stared at her once more. 'As I said, the choice is yours. For now.'

'I would rather die.' she replied.

Grimketil gave a quiet laugh. 'I took that choice away two weeks ago when I caught you. You're mine for life now. Yours or mine, whichever is shortest.'

'Then there are still choices.' Her mouth formed a mirthless smile, but it wasn't reflected in the beautiful blue of her eyes.

Grimketil was silent, then turned to the wall and picked up his staff. He held it lightly in one hand. 'I am hungry. Go and get my food, right now, or I will give you some encouragement.'

Rowena still didn't move, waiting a full ten seconds, until his knuckles grew white around the staff, before going to get his food. Between the kitchen fires and Grimketil's table, and unknown to him, it acquired some extra ingredients. She smiled secretly to herself, and thought 'One day my friend, one day soon, and we'll see who is teaching who.'

Back in real time, she looked at the rear of Grimketil's head and murmured softly to herself, 'One day. One day soon…'

The third of the mounted ladies glanced at her questioningly. She was a handsome woman, with short, light brown hair, blue green eyes set under strong yet feminine eyebrows, her expression strong and cocky.

Wulfstan sensed there was something different about her, but it took him a while to spot what it was. Her horse moved as if she wasn't on it, and she used no reins. In fact the horse had no reins at all, not even a bridle. It simply went where she wanted it to go. And there was something else unusual. Her dress showed off both arms to the shoulder, and she was powerfully muscled for a girl, especially her forearms. There was more to this one than met the eye.

Well, he'd probably find out more tonight at dinner. Assuming of course he was well enough to attend. Then he remembered. He could attend whether his body was okay or not. He smiled. What with being able to fly anywhere he wanted, go anywhere, see anything, hear anything, maybe this loss of body thing wasn't all bad after all.

Back in said body, Thomas was feeling a lot better. He'd chewed a good few willow leaves instead of the bark, mixed with apples this time to soften the awful taste. His head was as clean as it was going to get, and bound up carefully in clean bandages. The Queen had tucked him into bed as Ravena watched, trying not to show her feelings. His head rested on the table cloth, and he drifted off to sleep, watched over by Hengist and his friend.

Wulfstan floated happily above and around his new toys, and followed them into the town.

4 DINNER AND DESTINY

Thomas slept.

Wulfstan continued to follow the visiting entourage into the town and up to the Palace. He watched as they were greeted and everything sorted out. He watched the redhead and brunette brusquely ordered about their assigned tasks, including a couple of none too gentle clips around the side of the head from Grimketil. Both women rolled their heads slightly at just the right moment, converting solid whacks into glancing blows that only just disturbed their hair. Their faces remained impassive, no fear or subservience visible at all.

Eventually though, Wulfstan's keenness to explore the rest of his world took over, and he flew off to review his realm. By the time he finished his wanderings, it was getting close to dinner time. He floated back through the bedroom window, and went through to the kitchen, where he watched the cooks fussing and bossing, the spit boys sweating by the roaring fires as they slowly rotated the great lumps of mutton, beef and pork, the head cook chivvying and checking, and everyone else working hard in the heat and grease.

Out of the corner of his eye he spotted Ravena walking past the kitchen door, heading for the bedroom wing. For the first time in hours he wondered about his body. In truth he wasn't missing it at all. He was enjoying his new abilities, revelling in unimagined freedoms, and despite all those lovely cooking smells, he wasn't remotely hungry. But he knew that Thomas would be, so he hurried out after her.

He overtook her halfway down the corridor, and flicked into the room. Thomas was still sound asleep, his bandaged head quiet on the pillow. The washing and bandaging had been done well, and there was just the merest trace of blood showing on the outside.

'Dinner time!!' Wulfstan shouted, with schoolboy glee.

Thomas woke with a start, just as Ravena entered the room.

'I'm sorry Your Highness,' she said, 'I didn't mean to wake you.'

He yawned. 'No problem. It must be about dinner time anyway.'

She looked at him quizzically. 'Shall I have some food brought in?'

'Let's go to dinner Thomas!' pleaded Wulfstan. 'There are guests and I think there might be some fun.' Thomas could sense the boy's grin.

'I think I would rather get dressed and come to dinner with everyone else.' he told Ravena.

She clasped her hands in front of her, frowned a little, and said 'I'll go and get Her Majesty. She wanted to be told when you woke. She will make the decision.' And without waiting for Thomas to try and counter her, she bowed, turned, and was gone.

He laughed. 'I think she's still annoyed with me about the sheets and everything. What have you been up to while I've been asleep nursing your headache?'

'I've been flying everywhere! Looking at everything, right through the town, and out and about in the countryside! You were right. It's wonderful being outside the body. I feel I can do anything!'

Thomas nodded. 'Yep. I think if we can learn to get on with each other, we could have a lot of fun together. And we'll also have to learn to live with these unscheduled body swaps until we find out if we can control that.'

'I'm perfectly happy out here thanks. You can keep the body, and the sore head.' grinned the boy.

'Hm. You say that now, but you're going to get bored just talking to me. So let's leave it open for now. Why did you say dinner might be fun?'

Wulfstan told him everything about Grimketil and the three women, finishing just as the Queen walked in with Ravena.

'Ravena says you think you are ready to get up and have dinner with everyone?' she asked.

'Yes mother. I feel fine now, and very hungry.'

'How badly does your head hurt?'

Thomas grimaced a little. 'It still hurts, but a lot less than it did this morning. My sleep seems to have done me a lot of good, and I don't think I'm bleeding anymore.' He raised his hand gently to his bandage.

The Queen moved quickly to him and checked it herself. 'Yes. The blood has not come through.' She checked underneath him, turned to Ravena and smiled. 'And no blood on the sheets or pillows either you'll be pleased to know.'

She got a slightly pinched smile and a nod in response.

Thomas laughed lightly. 'Thank you for looking after me Ravena. I know you were worried about mother's linen.'

The smile vanished, but he got another nod.

Ravena spent the next half hour getting Thomas ready for dinner. His head bandage was changed for a fresh one which Thomas checked carefully for dirt. Grumpily Ravena explained that it had been boiled while he slept, and dried in the afternoon sun as she knew he'd "fuss".

She dressed him in woollen trousers, a linen undershirt, and a blue tunic gathered at the waist with a leather belt on which hung a knife. Leather shoes completed the ensemble.

Grateful for the time to think, Thomas let her get on with it in silence. He was once again wondering why he wasn't really, really scared.

'I should be! Shouldn't I? I mean, hauled out of my own body and time, now sharing someone else's body in another world. Things don't get much more scary than that, surely?' he asked himself.

Yet he didn't feel at all frightened. Once more he told himself that he'd been on his way to heaven when he became welded to Wulfstan, so that was good. If he continued to be himself, when this body died, he'd be on his way there again.

'And there's no feeling more secure than that!' he smiled to himself. Then he positively grinned. Well, if he was back in time, and a prince to boot, perhaps he could do a bit of good between now and the next ascent?

Then again, maybe not? He knew about the theories of causality, of butterflies and hurricanes. He also knew there were theories of multiple parallel universes. But the point was, all of them were just that, theories, or more accurately speaking, hypotheses, as none of them had actually been tested out.

In the end he decided he could only be himself, try to do no harm, and let the universe take care of itself the way it always had. And after all, isn't that all anyone could ask of anyone else? It seemed to him that whenever people did something different to that, things invariably went horribly wrong.

At last he was ready, and stood up ready to go to the hall. The Queen came in leading Hengist. 'Your father has ordered that Hengist serves you at dinner so that everyone knows about his punishment and new status.'

Suddenly, Wulfstan was back in the body and Thomas was kicked out into the fire. He skittered away instinctively, but was relieved to realise he hadn't been burnt.

The Queen raised her hand as Wulfstan's face creased in anger, and strong words rushed towards his lips. 'There's no use fighting this one Wulfstan. He said that if you make a fuss he will reinstate the original sentence.'

Wulfstan looked up at Hengist. 'Hengist, I am so sorry. I want you to live so that one day you can be free again, but what is your own wish?'

Hengist was still for a moment. 'I have always served you Your Highness, as best I could. Today will be no different, because I have your love and respect. What others think is not my concern.'

'Then you are a truly great man,' said Wulfstan, 'and truly a great friend. Please, take my hand and help me in to dinner. Ravena, thank you for your help and kindness this afternoon. Would it be possible for you to help Hengist tonight? There will be a lot that he won't know how to do, and I want him to suffer as little embarrassment as possible.'

Ravena looked at him with new respect. 'Of course my Lord, if the Queen permits it.'

The Queen looked thoughtful, smiled, and said 'I do not think the King will recognise you Wulfstan. That knock on the head has thumped a bit of adult wisdom into you. Yes, you can have Ravena for the rest of the night.'

She turned towards the serving girl so her face couldn't be seen by the others and winked. 'I think you'll have your hands full!'

When Wulfstan arrived in the hall, supported by Hengist, and followed by Ravena, everyone else was already seated. There was much laughter and back slapping going on, and beer horns already being quaffed, but the gaiety washed quickly away as the guests became aware of the new arrival.

Wulfstan headed for his chair, third in from the extreme left of the royal table. Hengist managed it for him, while Ravena poured him a drink. To his left were his younger sisters Eadburgh and Ealfflaed, who greeted him with smiles. To his right was Jaenberht the Archbishop of Canterbury, then the Queen, the King himself, Wulfstan's older brother Ecgfrith, and three thegns. Completing the royal family group was the baby Alfthrytha, being wet-nursed behind the Queen.

Offa stared pointedly at Hengist.

'Let all here know,' he said to the whole room, 'that Hengist has been stripped of all rank for trying to kill my son this morning. Prince Wulfstan has taken ownership of all of Hengist's land and property, and Hengist is now his slave.'

The room was completely silent. Most looked at Hengist with sympathy and affection. But not all. In the middle of the bench down the left side of the room was a tall, broad and well made man. He was grinning in delight.

Wulfstan thought to Thomas. 'That's Grimketil, the cocky horseman I was telling you about.'

'Well, well, well.' said Grimketil. 'How are the mighty fallen, Hengist? First, I steal your true love from under your nose, and now you've lost everything else! How delicious!' As he threw back his head and laughed, his entourage followed his example, sending catcalls and hoots in Hengist's direction.

'Look at the brunette with the long hair next to him.' said Wulfstan in a soft whisper, even though he knew nobody else could hear him. 'That's Wulfwynn. She used to be courting Hengist, until Grimketil kidnapped her and forced her to marry him. He doesn't even like her, let alone love her, but he and Hengist have been rivals since they were children, and Grimketil did it just to spite him.'

'Now, now Grimketil,' said Offa with false rebuke, 'it does not do to delight in the misfortune of others.' Then he grinned broadly, 'But given your history, I think an exception can be made!'

At that, Grimketil and his entourage laughed, hooted again, and banged their fists and knives on the table in delight. Hengist maintained an expressionless and dignified silence throughout all this, but it was too much for Wulfstan. He jumped to his feet and glared at Grimketil.

'Hengist may now be a slave, but he's a better man than you are, and always will be! He's never kidnapped an innocent person to force into marriage, just to spite another! He's worth ten of you, you foul little man!'

Once more the room plunged into an astonished silence, Grimketil's face frozen in disbelief. Behind him, a beautiful, red haired, young woman burst out laughing. Grimketil threw himself to his feet in a rage, spun, and crashed his open hand into the side of her head. 'Go and get me a fresh beer!!!' he shouted.

The suddenness of the blow caught her by surprise and she tumbled to the floor. The room was completely silent. Everyone there knew the blow had really been meant for Wulfstan, but to hit the King's son? Well Hengist was a living warning about where that could lead you.

The girl got slowly to her feet. She turned to face Grimketil, her face completely neutral as she ran her hands through her hair to straighten it. She gently stroked where his hand had fallen, nodded, and left the hall for the kitchen, past the available beer barrels.

'Get after her Thomas!' cried Wulfstan, 'Make sure she's alright.'

'Right!' said Thomas, already floating off in pursuit.

Wulfstan glared at Grimketil, who scowling around him, sat down once more amidst his cronies. What a perfectly revolting man!

The redhead walked purposefully to the kitchens. Thomas watched her ask where the strongest beer was kept, and then four fifths fill a new horn with it. As she walked back towards the hall, she ducked swiftly into a small storage area, looking around to check that nobody was watching, and squatted down, one hand in the straw of the floor. Thomas watched in astonishment. When she next walked down the corridor, the horn was full.

'You'll never guess what she's done!' he cried delightedly to Wulfstan.

'What has she done?'

Thomas whispered, amidst many giggles. Wulfstan grinned.

'Grimketil!' he called out.

Grimketil broke off his conversation in surprise. 'Yes Your Highness?' he asked carefully.

'No hard feelings? How about a toast to the future? Would you match me horn for horn?'

Grimketil was perplexed, but accepted the beer horn the redhead was proffering him. 'To the future!' he called out, raised the horn, put it to his lips and drank it dry.

Wulfstan smiled, Thomas roared with laughter, the redhead's eyes flashed in grim satisfaction, and the King beamed his approval. Wulfstan raised his own small, child's horn and drained it, eyes locked on Grimketil. 'To the future indeed.'

The redhead took Grimketil's horn, and returned to the kitchen. When she came back, it was full once more and Thomas was almost unable to speak for laughing.

Behind her came a string of servants bringing in the food, and the feast began in earnest.

The King had a pigeon, the Queen some slices of beef, and the Archbishop was salivating over a whole roast goose, stuffed with a pigeon, that was in turn stuffed with quail.

Grimketil took a huge chunk of roast leg of lamb, and put it on his trencher, a large piece of bread that acted as a plate to soak up the gravy and sauces. Thomas noted that everyone had trenchers except the royal table, which alone had wooden plates.

Forks were completely absent. Everyone ate with their fingers, slicing things down to a manageable size with their own knives.

Also absent was almost anything that looked like a vegetable. There were various soups available that did have vegetables in them, but most everything else was meat.

Wulfstan took some roast pork and crackling. The pork was delicious, and Thomas was able to savour it too. There was something about meat roasted over flame that was so much tastier than meat cooked by electricity, and definitely better than anything that ever came out of a microwave!

Then Wulfstan took a bite of crackling. This was a mistake. The flavour was exquisite, the fat under the crackling igniting his taste buds. It was just gorgeous, but the crack and crunch as his teeth plunged through it caused his head to ring like a bell, and his face creased like an anguished prune.

'How is your head?' asked Eadburgh, her face genuinely concerned. 'Mother thought you were going to die!'

'Yes! We all thought that!' cried Ealfflaed, her five old voice high and shrill.

Wulfstan's face relaxed as the pain lessened again. He put the remaining piece of crackling back down on his plate. 'It's true. It was a close run thing. Today I've been to places I never thought to be until I died, and yet I came back.'

'What do you mean?' Eadburgh asked.

He told the girls the whole story, leaving out the fact that there were now two people living in his body. Their eyes were wide with disbelief by the end, and Ealfflaed's mouth was hanging open.

Archbishop Jaenberht had been listening from his other side. 'Are you saying you almost got to heaven, then fell almost to hell, yet were saved and brought back here by an angel?'

'I don't know if it was an angel your grace, but yes, that's pretty much right. It's nice to be back!' Wulfstan grinned.

'But this would be a miracle!' cried the Archbishop. Then added quietly, with a suspicious glance, 'If it were true.'

Wulfstan met his gaze. 'Why would I lie about such a thing? I am a royal Prince. I have money, land, connections, influence, family. I lack for nothing.'

'Would you be King some day?' asked Jaenberht slyly.

'Oh I see what you mean your grace.' smiled Wulfstan mirthlessly. 'You are suggesting that receiving a miracle might make me seem a better choice to succeed my father than my brother? Is that it?'

A political animal, the directness of the question stunned the Archbishop. To his right, the King and Prince Ecgfrith were looking at him, their expressions giving away nothing.

'The King has always said he wants my brother to succeed him. Ecgfrith is a fine man, wise, with a good soul. He will make an excellent king, and I will be proud to serve him, and do whatever he asks of me. I don't need miracles to do that. I just need to be myself.' said Wulfstan simply.

'Then,' said the Archbishop, 'perhaps as God has seen fit to return to you the gift of life, you should think about joining the Church?' He smiled unctuously.

'This is a trap!' warned Thomas. 'Once you're in the Church, you'll be under his control, to be used against your father!'

Wulfstan nodded thoughtfully. 'Does anyone really know the mind of God? Perhaps I'm back for some other purpose? I think I need more time before the answer becomes clear, so thank you, but no, I do not wish to join the Church. At least not now.'

Jaenberht stared. 'You are a most remarkable ten year old, even for a prince of so great a king as your father.'

King Offa growled past the Archbishop's shoulder. 'Remember Wulfstan, that as a prince you have the choice of warrior or priest.

That's all. Do you think you're up to being a warrior? You've shown no seriousness about anything up to today, and not much ability either. Not like your brother here.'

Wulfstan stiffened in shock and shame, stunned into silence. In an instant Thomas was back in the body, and Wulfstan was watching miserably from the ceiling. Thomas was extremely glad he'd been paying attention!

He took a deep breath, deliberately relaxed his face to a gentle smile, and met the King's gaze. 'Your Majesty, I am but ten years old, a child still. My voice has not yet broken. It is true that I have played, and not yet been very serious, but watch the young of any animal play and you will see it learn. The kitten catching a grasshopper is learning to hunt real prey. A lamb playing jumping jacks with its fellows is learning to dodge a hunter. A puppy wrestling its littermates is learning where it stands in the pack, and how to fight for its place. Children are no different, other than that each child has to learn based on where in society its parents lie. As the son of the King I have more to learn than most, and so yes, I played.'

King Offa was looking perplexed. 'But…'

'I have not finished yet Your Majesty.' smiled Thomas. 'I am ready to take my place if you are ready to allow it. I can run a manor more effectively than any man in this room. I can lower the sickness and death rates of the people who work in that manor to lower than anywhere else in the kingdom.'

'Hah!' spat the King. 'And can you defend it boy? Against all comers?'

The hall was completely silent now.

Thomas marshalled his thoughts. This was serious. It wasn't a word game, but it was a game of some kind. Where would it lead? Well, nothing for it now. 'If I can select my own warriors, have a year to train them, have them properly equipped, then yes, against all comers of an equal number.'

'Excellent!' boomed the King. 'In that case you and I will have a bet. You and your chosen ten will have your year. I will pay for everything you want, then you can fight Grimketil and his ten best warriors. Winner takes all. If you win, you take Grimketil's lands. If he wins, he takes yours.'

Thomas frowned. 'And what would happen to the loser?'

Offa smiled 'He dies in the battle of course.'

Again the room fell completely silent, only the crackle of the flames was evident.

'Of course you could withdraw your boast,' added Offa, 'but then you would be no Prince of mine!'

Wulfstan had recovered his fire and snarled at Thomas. 'Say yes!'

Thomas forced a small laugh. 'Then we have a deal. When do I get to choose my ten men?'

'You can start any time you like.' came the reply. 'But who said anything about men. You can have slaves. Your pick of any you want, and I will pay for them.'

'Fair enough.' said Thomas, glancing at Hengist who was smiling at Grimketil fixedly.

'Not so fast. Now it's my turn to not be finished, my young clever clogs.' The King's smile was truly malevolent now. 'Female slaves only! You can have girls if you are so truly wonderful. Do you still accept?'

Wulfstan wailed in horror. 'My God!! What have we done? You must renounce it! Say you were joking! Anything! My honour will be thrown in a pit of filth and trampled!'

'And that worries you more than dying?' snapped Thomas.

'Yes of course!'

The whole room was now in an uproar of laughter, hoots, catcalls and the crashing of knives against tables.

Grimketil's redhead was reaching past him to place more mutton onto his trencher. Out of pure spite he lifted his hand and prepared to smack her face down into the table.

She'd seen it coming though, and ducked back out from under his arm. The hand flew past its target and smashed into edge of the table. Grimketil's knife spun into the air with the impact, spattering dark sauce over his face and shirt. Thomas laughed loudly. Grimketil glared at him, then deliberately picked up his knife, and moved purposefully towards the girl. She watched him carefully, spread her feet a little further, but did not retreat or attempt to run.

Grimketil's men rose from the table, and moved out to either end, blocking the gaps between the table and the wall, leaving no obvious escape. Grimketil lunged, his blade flickering wickedly on its way to its target. And struck nothing. The girl had once more dodged his blow, this time dropping to the floor and rolling out from under the table into the centre of the hall. With the fire at her back she rose to her feet.

'How brave you are my Lord, with all that strength, and that knife of yours. Brave enough to attack a noblewoman half your weight, and unarmed.' The sarcasm dripped like candle wax, searing his ego. She smiled mirthlessly, 'So come on great warrior, finish it, or are you too frightened to try now?'

But by now Thomas was on his feet and between them. 'That's enough! No more violence in the royal hall!' Then he grinned at Grimketil, before turning towards the King. 'It looks like the slaves in your realm are even better than your thegns, father. I think perhaps I could beat this man Grimketil with ten female slaves against him and his ten best men. I choose this lady as my first companion, if she'll have me.' He held out his hand to her.

The whole room erupted into gales of laughter. Grimketil himself slapped his thighs in mirth, and grabbed a fresh beer horn from the brunette serving girl behind him. Thomas waited for the laughter to die down, 'Well?' he asked her. 'If you say yes, and we win, you shall have your freedom. And if we lose, well anything's better than being under that oaf's control!'

She smiled for the first time since he had seen her, a true smile, warm, as warm as the flickering of the flames dancing off her hair 'I would be honoured Your Highness.' she said. 'I would rather die in your service than spend another day with this nothing of a man!'

Grimketil snarled, and hurled his knife at her. In mid-flight she knocked it aside with her hand, sending it spinning into the flames.

'When you kidnapped me, you took me by surprise, like a ferret, not a warrior.' she said, the softness of her speech catching everyone's attention. Then her expression hardened. 'From now on you will face me armed, and I will be ready. The next time we clash, it is you who will die!' she spat.

'Do not be a fool Rowena!' Grimketil cried in return. 'You have no chance against me. Withdraw your offer to the Prince and I will accept you back, with only a beating for your rudeness. But if you join him, I will certainly see you dead, and slowly at that!'

Rowena, hair flashing in the firelight, turned away from him, knelt in front of Thomas, and said but a single word. 'Please?'

Thomas took her hand, and raised her to her feet. 'I would be honoured to have such as you by my side. And also your friend,' he nodded, indicating the short haired brunette behind Grimketil. 'I sense she is something special too?'

'Yes Your Highness. She is Berthilda, a girl of great character, and a childhood friend. She would serve you well.'

Thomas held out his other hand to Berthilda. 'Would you also like to join me?'

Grimketil grabbed her shoulder. 'No! She would not! And she is not for sale!'

Thomas laughed. 'My father said any slave, and I want her, if she'll have me. Do you want to join me?'

Offa nodded slowly, and reluctantly Grimketil released his hold. She smiled, ducked under the table, and joined her friend. 'Thank you Your Highness.' she smiled.

Thomas turned to the King. 'Well, that's my first two sorted out. Thank you father.' And then returned to his seat as if everything was as it had always been. 'Hengist, Ravena, please make arrangements for any property they may own to be moved here.'

'They own nothing but their lives,' growled Grimketil, 'and even they are on loan! A loan I will collect in a year's time. But you'll have nothing else from me today!'

'Do you have anything?' Thomas asked the girls.

'No Your Highness.' replied Rowena. 'Even our clothes are his.'

'Which I would like back this instant!' came Grimketil's riposte. A loud coarse laugh erupted again from his table.

Thomas nodded, and whispered into Ravena's ear. 'Ravena, will you please go into mother's linen box, and look for the dresses she is not going to wear again. Find one for each of these two ladies, and some shoes if possible. If you can make them both look really glamorous, bring them back in to me. Otherwise, they can stay in my room and have their dinner there. Tomorrow we can make arrangements for clothes of their own.'

Ravena, who was looking stunned at everything that had happened, nodded and began to turn away, beckoning to the two girls to follow her.

'Ravena?'

'Yes Your Highness.'

'Would you like to join me as well? I know you're happy in your position, but if you want to join me I will set you free after the fight in a year's time, with money and a position. You don't need to answer now, but I mean it. I would be honoured to have you, if you're game to try.' He smiled. 'If you accept, find a third dress, and come back in wearing it.'

Ravena gasped. The Queen looked at her questioningly. Ravena moved quickly behind the royal table and whispered into the queen's ear. The Queen smiled, nodded at Thomas, and said 'With my blessing, whatever you decide Ravena.'

The three women and Hengist left the hall to a hubbub of conversation, a mixture of hushed chat, soft laughter, and earnest debate.

Wulfstan was still steaming mad. Thomas could feel the waves of disapproval radiating through his body. 'What's the matter?' he asked.

'They will have no chance against Grimketil and his men! We'll have a year of being laughed at by everyone, and then we will die! How could you be so stupid?'

Thomas thought for a moment. 'And the alternative was?'

Silence.

Thomas spoke again. 'Your father made it quite clear that there was no way to refuse his challenge. He basically said you were no son of his if you didn't accept.'

More silence.

'In any case, don't think for a moment that we are going to play by the accepted rules. I have knowledge about weapons, tactics and strategy that they have never even imagined. We will win, and when we have, your name will be on everyone's lips, for the right reasons. You may even become King yourself!'

No silence this time. 'What do you mean? What do you know?!'

'Your people fight on foot. We will not. Your people fight with spear, axe and sword. So will we, but we won't fight in the same way. Plus, we will have new and different weapons that Grimketil will never have seen.'

'But we can't do that! Father will never allow it. He'll force us to fight as our people expect us to fight, or there will be no honour in winning!'

'Our victory will be so overwhelming, that the people will think you magnificent!'

Wulfstan swore. 'You're not listening! The King won't let us fight differently. We won't be allowed to use your new ideas!'

Thomas laughed. 'Oh I think he will. If he tries that, I will ask him in public, if this is the way a great king behaves, to change the rules of the game after he has made his wager, to guarantee he wins. He will have no choice.'

More swearing. 'He is the King! He can do anything he wants to do! And that includes beheading his own son when he has gone far beyond acceptable bounds! We… will… lose.'

There was a short pause. 'Well,' said Thomas, 'the die is cast now. If you continue to think we're going to lose, then we probably will. How about trying to think about the possibility that we might actually win? Then it becomes possible. What do you say?'

This time the swearing went on for much longer. Thomas let it burn itself out. Eventually there was silence again.

'Well?' asked Thomas.

'Alright.' came the rather sulky reply. 'I don't have a choice do I?'

'Of course you have a choice.' said Thomas 'We all have this choice, every day of our lives. What the world gives you each day is what the world gives you, and there isn't always much we can do about that. But how we respond to it is a choice, our choice, and we can always control that if we want to. Look at Hengist. He has been treated so unfairly today that he'd be justified in being miserable, depressed, or screaming with rage, or running away, or taking his own life. He could have done any of those things. Instead he chooses, and I emphasise that word, chooses, to behave with dignity and grace, and to look forward to a better future. I am certain he finds that hard to do, but he chooses to do it because he believes it is the best way to respond. So yes, you do have a choice. But it has to be your own free will.'

Again there was silence. But this time the waves of disapproval and anger diminished, and a sense of tranquillity entered the body. The silence continued. Gradually Thomas could feel different sensations flowing through his frame, an excitement building in the pit if the stomach, his right arm trying to give a victorious arm pump, and finally, the full on wash of warmth that comes with an endorphin rush.

'You're right. I'd never thought about that before. I thought it was all just the will of God, and that was it.'

'Let me tell you a story.' said Thomas. 'Once upon a time there was a deeply religious man who lived in a hut on a small island. One day a storm arrived, and the river began to rise. A man came galloping downriver on a horse, and called out that there was much rain upstream and that there was going to be a flood. He said the man should come off the island now, while there was still time. The man refused, saying that God would protect him. The river continued to rise. The village folk came to the bank of the river with a long rope. They offered to throw it to the man so that they could pull him to safety. Again he refused and said that God would protect him. The river continued to rise, and the man had to climb onto the roof of his hut, which shivered and shook with the water hammering into it. An enormous tree trunk came sliding down the river, and by great good fortune, hit the largest bit of the island still above water. It juddered to a halt, before spinning slowly around, and sliding parallel to the walls of the hut. The watching villagers urged him to jump onto it and be carried to safety. Once more the man declined, saying that God would save him. The tree floated free, and washed away. A few minutes later a great wave came down the river and slammed into the hut. The little building crumpled with the blow, broke up, and was carried into the torrent. For a few seconds the man floated on the thatch roof, his face a mask of terror, and then he fell through into the water. The last the villagers saw of him was one arm raised in appeal to the heavens.

'When the man arrived in heaven, God greeted him warmly, but the man was bewildered and confused.

'"My Lord, why did you not save me? I thought you would come to my aid."

'"My son," said God, "I gave you eyes and a mind that could see the river was rising. I sent a horseman to warn you with words. I sent the villagers with rope and advice. Lastly, I sent you a tree, even placing it so you could step easily onto it and be carried to safety. Just how much rescuing do you need?"'

Wulfstan laughed 'And the moral of the story is?'

'Easy.' said Thomas. 'God helps those who help themselves. A big part of that is choosing how to react to things. And it is always a choice. Even when there is no apparent good choice, there is still a choice, the choice to be true to yourself and to those you love. I believe I can feel the choice you've now made?'

Wulfstan laughed again. 'Yes. I am with you now. What a difference it makes to have done it too! I actually feel different! I am excited about what we are going to do!'

Then suddenly they swapped again, and Wulfstan's grin became real on his own face.

'I'm off to listen in on what Grimketil and his men are talking about.' said Thomas. 'Have fun.'

Sensing Thomas's departure, Wulfstan looked across to Grimketil's table. Grimketil's face was, well, grim. That was the best word for it. He was deep in conversation with Ward, his right hand man. Wulfwynn was silent, nibbling on a pigeon leg, eyes staring into space. She seemed very much alone.

Looking around the rest of the room, he could see a lot of animated discussions going on. No need to guess what most of that was about. Here and there he could see hands slapped or shaken, indicating wagers being made, almost certainly on the fight to come.

For the next ten minutes he talked exclusively with the little girls, who wanted to hear every tiny detail about his adventure. Jaenberht did his best to eavesdrop as much as possible, but he missed a lot when he had to turn away to talk to the King.

Then Rowena and Berthilda walked back in, followed by Hengist and Ravena, silencing everyone. Despite the short hair style denoting their slave status, they looked glorious, majestic even. Rowena was wearing a long flowing dark blue gown, trimmed with white fur. Even without jewellery she looked stunning. Berthilda wore a deep red gown that poured over her shoulders, hiding her perfectly toned arms. Yet despite the sumptuousness of their clothes, it was their carriage and bearing that made the real difference.

Confident, secure of their place in their Prince's affections, they radiated a presence greater than all but the King and Queen. Wulfstan turned, and rose from his chair to greet them. 'You both look magnificent! Welcome to your rightful places.'

He was rewarded with two deep smiles, and four sparkling eyes.

Behind them, Hengist was his usual impassive self. Ravena, as dignified as possible, was holding their old slave girl clothes in her arms. She shook her head in reply to the question on Wulfstan's face.

He nodded in understanding. 'Ravena, please return Grimketil's property to him.'

She nodded, and walked quickly across to Grimketil's table, and offered him the cloth bundle. Snarling at her, he snatched it from her arms, scowled angrily at Rowena and Berthilda, and threw it onto the fire.

'You'll both follow them in a year's time! Make the most of now, because your future is short indeed!'

Both women simply turned away from him to look at Wulfstan. 'What would you have us do now?' asked Rowena.

Wulfstan thought for a moment. Then he beckoned her head down to his, and whispered into her ear. Initially she shot back to the vertical, looking shocked and fearful, but he grinned, gently took her hand, and with the softest of pressures once more brought her ear down to his mouth. When he had finished, her steely smile was once more in evidence. She took Berthilda's hand, and started to lead her out to the kitchen.

'Oh Rowena?' called Wulfstan.

She turned back towards him. 'Yes Your Highness?'

'I'll have one too please.' Then he winked. 'But not your special strength brew.'

She nodded, face impassive.

They returned with a horn of beer in each hand. Rowena handed her small one to Wulfstan, then led Berthilda across to Grimketil's table.

Startled, he recoiled a little. 'What is it? What do you want?'

'The Prince has asked us to render you and your two leading men one last service, a sort of goodbye, until we meet again in a year's time.' and she proffered him her remaining horn.

Still bemused, he accepted it while Berthilda handed her horns to the men on either side of him.

'I thought Grimketil,' said Thomas as the women walked back towards him, 'that you should be allowed one last service from these two wonderful ladies, a parting gift if you like. As it's beer you seemed to send them for most often tonight, that's what I chose. One last toast?' and he raised his horn.

Grimketil paused, then nodded to his two men. The three raised their horns to Wulfstan, who raised his in turn.

Thomas whooped in delight.

5 FIRST STEPS

After the feast, the five of them returned to the room Thomas had slept in during the day. Wulfstan had Ravena arrange for the delivery of three more palliasses, along with pillows and blankets.

He undressed and climbed into the bed, pulling the blankets over himself.

The girls took off their gowns, laying them carefully on top of the big carved chest at the foot of the bed, before claiming the two palliasses next to him.

Hengist placed his palliasse across the closed door and went to sleep still dressed, his sword close by.

Wulfstan wanted some answers from Thomas before he went to sleep.

'How are you going to win with girls? What do you know about running a manor? What actually are you? When - ?'

Thomas cut off the stream of questions before Wulfstan got up too much of a head of steam.

'Woah there! One at a time lad. Let's start with what I am. I come from the twenty first century, and I'm a museum curator.'

'What's that?'

'Someone who knows a lot of stuff about the past, who can look after things, and teach people about them. That's why I seem to know so much.'

'You're from the future? Is it a lot different to here?'

'More different than you can possibly imagine.' laughed Thomas. 'But you'll see some of it soon.'

'Why is that?'

'Well, to run a manor better than anyone else, I am going to bring in a few new things you won't have come across before.'

'And winning the fight?'

'Same reason. I know different ways of fighting, and how to make weapons people have never seen in your world.'

'Can you do that on your own?'

'No.' Thomas admitted. 'And that is a bit of a challenge. Finding the right kind of girl is going to be hard enough. We also need to find people I can teach, who can not only do what I need them to do, but can then teach more people in turn. That's going to be hard. It's also going to take money, a lot! I have some ideas about that too, but it takes money to make money and we don't actually have any.'

'What sort of ideas?' Wulfstan grimaced. His head was still hurting him a lot.

'I don't know which ones will work yet. I need to find out a bit more first. Perhaps we should discuss this tomorrow? I really think you need to sleep now, and give that head a chance to rest.'

Wulfstan wasn't too keen on that suggestion, but another wave of pain overcame his reluctance. As he drifted off to sleep, Thomas went out to watch the barn owls hunting, something that kept him fascinated until dawn.

The four with bodies to look after all slept well. Even Hengist managed to find enough peace within himself to drift off.

During breakfast the following morning, Wulfstan found out a bit more about Rowena and Berthilda.

'My father is a thegn near Nottingham, and Berthilda's father is our neighbour. We've been friends our whole lives.' said Rowena.

Berthilda chipped in. 'We did everything together, learning to ride, to shoot, to use knives. Just like the boys. Our mothers disapproved, but our fathers made allowances.' She grinned. 'We got to be better than the boys at some things, especially archery and riding.'

'Well, you did!' riposted Rowena. 'I'm not as good as you.'

'You're better with a knife.' said Berthilda.

Rowena considered this, before nodding. 'I suppose that's true.'

'So how on earth did Grimketil manage to get his hooks into you?' asked Wulfstan.

'We were swimming in the river, about a mile from home. He and his men caught us unawares and there was nothing we could do.' said Rowena frowning.

'But why didn't your fathers do something after you were taken?' asked Wulfstan.

Berthilda sighed sadly. 'Grimketil made sure we knew that if one of us tried to escape, he'd kill the other. When he cut my hair, one of his men had his knife to Rowena's throat. Then they held the knife to mine when they cut hers. He kept us apart a lot of the time, so we never found an opportunity to try and escape together.'

Rowena closed the loop. 'It was only two weeks ago. Our fathers are busy maintaining the defences up there. They'll assume the Northumbrians have taken us. They haven't been to court since then and so won't know about Grimketil.'

'Ye gods.' said Wulfstan. 'Won't your fathers kill him when they find out?'

Rowena shook her head. 'Unlikely. Grimketil is a favourite of the King. You saw that last night. And Grimketil's warriors are better than my father's. He wouldn't stand a chance.'

Wulfstan frowned. 'Well then, we must get a message to them to let them know you're okay, and what's afoot. And that they aren't to do anything, or we'll lose our bet! They can do what they like if we lose, but we'll try to make sure that doesn't happen.'

After breakfast Wulfstan led them all out into the marketplace. He equipped both girls with new underdresses, dresses and shoes. He'd had to borrow some temporary clothes for them from Ravena before they went out, as the only clothes they had were the two gowns, which were hardly appropriate for wading through the doings of animals, and other filth that littered the marketplace.

Under Thomas's urging, and much to their surprise, he also bought each of them a complete set of men's clothing, explaining that dresses were not going to work well for what they were going to be doing.

Last on the clothing front, he bought a complete set of new clothes for Ravena as a thank you present. They were much nicer than the ones she already had.

He sent the bill for all this to his father.

Then they visited the arms merchants.

'This lady will be in charge of choosing our bows.' he said to the man, indicating Berthilda.

The merchant came back with some very polished looking weapons. Berthilda looked at them carefully. She turned them over in her hands, one at a time, looking at the grain and the knots. After stringing what she assessed as the best of them, she took a practice shot at a target thirty yards away. She shook her head.

'Very pretty.' she said. 'Just not as good as we'd like. Something with a bit more strength in it please, and with more consistent feel.'

The merchant blustered. 'With all due respect missus, that's a fine bow for a woman! The most handsome of my entire stock!'

She looked him firmly in the eye. 'I don't care what they look like. I care how they shoot!'

The merchant wasn't done yet. 'But do these other ladies have your strength missus? Can they pull a stronger bow?'

She nodded. 'A fair point. They will, with practice. Better bows please, or we can always ask your competition.'

The man gave up. 'As you wish missus. As you wish.' He came back with four rather ugly looking bows. 'These are finest English yew. I'm sorry I don't have any Scandinavian at present. In fact nobody does. These are the best I have for war.'

Berthilda tried a few practice shots. All but the first went straight into the bullseye at thirty yards. She nodded with satisfaction. 'Much better. A bit strong for the others I admit, but they'll manage with a bit of practice. We'll have four quivers of broadhead arrows, and two with bodkin heads for each of us.'

The bodkins were unusual in that the heads were simple points, especially made to pierce armour. Wulfstan was impressed. 'You really do know your stuff Berthilda.'

She grinned. 'I know how to shoot well too!'

'So I saw!' he said. 'I hope you are also a good teacher because you'll need to train us all up to your standard.'

She beamed with pleasure at this display of trust and respect. 'What a difference a day makes!' she thought.

Wulfstan sent the bill to Offa…

'Now," he said, "I believe you're a pretty good horsewoman too. Let's go and choose our mounts.'

Being the palace marketplace with the King in residence, some of the finest horses in the country were there. They did an initial check of all three horse merchants to see just what was on offer, before they settled down to the selection process.

'We'll start with one for you Hengist.' said Thomas.

'But I already have a horse Your Highness.' said Hengist.

'That's true, but he's your personal mount. I'm going to get you one specifically for our challenge. That way, if anything happens to it, you'll still have your own. Now, go and choose one, and don't worry about the money. You can get your own back on my father at this point!' he laughed.

Hengist grinned, a little sheepishly, then picked out a beautiful piebald stallion that at 14 hands was one of the biggest in the country. He also seemed to have a mind of his own, but Hengist was confident he could handle him.

Rowena fell for an almost pure white gelding. The horse was beautifully muscled, yet gentle in nature. When she was astride it, with her glorious red hair and pale complexion, the effect was otherworldly.

Berthilda chose a lovely roan gelding with three white feet. He wasn't quite as good looking as the other two horses, but handsome enough and Berthilda sensed something in him. He in turn seemed to bond almost instantly with her.

That left Wulfstan, but at this precise moment he found himself outside the body again, watching Thomas.

'Bother! I could get really tired of this!' he shouted. 'Oh well, we both want the same one, so go get him Thomas.'

From the moment they'd seen him, Thomas and Wulfstan's hearts had settled on an almost pure black gelding. Its muscles rippled under the sheen of its coat as it stood proud and aloof, held by the merchant's servant.

The boy was bored and began to play a game, tossing the end of the lead rope into the air and catching it in the same hand. The higher he tossed it, the less accurate he became, and eventually he got it wrong. The end knot landed heavily on the horse's nose, causing it to flick its head in alarm. The boy took the blow full in the face and was sent flying. The merchant rushed up and prepared to strike the horse with his whip, but Thomas leapt between them and held up his hand to stop him.

'Your Highness!' called Hengist. 'You should stay back! He could flatten you!'

Thomas turned slowly to face the horse, who watched him warily. He held out his hands in front of him, open, showing he had nothing in them before taking a step slowly towards the animal. The horse stepped skittishly away, keeping the distance the same.

Thomas cocked his head to one side, dropped his shoulder, and snaked his head gently towards it.

The horse stood still, watching carefully.

Then Thomas turned his body so he was parallel to the horse, and again cocked and snaked his head.

The horse remained still.

Another couple of rounds of this and Thomas was next to the horse. He held up the back of his hand, limp, so the horse could smell him. It began to nuzzle him gently, and in turn allowed Thomas to softly stroke its nose.

Within a minute it was calm enough for Thomas to nestle his forehead into its neck. The horse lowered its own head over Thomas' shoulder, and closed its eyes in pleasure as the little human scratched it behind the ears.

'We'll take him.' said Thomas.

The others were watching him with astonishment. He shrugged his shoulders with an embarrassed smile. 'I just behaved like a horse. I used my body like another horse would, and he understood I meant him no harm.'

'But where did you learn how to do that?' asked the merchant. 'It's like magic!'

Thomas shook his head. 'No. Not like magic. I've been watching horses for a long time, and learned how they behave, how they move. I thought that if I tried to speak their language, it might help, and it did. Berthilda does it too if you watch her. That's why she's so good with them. They trust her.'

'I do that?' asked Berthilda.

'Sort of, only you're much better than I am. For you it's a natural thing. You're just not aware you do it. But how many others can ride with no reins? Very few. The reason you can, is that they trust you, and you're directing them with your legs. That's all they need from you. It's a gift, but it isn't magic.'

They went on to buy another ten horses, eight for the other girls he would have to find, and two heavier ones for reasons he kept to himself. The merchants couldn't believe their luck.

Wulfstan had been busy throughout, checking out the horses' feet, making sure they hadn't been gingered up for the punters, and reporting back everything he found to Thomas.

'Why did you buy them all before we have the other girls?' asked Rowena.

'Because the court moves on soon, and these merchants will move with it. If we want the best horses we have to buy now.' Thomas replied.

Then they went on to buy a sword each. Thomas was dismayed, but not surprised, at the poor quality of the metal, amazing Hengist with his ability to spot the flaws. Swords were relatively rare in the Dark Ages, and very expensive, but the court market tried to cater to all tastes. Anglo Saxon swords were made for slashing, weighted towards the point to increase the impact of the blows. You needed to be very strong to use them, much stronger than Wulfstan and the girls, but Thomas had plans.

Meanwhile, Wulfstan had left the market and was hovering in the King's chamber when the first of the bills arrived, carried by a steward. Offa's eyebrows rose a little when he was told the amount, but he paid up without a murmur.

He was less sanguine about the second, and by the time the tenth, eleventh and twelfth had made their appearance, he was incandescent. They were for the fourteen finest horses in the market. An astronomical cost!

'Bring that wretched brat to me this instant! ' he roared.

'What's the matter dear?' asked the Queen, who had just walked into the hall.

'Your son is spending gold and silver as if it's water!!! And he's sending me the bills!! How dare he mislead the merchants in this way?!? How dare he assume I'll pay for his latest games?!?!'

The Queen cocked her head to the right, her eyes twinkling. 'Are the bills for things to equip him and the girls?'

Offa paused in mid rant. 'Yes! So what?'

'Well you can hardly complain dear. You told him you would not only buy whatever girls he wanted, but would also pay to equip and train them. You placed no conditions on that, but you did put him in a position where he will almost certainly lose. So, you can hardly blame him for getting the best he can find.'

Offa looked angrily into her still twinkling eyes. His glare would have terrified any other person in the land, but she knew her man, and fearsome monarch though he was, she knew he loved her above all else and would never harm her. More than that, he trusted her judgement. It helped him to keep his balance.

Finally, his face broke into a laugh. 'Alright Cynethryth! You're right. What does it matter? There's plenty of gold after all. Let him have his trinkets. But I'll make him eat humble pie when he caves in and begs pardon for his stupid pig headedness.'

The twinkles continued. 'Oh I don't think he'll cave in dear. I believe he has every intention of winning the bet, and surviving. That knock on the head has changed him more than you could ever guess. He's all grown up now, a man in mind, intelligent, wise, and determined. I think he's going to win.'

Offa's mouth dropped open. 'You're serious! But he can't! Grimketil's the best! Wulfstan couldn't beat Grimketil with trained soldiers, let alone a bunch of untrained girls!'

'You didn't see him last night before the feast. He was strong and firm in ordering the treatment he received. He treated Hengist with deep compassion, love and support, as one best friend to another. Not only that, he was wise in his words and actions. He even wormed his way into Ravena's affections, and you know what she really thought of him up to yesterday! You're too hard on him. He's always been a bright, intelligent, and loving child, but now he's become someone you'll be proud to call your son.'

Offa's jaw continued to hang open. Collecting himself he asked 'So, do you think I need to rescind Hengist's punishment? Take back my bet with Wulfstan?'

It was Cynethryth's turn to think. She turned away and looked into the flames of the fire. 'I don't see how you can do either of those things, even though I would wish that you would. To rescind Hengist's punishment would probably make Grimketil think he can strike Wulfstan and get away with it. Wulfstan really pushed him last night. Grimketil lost a lot of face, two of his favourite girls, and he's very angry about it all. And since having his morning beer, he's been in an even worse mood, wandering about trying all the barrels he can find, even your special ones. I have no idea what that's all about, but he was swearing under his breath the whole time.'

'Secondly, I don't think you can call off your bet without making it look as if you made a foolish mistake last night. Jaenberht would revel in that at the next synod when he wants to manipulate you.'

Offa came up behind her, and put his arms around her, clasping his hands gently but firmly over her tummy. He pulled her lovingly into his chest, and dropped his face into her hair. She smiled, and stroked the back of his hands. For a full minute they stayed together, her scent filling his world, as he mulled things through. He kissed the top of her head, and gently turned her to face him. 'So what do you think I should do?'

She kissed his cheek. 'Give him your full support. Buy him what he asks for. And encourage him. Don't belittle him again, especially not in public. And just maybe, once in a while, you might tell him you love him. I know you love him, but you've never told him, nor shown it in any other way, and I don't think he knows.'

Their eyes rested together, a few inches apart. Ever so slightly, he nodded. Then they kissed. For a long time.

Wulfstan was astonished. He'd never seen his parents so tender together. And he'd genuinely never known that his father loved him. He'd always been terrified of Offa!!! Hardly a smile, little encouragement, harsh words, nothing Wulfstan did was ever good enough. And now. And now. And now, he knew. He knew his father loved him.

For an instant fear and jealousy ripped through him. 'He doesn't love me! He loves Thomas, and what Thomas is!!' And then he remembered his mother's words "I know you love him..." and knew his fear was groundless. Then regretfully, but respectfully, he left them, to go back to the marketplace.

'Wulfstan!' came a boyish cry.

Thomas looked up. 'Hello?'

Wulfstan was just exiting the Palace window, but instantly he was back in the body, covering the three hundred yards in less than a second. Much to his surprise, Thomas was booted out the same distance on the other side, and it took him a moment to get his bearings.

Ethelwulf ran up, puffing away. 'I thought you were dead yesterday! How have you recovered so fast? Hengist! How are you? Are these the two ladies everyone is talking about? And -'

Wulfstan laughed, and gave him a big hug. 'Everything's just fine! It's going to be alright! Let me introduce you to everyone.' And for the next fifteen minutes they talked and jabbered like the boys they were.

Thomas watched from afar, thinking about their latest body swap. This was the first time it had happened when the outside person was a long way away, and it could lead to trouble if it happened in the middle of a conversation. He floated up to the treetops, where he lay on his back and thought, meditating on a kite soaring high above.

Hengist and the girls continued to shop as the boys walked beside them, then Grimketil came around the corner with four of his men. Seeing Hengist still armed, Grimketil lost his temper.

'Slave! How dare you carry a sword in the marketplace?!' he screamed, drawing his own from its scabbard. His four cronies raised their spears, fanning out to block escape.

Wulfstan spun around. 'Bows! Load and prepare to draw! Shoot on my word!' and stepped to Hengist's side.

Berthilda had her arrow nocked and ready in seconds, Rowena a little behind. Hengist instinctively drew his blade.

'How dare you threaten a thegn, slave?!?!?' screamed the enraged Grimketil, still advancing rapidly, sword waving with intent.

Wulfstan leapt in front of him, unarmed. 'Would you kill an unarmed prince in the marketplace Grimketil? What would my father do to you after that?'

He turned his head and screamed at the men to his right. 'You two! Stop where you are or I'll let my ladies drop you where you stand!' And spinning his head to the left he added 'And that goes for you two too!'

Startled, they did, looking at Grimketil for their next move.

The thegn's face was white with anger, the veins on his forehead bulging and throbbing. He glared with pure hatred at Wulfstan. 'What did you tell that redhead to put in my beer last night?!?! I know from this morning that whatever you had her give me wasn't just beer! What trick were you playing?'

'Put your sword away Grimketil. And have your men lower their spears. And then we'll talk beer.'

Grimketil nodded angrily to the men, who withdrew to his side and rested their weapons on the ground.

When Grimketil's sword was safely back in its scabbard, Wulfstan turned to his flame haired companion. 'Rowena, Grimketil thinks you and I conspired to put something in his beer last night.'

Rowena, bow still in hand, but lowered and undrawn, said 'Last night I gave him the same kind of beer I have given him since the day he kidnapped me. Nothing different except it was from the King's best barrel. That's the truth.'

'I tried that barrel this morning and it tasted completely different!' Grimketil cried.

'You drank out of the King's own barrel?' asked Wulfstan, pretending to be serious. 'Does he know?'

Grimketil jerked his head, and said nothing.

'He might be quite annoyed about that… You really should have asked his permission.' Wulfstan's smile was as sweet as could be. 'Perhaps though, we should say nothing about it, for your sake. What do you think?'

Grimketil was shaking with the realisation that he was in someone else's power for once. He nodded, uncertainly.

'Excellent!' soothed Wulfstan. 'I think perhaps Rowena has a special gift when it comes to beer. It's simply that you'll never have her pour you one again, and you're already missing it. Nothing more than that I think. Don't you agree?' Again the gentle smile.

Grimketil swallowed, nodded in a jerky sort of way, then bowed clumsily to Wulfstan, turned and walked off, taking his men with him.

'One thing's for sure Rowena,' Wulfstan said, 'he'll have to really experiment to find out how you make his beer so special!!'

He, Rowena and Berthilda doubled up in laughter. Hengist looked on perplexed until Rowena took pity on him, and whispered into his ear. Disbelief spread across his face.

'No!? Really? No!! You're joking surely? For how long did you do that? Every single time!!?? How did you…' until he stuttered into silence. And then he too threw his head back and roared in appreciation.

'What? What is it you're all laughing at?' demanded Ethelwulf, unhappy at being the odd one out.

'I'll tell you when you're older!' laughed Wulfstan. 'Come with us back to the Palace.'

Suddenly he was aware that Thomas was back. 'Hello my friend! How are you? What have you been up to?'

'Oh, just floating around, watching the birds. I saw what you just did. Most impressive. What were you up to before the last body swap?'

'I was watching my father get cross about all the money we're costing him today. And finding out how he really feels about me.'

'And that is what precisely?' asked Thomas.

Wulfstan told him.

'That's brilliant.' said Thomas. 'You must be really pleased about that.'

'I am.' agreed Wulfstan. 'For the first time in my life, I'm truly happy.'

6 MANOR FROM HEAVEN

They spent the rest of the day getting ready, and after a good breakfast the following morning, they set out for Hengist's manor, ten miles to the west. Thomas was relieved that after the marketplace altercation the previous day, Grimketil and his men had left for his own manor thirty miles south east of Tamworth.

The four of them made an interesting sight, the women in particular triggering a lot of chatter because they rode in their male clothes and not dresses. Berthilda once more used no bridle or halter, her rich roan horse responding to the subtle movements of her weight and legs. Thomas was astonished that she'd been able to bond with her new mount in less than a day, and that it was so responsive to her commands.

For himself, it was a new experience. Fortunately, Wulfstan's body's muscle memories and training made much of it automatic, and despite Thomas never having sat on a horse before, he found he could ride quite well. It was interesting that he and Wulfstan seemed to share the physical skills they each knew, yet their conscious minds and detailed memories remained separate. Thomas wondered how it all worked.

Connected by the lead ropes the other horses followed along, including Hengist's who was enjoying not having a load for a change.

Wulfstan floated above, watching everything unfold. Once they were clear of the town he scouted ahead and off to the sides of the road, checking out the hedgerows, the forest edges, and even the condition of the crossings long before the party arrived at each river or stream.

The road itself was pretty basic, little more than a dirt track. Thomas thought it must get very boggy in winter, probably impassable to carts, but the countryside was beautiful. Sometimes there were fields of grass, sometimes of crops, and often there was forest. Everywhere there was birdsong, and high above soared the kites, hawks and other birds of prey. Thomas simply revelled in his new young eyes. He'd regretted the deterioration in his eyesight as he'd got older, but as it happened over a long time he hadn't realised just how huge the loss had been. Or perhaps he'd never ever had a set of really good eyes? Well, he had them now, and he certainly wasn't going to take them for granted!

He was thoughtful too, primarily about the King and Queen. They'd had a truly royal send off. The Queen had been lovely, not just a doting mum towards Wulfstan, but warm to all of them. And Offa himself had been a real surprise. The hostility and temper of the previous night had vanished like the mist on a sunny dawn. He'd given Wulfstan a great big hug, not a bone crusher to show his own strength, but a warm, enveloping cocoon.

There had been farewell gifts too. The girls got to keep the dresses Ravena had sorted out for them the night before, and Wulfstan was given a beautiful small sword. It was the right size and weight for him, but Thomas thought it looked more impressive than effective. Then again, it was a status item, not intended for use, so that was okay. And of course there was the money. Offa had tried to head off his losses by giving his son two saddle bags of the stuff, imploring his young lad to use it wisely. Thomas silently noted that he hadn't been told to pay everything else out of it, so thought he would still send the bills for his remaining girls on to Offa wherever the court was.

And that was a key point. The Mercian court, always itinerant, was itself on the move again. Offa was off to the south east to show his face and collect his tributes. To be a king meant traveling around showing yourself to your people, an almost constant round of travel. He had the occasional week or two in his beloved palace at Tamworth of course. He enjoyed that. The palace was famous across Europe, and he enjoyed knowing that too!

What it meant for Wulfstan and Thomas was that they were on their own. There would be no kingly backup available if they needed it.

Wulfstan bobbed happily along. He couldn't remember being so happy ever before. He'd started the day in the body, but when it came time to leave his parents, he'd found himself staying where he was as the horse moved out from under him, and Thomas took over. He'd stayed until he saw the party leaving Tamworth, whereupon he took up his scouting duties with some reluctance. Happily though, the warm glow never left him.

So all in all it was a good ride to Hengist's manor, but the mood was about to change.

They entered from the south, the road meandering through a dozen or so huts before approaching a T intersection.

'That's the hall straight ahead, with the kitchen over to our left.' said Hengist. 'The servants' quarters are those two buildings to the left of that -'

At that moment, two men came running down the road in front of those very buildings, one chasing the other. Startled by the riders' appearance, the one in front stumbled and fell In an instant his pursuer was standing over him, lashing down with a thin branch ripped from a tree, causing the fallen man to scream in pain.

Thomas urged his horse forward, crying out for the man to cease and desist. Startled, the aggressor looked up. He didn't recognise Thomas, but did recognise the wealth and status his horse and dress implied. He reached down, grabbed his victim by the neck and dragged him to his knees, where he held him fast.

He relaxed a bit when he saw Hengist riding up behind. 'Welcome home my Lord!' he cried.

'What's going on Cuthbert?' asked Hengist.

'This wretch refuses to pay me my tithe!' said Cuthbert angrily, shaking his victim. 'I have asked for it three times now, and always he makes the excuses. He claims to have managed his affairs so badly that he cannot pay. I say that he needs to be taught respect to the Church of our Lord!'

Hengist turned in his saddle to face the others. 'Cuthbert is the village priest. Ashlin,' he said, indicating Cuthbert's victim, 'is a farmer who tills the fields at the edge of the river.'

'Let him go Cuthbert.' said Thomas.

Cuthbert looked at Hengist, who nodded in reply. Cuthbert did let his victim go, using the gentle technique known as throwing your enemy to the ground where Ashlin sprawled, groaning.

Thomas leaned forward 'So we are talking about a Church tithe, a tenth of one's income to the Church, yes?'

The man nodded miserably.

'And why can you not pay?'

Ashlin looked up fearfully, glancing sideways at Hengist. 'Half my land was washed away in the winter flood, with most of my tools and grain. I have barely enough food to feed my family, no spare seed to plant for next year, so none left over for the priest and his church. He can beat me as much as he wants. There is nothing to give.'

The priest scowled angrily. 'It is God's will, punishing you for being so wicked!! Only paying your tithe will wash the sin away that caused your land to be taken.'

Shocked, Thomas asked 'Are you suggesting that God took his land on purpose, to punish him for something? And that you are therefore entitled to make his family starve as part of the same deal?'

'Of course my Lord.' replied the priest. 'God's will is in everything.'

Thomas looked at him, mouth smiling, eyes hard. 'Then that must include me too. I am the new owner of the manor, and using your own logic, in the name of God I excuse this man of his tithe. The Church is surely there to nurture and grow our people, not to see them starve. To encourage a just world, and not to inflict injustice itself. To offer mercy where mercy is deserved, and not to inflict punishment where none is merited. Don't you agree?'

Cuthbert looked startled. He turned questioningly to Hengist, who nodded. 'This is Prince Wulfstan, son of our King, and the new owner of the manor.'

'Your Highness,' said Cuthbert, 'the tithe is taken very seriously by the Church. It is not just a gift to the priests and monks, not just to the Church even, but to God himself. It is not to be discarded lightly. I must insist upon my rights.'

Thomas looked thoughtful. 'This village has about 30 households, plus Hengist's and mine. That means you collect thirty two tithes, or to put it another way a full tenth of all the manor's income. That's just over the annual income for three families in total. Correct?'

'Yes Your Highness.' replied Cuthbert.

'I assume there is just the one priest, plus a servant or two to help him. Correct?'

'Yes Your Highness.' repeated Cuthbert.

'That makes less than a standard household, with more than three times the income. What do you do with it all that you cannot excuse a starving man from his obligation?'

Cuthbert thrust out his chin 'Some of it goes towards saving for the building of the new church, once you have gifted the land for it. Some goes to pay me for the writing and numerical skills I provide to you and the manor. Some goes to support the poor, and the rest goes to the Archbishop for works that enhance the glory of God.'

Thomas's fake smile faded away until the mouth matched the eyes. Cuthbert maintained his pugnacious pose, but could not help a little shiver of unease looking at this strange boy.

'Well master priest, Ashlin would currently appear to be a member of the poor, and I cannot remember any story of Jesus taking food out of anyone's mouth. In fact, if I remember rightly, he did more for the glory of God by his good deeds, than by anything he built or bought. I cannot think that Jesus would agree with your actions, and I cannot agree with them myself. Mercy will be granted in this instance. The man is excused his tithe this year. Tomorrow Hengist and I will meet with the village and discuss what can be done about his land, so he can perhaps meet his obligations in future.'

As Thomas gently urged his horse to walk on, Cuthbert burst out 'With respect Your Highness, the tithe is not yours to forgive! It is the Church's debt, not yours!'

Thomas stopped his horse, staring straight ahead, not looking at the priest. 'If forgiveness of the tithe is truly within your gift, and I do not yet accept that as fact, I would urge you to remember that the gift of land for your church is within mine. Perhaps the best piece to choose may be the part that was washed away from this man's land. After all, according to you, God has already claimed it, so perhaps that is God's will also!!'

He finally twisted to face Cuthbert, his face red with anger, 'And the decision as to whether or not you are the right priest for my people definitely lies with me, despite what the Archbishop may think!'

Cuthbert cowered away from this attack.

Thomas was shouting now, his anger overwhelming his judgement. 'How dare you, as a representative of a gentle, kind and good man such as Jesus Christ, threaten to starve a fellow's family on the basis of an accident of nature, just so you can have more money that you do not even need?!' Spit had formed in the corners of his mouth now, the redness in his cheeks faded into white.

Cuthbert, his own face white with fear, reeled back from the onslaught.

'Fortunately for you I do not claim as you so arrogantly do, to know the mind of God! I only know my own. You may have tonight to reconsider your position.' continued Thomas, beginning to calm down a little. 'Tomorrow we will discuss it in a calmer manner, in front of the village. And we will decide whether you will continue to be the priest here. Now go!' he hissed.

Cuthbert stumbled backwards a few steps, but came up short as he turned to leave. Half the village was there, watching. He saw no support in the faces. Humour? Yes. Grim satisfaction? Yes. Fear? Yes. But support? None. Love? None.

Trying to maintain his dignity, he pushed through them, heading back from whence he'd come, face set in what he hoped was a neutral expression. The murmur of chatter and soft laughter kept him company back to his hut.

Thomas felt his rage abate as he watched the priest's retreating back. 'Wulfstan?' he asked.

'I'm here.' said a clearly shocked Wulfstan. 'Do you fight with every person you meet?'

'No. But I see no reason to tolerate bullying when I'm in a position to stop it. Can you please go and follow that priest creature and see what he gets up to? I don't trust him.' said Thomas.

'On my way.' said Wulfstan, as he floated slowly after the man of God.

Thomas looked around him. The people were watching him with keen interest, glancing to Hengist, and back to him again. He would need to settle things with them before anything else could be done. He sat upright on his horse, and bowed to them.

'Good people,' he said, 'as Hengist confirmed, I am the new owner of the manor. The situation is temporary, and Hengist will continue to run it until it returns to him. I am Prince Wulfstan, son of Offa, King of Mercia. I have a task to complete for the King, that of raising a troop of fighters. This manor will be our base to do that.'

The villagers nodded. One spoke up, a slim, elderly man, face deeply lined, his hair a dirty grey. 'When will they be joining you oh Prince? And where do you want them to stay when they are here?'

Hengist leaned towards Thomas and said 'This is Alfred, the wisest man in the manor. He usually runs the place when I am gone.'

Thomas threw out his left hand. 'I have already found two of them Alfred, these ladies here. Meet Rowena and Berthilda, my companions.'

A round of startled muttering erupted from the villagers. Alfred raised one eyebrow. 'Female warriors Your Highness?'

Thomas met his gaze and smiled. 'Yes indeed my friend. The King and I have a bet. He has challenged me to collect and train ten slave girls, and then beat Thegn Grimketil and his men in mortal combat. Rowena and Berthilda have volunteered to join me.'

The chattering subsided. He could see a number of the men casting appreciative glances over Rowena and Berthilda. That had to be nipped in the bud too, before anyone did something they would regret.

'Ladies and gentlemen of the manor,' he said, 'I wish you all to be quite clear on one thing. Although these two ladies are legally slaves, they are also my chosen companions. They are entitled to bear arms at all times. They are also entitled to be treated with the greatest respect, again at all times. When either of them asks something of you, assume they are asking on my behalf. I will expect you to comply.'

Now there were frowns appearing on some of the faces.

'Your Highness,' said Alfred, 'female warriors are, not common. This is new to us. Slaves ordering freemen and women to do things is also new to us. It is likely mistakes will be made, and misunderstandings to occur. And how will our own slaves behave when they see what rights your companions have? Will this not sow discord in the village?'

Thomas nodded. 'Fair questions Alfred. They will be free women in a year's time, not slaves, so think of them as that if it makes things any easier. Secondly, the villagers are used to doing what you tell them because you are Hengist's representative. This is no different. You can tell by their clothes and their bearing that Rowena and Berthilda have high status. Their hair will grow longer from now on, so they will look more and more free as time passes. There should be no reason for trouble.'

Some of the men were still looking angry and unhappy. Thomas spread out his arms, palms up, and beamed at them. 'My friends, I do not want to impose anything upon the free men and women of this manor that they do not desire.' That generated more head nodding. One of the still grumpy looking men started to open his mouth.

'So, as I wish to be surrounded by people who want to be with me, I will allow any free man or free woman to leave the manor to go and live somewhere else if they have a problem with any of this. I can arrange exchanges with other manors. Just let me know if you wish to do that. You don't have to decide now, you can do it whenever you want.'

There were mouths open now. The grumpy looking one had slammed his shut. Alfred just quietly nodded his head.

Thomas looked around to Hengist. 'Is there anything else you would like to add?'

Hengist nodded towards the horses. 'I think they need to know the responsibility everyone will have to look after the horses.'

'Quite right. Where will they be stabled?'

'Behind the hall. The stables and the barn are both there. There is a field between the stables and the river where they can graze and run before being settled for the night.' said Hengist.

'Can I leave that to you and Alfred?'

'Yes my Lord.'

'Excellent. And where is it best for us to live and to sleep?'

Hengist indicated the two huts immediately to their left.

'These are the guest houses, but perhaps in the circumstances we might be better off all living in the hall? I have one part walled off as my own quarters, but the rest is all one big room. If you would like to go and look things over to see if it's to your satisfaction, Alfred and I will see to the horses and baggage.'

Thomas nodded, and dismounted. He walked to the front of his horse, stroked its nose softly, and tickled it behind the ears. 'I'll come and see you soon, and make sure you are all comfortable and well fed.' The horse nuzzled him gently in return before Hengist led him away.

Thomas addressed himself once more to an astonished Ashlin. 'Do not worry about your tithe. It is either forgiven, or the manor will pay it on your behalf. And do not worry about the future either. Somehow we'll make a space for you and your family.'

Ashlin smiled nervously, and nodded repeatedly. 'Thank you Your Highness! Thank you!'

'You're welcome. Now off you go home and tell your wife and children they can sleep peacefully tonight.'

Ashlin did one more nervous bow, then turned and ran off towards the river. Thomas watched him go, then turned to his companions.

'Rowena and Berthilda, come with me please. Let's look at our new home.'

The three of them walked towards the door of the hall, in front of which was a cluster of young children. Thomas gave them a friendly smile, and said. 'Hello. I'm Prince Wulfstan. What are your names?'

Shyly, a little boy with a fresh scar across his forehead returned the smile and answered, 'I'm Sigeberht. These are Oscar and Oswin my brothers, and these are Grimhild and Gundy, my sisters.'

'Pleased to meet you all.' said Thomas. 'How did you get that scar Sigeberht?'

The boy blushed. 'The priest hit me with his stick because I said a prayer wrong in church.'

Thomas was stunned and shook his head in bewilderment. 'You were reciting a prayer in church. You made a mistake, and Cuthbert hit you across the face with his stick, hard enough to break the skin and leave a scar?'

Frightened, Sigeberht withdrew his hand, and nodded fearfully.

Thomas took a deep breath, and slowly exhaled, trying to calm the fury that was bubbling back up to his lips. He smiled into Sigeberht's face, and gently retook his hand.

'Well then,' he said, 'let's see what we can do about that shall we? I have a task for you and your friends here, to be ready for me to use before breakfast tomorrow. I want you to find and collect one small very dark stone for each person in the village, and one very light stone. I want to make two piles, one very clearly dark stones, and one very clearly light stones. I don't want any confusion as to whether a stone is light or dark. And I mean one for every man, woman, boy and girl over the age of 6 in the village. Include free people and slaves. One light and one dark for everyone. And bring them to me when you have done it. Understood?'

He smiled again, looking into each of the four faces.

'Do you understand?' he asked again.

'Yes sir.' They cried in unison.

'Good. Then off you go! The sooner you start the sooner you finish. Oh, and if your parents ask what you're doing, tell them the Prince has given you a very important job to be done by nightfall.'

He laughed as the five children took off towards the river.

'What are you going to do?' asked Rowena.

'I'm going to give people a lesson in ancient Greek.' grinned Thomas. 'Come on, let's look at this hall.'

7 FOUNDATIONS ESTABLISHED

Wulfstan floated off after the priest, who managed to maintain his dignity all the way back to his hut at the very end of the lane, opposite Ashlin's. Once there however, Cuthbert let loose a string of curses so strong that his two slaves cowered as far away from him as the little building allowed.

The priest picked up a hand axe, and smashed it as hard as he could into a branch stacked next to the open fire in the middle of the room.

'That little runt! Prince or no prince, I know how to deal with him!' he swore as the branch split into two and flew into the darkness. Down the axe came on the next branch which splintered into matchwood. 'I'll kill him!' he seethed.

The female slave gasped.

Cuthbert froze.

Suddenly aware that he had uttered treason in the hearing of others, his whole demeanour changed. The angry uncontrolled rage was kicked aside by the cold blooded knowledge that there was only one way to ensure silence. His grip hardened around the handle of the axe, and he turned to face the cowering woman. He managed a single step before she made a bolt for the door.

'C'mere!' he screamed at her. 'Don't you dare run from your master!'

Skirts flying, mouth open in terror, she burst from the door and into the lane, running as fast as she could, with Cuthbert hard on her heels, his face twisted in fury. Behind him, the male slave slipped quietly out of the door and headed in the opposite direction, west across the fields, and into the forest.

Air searing into her lungs, legs pistoning, the woman knew it wouldn't be enough. He would catch her and that would be that. Cuthbert was equally certain of this, and he was already closing the gap. Other villagers jumped to the side as the pair tore past. Nobody tried to stop her. Nobody tried to save her. Why would they? She was his property and he could do what he liked with her. And he was the priest. Who would go against the one who stood between you and God?

As she approached the hall, five small children ran out across her path, laughing and giggling. She jinked to her left, just missing them, and heard an angry shout from the hall.

'Cuthbert!!!! Leave her alone!!! That's an order!!'

Hope! Maybe there was some! She jinked again, this time to her right, but her foot slipped on the ground and she was down, skidding through the manure that spattered the road surface. Cuthbert's foot thudded into her back, but it wasn't a kick. He'd been caught by surprise, and simply ran into her. In a heartbeat he was face down in the muck himself, cursing and swearing. First to go down, the slave was first to get up too, fear driving her forward. Desperately she looked at the door to the Hall, made up her mind and went for it. Flat out once more, she bounded into the doorway, running straight into a little boy coming out.

Thomas was knocked flying by the impact, and bounced across the room and into the wall.

The woman went tumbling along the floor, coming to a halt just in front of the great fireplace. She rolled onto her back and saw her would be killer bound through the doorway, axe raised high above his head. A shout of triumph erupted from Cuthbert's throat as he rushed forward, eyes fixed upon his prey. She screamed! There was a blur from her left and a body thudded into the priest, knocking him off his feet. The pair of them crashed past the hearth to land on the floor in a jumbled heap. The scream of triumph turned instantly to one of fury. Cuthbert grabbed his assailant's arm with his left hand and forced it to the floor. He raised his right, the axe poised high.

'Halt! Or I'll shoot!' came a cry from behind him. He hesitated. Looking over his shoulder he saw Rowena, bow drawn back, a broadhead arrow pointing straight into his face.

'She means it.' came Thomas's voice.

The world froze for Cuthbert. He looked down to see Berthilda glowering back at him.

'Let me go priest!' she spat. 'If you don't, my friend will end your life in an instant.'

Cuthbert did nothing until he saw Rowena's arms beginning to quiver with the strain of holding the bow, then let the axe fall to the floor. It missed Berthilda's fingers by less than an inch. Eyes still locked, he let her go, and slowly stood up. He didn't offer to help her to her feet. Nor did he apologise.

He looked at Thomas, his clasped hands twisting together. 'It seems my clumsy slave has committed a serious offence by knocking her Prince to the ground. I will take her away and punish her for that, and for the other things she has done this day.'

Without waiting for a reply, he stepped toward the slave woman, who scurried away backwards on her elbows, mouth wide in terror.

'I think not Cuthbert.' came the soft voice of the Prince. 'Please do not touch her, or you will die.'

Cuthbert stiffened. 'Your Highness? She is my property, and my responsibility. She must be taught her duty.'

Thomas shook his head as he walked towards them. Ignoring Cuthbert, he offered his hand to the woman. 'Please. Get up off the floor. It was clearly an accident. You never meant to flatten me.'

The woman stared at him open mouthed, still too terrorised to respond.

'Come lass.' soothed Thomas. 'Nothing will happen to you now. Come. Take my hand and stand up.' He smiled his biggest, warmest smile.

'He was going to kill her Thomas!' cried Wulfstan, finally finding a gap in the conversation.

'I could tell.' said Thomas. 'Why?'

'Because he was swearing and cursing once he got home, and threatening to kill you. I think he was frightened she might tell someone.'

Thomas bent down towards her. 'Why was Cuthbert chasing you so hard my dear?'

In the face of her terrified silence he sighed. 'Come, come. It gets boring looking into an open mouth. Why was he trying to kill you?'

Finally she found her voice. 'He...he...he... said bad things about the Prince. He said he would kill the Prince. He didn't know I was there when he said it. But when he saw me, he came after me with the axe! So I ran!' Tears burst from her eyes.

Thomas looked at Cuthbert. 'Well?' he asked.

'She lies!' hissed Cuthbert. 'She tells lies all the time! She is a useless servant, constantly needing correction!'

'Yes…' murmured Thomas, looking at her carefully. 'A black eye, bruises around the mouth, burns on her upper arms, broken finger nails. Skinny and underfed. Starved even.'

He looked again at the priest, shaking his head in bemusement.

'Just what kind of man of God are you Cuthbert? Do you think violence is the way of our Lord? Do you think that being a priest gives you the right to do anything you like to anyone else? Do you think that to be cruel is to be godly?'

'She is a slave! I can do anything I like to my own slave, even kill her! And that is what I am going to do!' He looked defiantly at them all. 'The law says I can, and there is nothing you can do about it!'

'Yes there is.' said Thomas, so quietly they could hardly hear him. He took out a small purse and removed a coin.

'Here's three times what she is worth if you tried to sell her on the market. I am buying her off you, with immediate effect.' He handed the coin to a mute Cuthbert.

To the woman he said. 'Please get up, and stand behind me.'

She scrambled quickly to her feet, and without taking her eyes off the priest, scooted in behind her new owner.

Cuthbert shook his head helplessly. 'You have no right. Not even a prince can flaunt the law. She is mine. You cannot do this.'

'I can, and I have.' said Thomas firmly. 'And what is more, you are banned from ever owning another slave. For the rest of your life. If I catch you owning a slave in Mercia, I shall deal with you severely.'

Cuthbert scowled, but moved towards the door, his fist twitching towards the slave as he went. She squealed, and cowered further behind Thomas.

'He has a male slave too!' said Wulfstan. 'He ran off into the woods.'

'Wait Cuthbert. I believe you have a male slave also? Here is a coin for him as well. I am buying him from you. If you see him, send him to me.'

Sulkily the priest took the coin and shuffled towards the door once more.

'I'll see you tomorrow Cuthbert.' called Thomas after him.

The priest's back gave away nothing.

Shaking his head, Thomas addressed his new acquisition. 'What's your name miss?'

'Sherelda, Your Highness.' she quivered.

'Well Sherelda, I think we need to get you cleaned up, properly fed, and some new clothes. Rowena and Berthilda, could you please find people to show you where everything is, and see those things are done? I want you both to stay with her at all times between now and when we deal with Cuthbert tomorrow morning. She must be protected every moment until then.'

'Yes Your Highness.' nodded Rowena.

Hengist came running in, panting with the exertion. 'Your Highness! They say Cuthbert went mad and attacked you!'

Thomas rested his hand lightly on Hengist's arm. 'Not me. He was after someone else who just happened to run into me. Do you know Sherelda?'

Hengist stared at the slave woman. 'Not well. She's Cuthbert's slave isn't she? But she was hardly ever out of his hut.'

'I've just bought her from him. Very much against his will I may say. He was intent on killing her because she overheard him threatening to kill me.'

Hengist started. 'No! Surely not? He's not so stupid as that?'

'Just how long has he been priest here Hengist?'

'About two months now.'

'Why did you keep him? He's vile!'

Hengist shrugged his shoulders helplessly. 'The Archbishop himself appointed him, and made it plain that it was an honour for us to have such a dedicated man of God to minister to us. I didn't see how I could go against that.'

Thomas scowled. 'Well I can, but we'll do it fairly tomorrow. In the meantime, for everyone's protection I want Cuthbert placed under an armed guard tonight. He isn't under arrest, and is to be well treated. I just don't want him attacking, or even threatening anyone else until tomorrow. Especially as he's just across the lane from Ashlin and his family.'

'He's gone back into his hut now, and he's very quiet.' said Wulfstan in his ear.

'Not throwing things around the place? Not cursing and swearing? Not threatening anyone?'

'Nope. Quiet as a lamb.'

Hengist called over one of the adults. The man's eyebrows rose a little in surprise at what he was being asked to do, but he nodded and went away at a trot.

'It will be done.' said Hengist.

'Excellent. And the horses? Let's go and see them. Oh, and get someone to bring Cuthbert's male slave to me as well. I've bought him too.'

He and Hengist walked across the courtyard, going down the left side of the barn to the stables.

Rowena, Berthilda and Sherelda walked over to the other side of the barn to where two women were chatting.

Wulfstan rose high above it all and looked over the entire manor. It was set on a peninsula jutting north into a bend in the river. The road they had arrived by, wound up the middle of the peninsula, past a number of huts on both sides, and then into the courtyard, with the hall straight ahead, the barn behind it on the left, and the stables to its right. There was nothing beyond them but the river, a hundred yards north, a grazing meadow in between.

Wulfstan followed the river west, moving upstream past the barn, the kitchen, the village water mill, and a sprinkling of huts, including Ashlin's and the priest's at the very end. Beyond that were strip fields, following the course of the river due west before it turned to the north, skirting the edge of a large wood.

Just this side of the trees, two men were pulling in a wicker basket fish trap. Diving down for a closer look, Wulfstan could see it was a good catch. Someone would eat well tonight.

Turning to look downstream he could see a blacksmith's smithy on the eastern edge of the peninsula, then a quay in the deep water of a left hand bow in the river. Beyond that were more strip fields, and another wood.

At the top of the peninsula, the river grew shallow as it swept around the village. He could see the five children splashing around as they sought out the lightest and darkest pebbles they could find without drowning themselves.

Just down from them, four women were knee deep in the water, washing clothes, chatting and laughing.

'The priest got a good talkin' to didn't he?' laughed one.

'Aye. Deserved it too, the miserable old bully.' scowled a second.

'Hush!' whispered the third. 'He might hear you. They say he has eyes and ears in every hut! And he has no mercy for anyone. He'll send us to hell!'

'Hah!' shot back woman number one. 'He's just a priest, not God himself.'

'He has God's ear, and that's just about as bad.' whispered number three.

'Maybe he has the devil's ear! I don't think he has anything much to say to God.' said the fourth.

Number three looked uncertain and frightened at this, but the other three's laughter was unconstrained.

'Well,' said number two, dunking another shirt into the water 'the Prince has his measure and no mistake. It'll be fun tomorrow I'm thinkin'. I for one hope he gets sent packin'! He's been nothing but misery since he got here. Not like Ceadda the old priest. He were a good un.'

'Well he's dead Maud! We can't have him back.' said number three, savagely wringing out a sock. 'And we have to have someone to do the ceremonies, and pray for us. What'd happen to us with no priest?'

'The Prince will get us another one Deirdre!'

'But what about in between?!' wailed Deirdre. 'What about our souls in between? No last rites, straight to hell. No weekly prayers, straight to hell. No-'

'Oh give it a rest Deirdre! You think God cares more about the ceremonies than about the people they're for. That can't be right!'

'Well that's what Cuthbert says!'

'And it isn't what Ceadda said! Remember poor old Ethel, swept away in the last flood? No last rites for 'er. No body to give 'em to! Ceadda said she'd be safe in God's house because she'd been a good woman, and God would never turn 'er away for want of a few words from him.'

'Well Cuthbert-'

Maud straightened up and put her hands on her hips. 'I don't want to hear another word about what Cuthbert says or thinks! He's an evil minded bully, and as ungodly a man as ever walked the village streets! Understand?' She cocked her head to one side, her expression fierce.

'Yes Maud.' said Deirdre meekly.

They fell into an awkward silence, and the tinkling of the river filled the void.

Between the washerwomen and the smithy, Wulfstan could see Sherelda getting a careful all over wash from Rowena and Berthilda. Each bruise was soaked gently in witch hazel, and she was loosening up, learning to trust these two slaves who were not slaves.

Wulfstan thought of his father's initial challenge.

"And can you hold it boy? Against all comers?" he'd asked.

Well? Could he?

Even to Wulfstan's young mind it seemed a very good target for raiders. With a palisade around the southern end of the peninsula it would have been easy to defend, but there wasn't one. The woods to the east and west meant they might get precious little warning of an attack. Northumberland was ostensibly friendly, and a long way away, but still within raiding range. More to the point, Grimketil was only forty miles south east, close enough for his mounted band to make trouble if he wanted them to.

With that thought in mind, he returned to Thomas, who by now was in the meadow north of the barn and stables.

Hengist, Alfred and Thomas were checking each of the horses carefully, making sure they were all settled and safe in their field. Later on they'd be brought into the stables where they could be guarded overnight, but for now they could run free and eat their fill of grass.

'Alfred.' said Thomas.

'Yes Your Highness?' said Alfred.

'As Hengist's trusted number two, I would normally ask you to dine with me on my first night here, but this situation with Cuthbert changes things. Tomorrow will be intense, and it is vitally important that you of all people are seen by the village to still be your own man. If you dine with me tonight, they'll think you're following my orders.'

Alfred looked at him reproachfully. 'As you wish Your Highness.'

Thomas shook his head. 'No. You don't understand Alfred. I am not snubbing you. I'm trying to protect you from what may happen tomorrow.'

He smiled. 'Look, I tell you what. Why do we not have a feast tomorrow night, with the whole village invited, and you at my table next to Hengist, so everyone can see you still stand tall?'

Alfred nodded uncertainly.

'Then it's agreed. You and Hengist can make the arrangements, since you know what we can afford. Agreed? Good!'

Bored, Wulfstan floated off towards the hall. It was as Hengist had said, a large building with a central fire place, but just the one room. There were benches and tables stacked around the edge, out of the way. At the farthest left hand corner, there actually was another small room, which wasn't just Hengist's private quarters, but contained his treasury, a strongbox with a stout lock into which were placed Wulfstan's own bags of cash.

Right at that moment, the hall was a hive of industry. Men were coming in and out with wood for the fire, the cooks were setting up their spits, women were cleaning and setting out the tables and benches, and two hefty men were setting up the beer barrels on each side of the room.

'Are you really sure you want to do that? The Archbishop will be livid!' Hengist asked as he and Thomas walked in.

'Which is my problem, not yours.' replied Thomas. 'We'll do it after breakfast. Send word to every household that the whole village will meet in the courtyard.'

They were interrupted by the excited arrival of 5 small people wreathed in smiles. Oscar handed over a bag saying 'These are all the light stones Prince Wulfstan!'

Gundy pushed forward proudly with her own bag. 'And these are the dark ones! We thought you might want to check we've done it right so we have time to fix it if we haven't.'

'That's very clever of you.' said Thomas.

The children beamed.

He poured out the stones onto one of the tables, in two piles. The colours were good, and there were the same number of each. 'I need one light and one dark for every person over the age of six in the village, including our own party. Hengist, can you please check that we have enough?'

Hengist counted them out. Or rather he didn't. As he flicked each stone, he said a person's name. At the end he nodded. 'That's right. With a few extras.'

'Good.' said Thomas. Then he pulled Hengist down so he could whisper into his ear. 'But why did you not just count them?'

Hengist looked surprised. 'Because I cannot count Your Highness. Nor read or write. Those are jobs for priests, not men! None of the men in the village can read, write, or count. Except Cuthbert of course. He does the accounts, and reads them to me regularly.'

'Ah yes.' murmured Thomas. 'Auditing the accounts, in action and in deed indeed.' Then he turned back to the children.

'Thank you my friends. Can I offer you a reward by inviting you all to dine with us this evening? You can bring your parents too of course.'

'Yes please!' came five excited voices all at once.

'Then off you go, chop chop!' The thunder of little feet seemed to echo off the walls for a long time after they had run squealing in delight to tell their parents.

'I think you have some loyal subjects there.' said Hengist.

At dinner that night, Thomas sat at the centre of the table, with Hengist to his right, and Rowena and Berthilda to his left. On the other side of the table, their backs to the fire, sat the five children, mother Lynette to their right opposite Rowena and Berthilda, and father Sighard to their left across from Hengist.

Sherelda sat on a bench tending the fire, quietly eating the best food she had ever had in her life. She glanced up at the Prince. Thomas looking between Oscar and Gundy, caught her eye, gave her a smile and raised his cup in salute. Shyly she smiled back, and nodding happily, waved a pigeon breast in reply.

The one person who wasn't there was Cuthbert's male slave Alcott, of whom there was no sign whatsoever.

For much of the meal it was Wulfstan doing the talking, through Thomas to the five siblings. Thomas couldn't relax though. It's hard work being a living ventriloquist's dummy, with a fully working face and body.

Hengist of course already knew Sighard the father, and they talked mostly of the doings of the manor.

Rowena and Berthilda were finding it harder going with the mother. Lynette was struggling to find where the hierarchies lay. Was she socially superior as a free woman? Or were they subordinate to her because they were slaves? Or did a Prince's slave outrank a free woman? Fearful of making a terrible mistake, she tended to say almost nothing at all.

Finally, Thomas leaned over towards her. 'Lynette?'

'Yes Your Highness?' she whispered.

'Rowena and Berthilda are only slaves according to the law. In every way that matters they are free women, like yourself. And at year's end they will be free in law as well. Treat them as equals. There are no status traps here. Just be yourself.'

She looked at him uncertainly, then turned towards her husband for reassurance. Sighard nodded. So did Hengist.

'I am sorry.' she said to Rowena and Berthilda, 'It is difficult to know how to behave.'

Rowena laughed. 'Everything is different with the Prince. As he says, just relax and be yourself. Here, have some of this excellent mutton.' and handed Lynette a choice chunk of rump.

After that, things were much easier all around.

Still acting mainly as Wulfstan's mouthpiece, Thomas had time enough to watch and learn. Oswin and Sigeberht were charismatic, outgoing boys, full of tales of fishing, hunting small game, and of course games.

Oscar, though smiling in all the right places, was mentally somewhere else. He was playing with the crumbs from his trencher, putting them into piles. At first Thomas thought he was just pushing them about, but suddenly he realised the boy was playing a numbers game. There was a pile of three crumbs, then another pile of three, followed by a pile of six, followed in turn by three piles of two each.

'Do you like numbers Oscar?' he asked.

Startled, Oscar looked up guiltily, and shot a glance at Gundy. Thomas noted for the first time that she was following along. She blushed.

'Nothing to be embarrassed about.' said Thomas. 'Tell me what you're doing.'

Sigeberht sighed, looked skywards like any big brother would, but he was smiling.

Oscar grinned sheepishly, and then started to explain. He pointed to the two piles of three. 'If I take these piles, and put them together, then they become the same size as this larger pile.' He pointed to the pile of six.

'And?'

Gundy leant across Sigeberht and pointed to the three piles of two. 'And if you push these piles into one big pile, that makes the same sized pile too!' She looked at Thomas, her face deadly serious.

Thomas nodded. 'Which means?'

Oscar butted back in 'It means that these piles on the left, the pile in the middle, and the piles on the right are all the same, even though they're different!'

'Excellent! said Thomas. 'Now, do you know what numbers they represent?'

Gundy's face fell. 'No. The priest says numbers aren't for little girls.' Her bottom lip trembled with indignation. 'But he wouldn't tell Oscar either!! He said only priests should know, and threatened to hit him if he asked again!'

Thomas laughed. 'Not true! I shall teach you myself.'

'Really?!' cried Gundy and Oscar in unison.

'Certainly. Let's do a little bit right now. See here.' and he took a pile of breadcrumbs himself.

'We start with nothing.' he pointed to an empty space on the table. 'And we call that zero.'

Oscar frowned. 'Why do you care about nothing?'

'If you sit down to dinner and have one loaf of bread put in front of you, but I take it away. What do you have?'

'Nothing.'

'And surely you want to know if you have something to eat or not, yes? See? You do care about nothing!'

Gundy nodded uncertainly.

Thomas put a single bread crumb to the right of the nothing space, and added nine more piles in order. 'Then we have one, followed by two, three, four, five, six, seven, eight, nine and ten.'

They nodded, faces keen with concentration. Even Sigeberht was paying attention now, and for the first time Grimhild was in on it too.

'So, looking at your piles Oscar, how many crumbs are in each of these piles?' he asked, pointing to Oscar's left.

'Three.' said Oscar slowly.

'And how many piles of three do you have?'

'Two!' shouted Gundy.

Thomas laughed again. 'So two piles of three make how much?' he asked, pointing to the middle pile.

Oscar looked at him carefully, then at the ten different piles. 'Six?'

'That's right. Well done.'

Oscar beamed.

'Now, how many piles do you have here?' he said, pointing to the piles between Oscar and Gundy.

'Three!' said Gundy excitedly.

'And how many crumbs in each pile?'

'Two!' they cried simultaneously.

'So three piles of two, also equal six. True?'

They nodded eagerly.

Thomas paused, until he had their full attention. 'So, if two piles of three equals six, and three piles of two also equal six . . .' he paused again to make sure they were fully engaged. 'That means that two times three equals three times two. True?'

Oscar frowned. 'But we already knew that.'

'You knew all three were the same, now you know what to call them. And you are also beginning to learn how numbers can be moved around, to let you do things in different ways.'

Sigeberht grimaced, 'But what use is that?'

'Well we're just playing with very small numbers now. How did you know you had the right number of stones today?'

'We listed all the people, just like Hengist did.' said Sigeberht.

'So you needed to know every single person in the village, plus us new comers before you could do that. Right? Now what would have happened if I had asked Berthilda here to collect the right number of stones?'

'She'd have to ask someone for help.'

'Right. But I now know that there are one hundred and eighty three people in the village. So if I tell Berthilda to collect one hundred and eighty three dark stones, and she knows how to count, then she can just go and do it. She doesn't need to know every single person. She just needs the number, and to know how to get there.'

'So numbers let you do things?' asked Gundy.

'Oh yes!' smiled Thomas. 'Let me show you what you can do with a bit of string and a few knots!'

Which took care of the next half hour.

Later on, after everyone else had gone to their own homes, and the women were making ready for bed, Hengist managed to get Thomas on his own. 'May I ask you something Your Highness?'

'Of course Hengist. Anything you like.'

'Who taught you your numbers? I don't remember anyone at court teaching you numbers.'

Thomas looked into Hengist's face. For once it was hard to read. He thought quickly. 'Nobody taught me Hengist. I listened to the clerics doing the palace accounts, and learned the basics from that. And I watched the builders and the stone masons at their work. But that bang on the head you gave me seems to have given me a lot more understanding for some reason. Perhaps a divine gift?'

Hengist returned his gaze, his own face still revealing nothing of his thoughts. 'Quite a gift.' he said simply.

There being just the one room, the bedding was arranged around the fire. One room for everyone, and one room for every function. There was virtually no privacy, not even for the most personal activities, but nobody much bothered about it. It was normal.

The word normal really just means, "That which me and mine do, most of the time." Nobody in the hall except for Thomas had ever had any privacy, and you don't miss what you've never had. Thomas just had to keep telling himself that!

Soon the hall was dark, with only the cacophony of sleeping humans to disturb the mice as they frolicked happily in the straw.

8 A MATTER OF CHOICE

The following morning saw the entire village assemble at the riverside, just upstream of the laundry.

Thomas oversaw the erection of two curving, parallel lines of brushwood fencing across the very top of the peninsula. The idea was that people would enter from the downstream end, do their voting in the middle where they couldn't be observed, and then leave by the upstream end.

The villagers were all assembled on its landward side, but to their puzzlement, the Prince had arranged them into groups. Facing the river, at the far left were the adult men. To their right were the adult women, then all the children, followed by the slaves at the extreme right.

Wulfstan had zipped around the perimeter of the manor, over two miles out from where the voting was being held because Thomas had asked him to check that there were no bandits or other miscreants lurking, ready to make mischief. There weren't so Thomas brought all the guards into the voting area so they too could have their say.

Thomas stood facing the villagers, Cuthbert and Hengist to his left. He raised his arms in welcome. 'Good people, thank you for coming. This morning,' he paused to glance sideways at a defiant Cuthbert, 'you will decide whether you want to keep your priest, or you will tell me that you want a new one.'

Cuthbert scowled at him, but said nothing.

'I arrived only yesterday, as you know. The very first thing I saw was Cuthbert beating a starving man. Less than half an hour later he was trying to kill a woman in my own hall, and in between I met a child that he'd beaten on the face for a trivial mistake during prayers.'

He paused again.

'I find these behaviours at odds with what I expect from a priest, but, I've been here less than a day, while you've had the pleasure of his company for a full two months. So I will be guided by your collective wisdom regarding what should be done. Today you will vote.' and so saying, he waved for two barrels to be brought in and placed between himself and the villagers.

'Each of these barrels is empty, and sealed, except for a single small hole in the top. Cuthbert, would you please examine the barrels and confirm to your satisfaction that they are just as I described?'

A highly suspicious Cuthbert examined each one carefully. He tried to open the tops and the bottoms. He checked for loose staves. Eventually he nodded his agreement.

'Thank you Cuthbert. The first barrel will be placed in the middle of the brushwood lane behind me. There is a cutout at the bottom of the brushwood so you can see that it is not interfered with in any way. The other barrel will be put close to the upstream end of the path. Each of you will be given a light coloured pebble, and a dark coloured pebble. One at a time you will walk through the path until you get to the barrel in the middle. If you want him to stay, you drop in the light pebble. If you think he should leave, you drop in the dark pebble. The remaining pebble, you drop into the barrel at the upstream end. When everyone has dropped their stones, the brushwood will be pulled aside, and the stones in the middle barrel counted. If there are more light than dark, he stays. If there are more dark than light, he goes.'

He paused once more. 'Any questions?'

He took his time, and looked carefully around the crowd, catching an eye here and there, but nobody said a word.

'Well, I've said that I didn't like what I saw, but it's only fair that Cuthbert be given the chance to say how he sees things. Cuthbert?'

Chin held high, Cuthbert glared out at those who would now judge him. 'I was specially chosen to be your priest, by the Archbishop of Canterbury himself. If you cast me out, you will be going directly against his wishes, and he will be very angry!'

There were ripples and murmurs in the crowd at this. Scenting blood, Cuthbert continued, his voice becoming more strident. 'He sent me to bring some discipline amongst you, and to beat it into you if necessary! I was dismayed to find you needed t so badly. If I have been harsh and beaten some of you, it has been only for your own good. That is what I have been sent here to do! If you throw me out, the devil himself will take hold of this village, without me to see him off!'

The murmurs now broke out into hushed, but intense chatter as people debated what had been said. Cuthbert's words had clearly struck fear into some of them at least. He allowed himself a smile of triumph.

Thomas held up his hand for silence. 'Thank you Cuthbert. You raise three good points. Let me address them in turn.' He raised his right hand, first finger extended and brought it down onto his left palm.

'Discipline means control over one's self. You cannot teach a person, or even an animal discipline if you lack it yourself. You are the most undisciplined man I have met outside an outlaw band! You lose your temper at the drop of a hat, and then you lash out at whoever is near you, using the word discipline to cover your own wickedness. All you've actually instilled to date is fear.'

Cuthbert was actually quivering with fury. His face bright red in indignation, his pupils mere slits.

'Secondly,' continued Thomas, not taking his gaze off him for a second, 'Given the behaviour I have seen in less than a day, you don't so much keep the devil out, as invite him in and give him bed and board! So I very much doubt the village is at risk in that regard, if we dispense with your services.'

Cuthbert had gone past red now, and was chalk white.

'Thirdly, the Archbishop may indeed allocate a priest to a parish, but the parish can decide if it wants to keep him. And if the Archbishop disagrees, then he can debate it with me directly, not the villagers. Do you have anything else to say?'

Speaking through clenched teeth, Cuthbert managed to get out 'You have no right to do any of this! The slave is mine and I can do what I want to a slave, even kill her if I want to! I did not choose to sell her to you, you took her! The tithe is a Church right, not yours, and you have no right to usurp that either! And Church prayers are my domain, not yours. You are trespassing on the Church's rights, on God's rights, and your soul will be damned for it!'

Thomas put a gentle smile on his face. It was a good attempt, but it didn't fool anyone. 'Slaves are a temporal matter, not ecclesiastic. The

King has given me the right to buy any slave I want from anyone, as part of my challenge. I chose yours and you have been paid three times her worth. I am within my rights. Sherelda is mine now.' He glanced across to her, where she was standing proudly between Rowena and Berthilda. For the first time she didn't look fearful. She even looked determined. Thomas continued.

'The tithe is indeed the Church's right, and who said you would be deprived of it? I just said Ashlin didn't have to pay it. The manor will pay his tithe on this occasion. The Church will lose nothing.'

'Lastly, prayers may indeed be your domain, but when you strike my people, that is my affair, and I take exception to it.'

He paused once more for effect, cocking his head to the right. 'So, I think we can say that none of your rights have been infringed to date. In fact you've actually made money on the deal!'

He shook his head in mock amusement. 'Anything else you'd like to say?'

Cuthbert scowled and shook his head. 'Do your worst!'

The chatter of the crowd broke out once more. Thomas immediately put up his hand and commanded silence.

'There will be no talking at all, between now and when all the stones have been cast. I will have complete silence until then. Do you understand?'

The crowd was a kaleidoscope of emotion. There was a lot of nodding going on, a few smiles and grins, a smattering of anxiety, and a cluster of deep frowns, but silence was maintained.

'Good. Thank you. We will vote in order. The slaves will each vote, one at a time. They can make their own call, and nobody will direct their slave as to how to vote, nor will they afterwards demand that their slave tell them how they cast their vote.'

He fixed the crowd with gimlet eyes. 'I am deadly serious about this. If I find any person coercing their slave on this matter, I will throw them out of the village. Do not try me!'

'Next will be the children, everyone between six and ten years of age, followed by the women, and lastly the men. Understand?'

Alfred raised his hand.

'Yes Alfred?'

'Your Highness, are we to understand that in this process a slave's vote caries the same weight as a child's, which is the same as a woman's, which is the same as a free man's? This is not our way. Surely only the free men should vote on such a serious matter as this?'

The silence was maintained, but there were many vigorous nods amongst the men.

Thomas bowed slightly. 'Another excellent question, as I am learning to expect from you Alfred. I understand what you're saying, but on this matter, everyone has a stake. The priest's power allows him to isolate the most vulnerable members of our community, be they man, woman or child, free or slave. Abuses can be easily hidden away, and covered up in such a situation. You free men are less exposed to the bullying, so you don't experience what it is like yourselves. Indeed, you probably have no idea what your women, children and slaves have been exposed to. How could they tell you?'

He stood erect and still. Alfred looked at him calmly, for what seemed an age. Then he nodded his assent. 'I see your point Your Highness.'

Many of the men took their lead from Alfred, but some were still shaking their heads, their faces unhappy.

Thomas relaxed. 'Good. Then let us begin. Slaves first!'

An old man stepped forward out of the slave group, accepted his light and dark stone from the guard, and stepped into the path. Everyone could see his lower legs when he got to the voting barrel. There was a short pause, then a loud echoing thunk, as the pebble hit the wooden bottom of the empty barrel. They watched his legs depart to the other end, where they heard another echoey thunk before he appeared out the other end. The guard there pointed him to an area well away from those who still had to vote.

Sherelda was next, stepping deliberately out from between Rowena and Berthilda. She didn't even bother to look at Cuthbert. She just walked quickly through, dropping her stones without even stopping at the barrels. Rowena and Berthilda followed just as swiftly, leaving her alone for as little time as possible.

It took just under two hours to get the one hundred and eighty odd people through the voting process. When it was over, they all walked back to the starting point, but this time as a village, in family groups and not in the voting blocks.

The brushwood was carefully taken away and the voting barrel brought out. The top was prised free, the wax seal being checked first to see it had not been tampered with. Then the stones were emptied onto a cloth covered table.

'Gundy and Oscar? Can you come here please?'

Brother and sister ran out from the crowd.

Thomas commanded 'Please sort the pebbles out into one pile of light and one pile of dark. Make sure you keep all the stones visible to everyone, and keep your hands above the table at all times so people can see them until the two piles are ready.'

Cuthbert looked on keenly. Although dismayed, because right from the start the pile of white was visibly smaller than the pile of dark, he had an ace up his sleeve.

'When they are finished Your Highness, I will count them for you, so you know the numbers.' he smiled warmly.

'No need Cuthbert.' grinned Thomas. 'I can count them myself.'

Cuthbert blinked. 'Your Highness?'

A huge laugh erupted from Thomas. 'You're not the only one here who can count Cuthbert! I have a far better knowledge of mathematics than you do.'

Thomas proceeded to demonstrate that mastery as soon as the children had finished. He created little piles of ten, keeping them visible to the crowd throughout, then added them up quickly to get the totals.

'Well Cuthbert, I make it one hundred and fifty two dark, and thirty one light. Time to go I think. Unless you think I have added them up incorrectly.'

Cuthbert was thunderstruck, the shock visible on his face.

'We'll look after you properly Cuthbert." said Thomas. You'll have a hand cart to carry your things. We'll give you some cash to safely cover your journey to wherever you want to go from here. And we'll give you plenty of food to take with you.'

Cuthbert shook his head. 'I'll need a slave, or at least an animal to carry my goods.'

'No Cuthbert.' said Thomas sadly. 'I've seen how you treat those in your power. You shall have no slave, and you shall have no animals either. I imagine you would be even crueller with animals than you are with people, so I cannot agree to that. That's why you'll get a good hand cart.'

Cuthbert began to expostulate, but Thomas held up his hand. 'I'm not going to debate this point Cuthbert. You get a handcart, and you will push it yourself. Hengist? Take Alfred and two others, to help Cuthbert to pack his belongings, then see him on his way please.'

Hengist gently took Cuthbert by the shoulder, the crowd parted, and the priest was led away. Only once he was out of sight did the hubbub of conversation break out, and this time Thomas let it run.

Wulfstan floated to and fro amongst them, listening to the chatter. The children were running around in delight laughing and chanting.

The priest did hit, the priest did smite.
The priest did spit and said t'was right.
The Prince said no, let there be light.
Now Cuthbert's gone, clear out of sight!

Again and again the verse sang out until one of the adults waved them gently away to play down by the river.

'Who came up with that Wulfstan?' asked Thomas.

'Grimhild. She's really good at verse.'

'Very impressive. In fact the whole family is impressive, each in their own way.'

Thomas glanced around. His eyes fell on the one group that didn't look at all happy, a small knot of 8 young men. They stood close together, faces frowning, brows furrowed, heads shaking and nodding alternately. He walked over to them.

'Gentlemen, you seem to be vexed about something. Please, feel free to say what you feel.'

One looked at him suspiciously. 'I am Fulton, and with respect Your Highness, we do not wish to say anything that might upset you. We have seen what can happen to those who do.' The man dropped his eyes to the ground.

'Oh come now Fulton. Alfred has asked me some very hard questions, both yesterday and today. But they were good questions, asking about important things that needed to be discussed openly. I now trust, admire, and respect Alfred as a man who will always tell me the truth, or challenge me when he thinks I may be wrong.'

'It's true that I don't think much of Cuthbert, but I let the village make that decision, not me. And I let each person do it secretly so they could safely do what they felt was right, without fear.'

Still looking at the ground Fulton mumbled 'That's why we are unhappy. It shouldn't have been everyone. It should just have been the free men making the decision.'

He raised his head, a mixture of caution and belligerence confusing his face. 'It took away our authority. It took away our respect.' His voice rose a little. 'It took away our manhood, and our rights as men! Imagine letting a woman have the same vote as a man!'

Thomas interrupted. 'This is Mercia, not Northumbria. Women in Mercia have always had rights of speech, rights of property, protected under law, and our kingdom is the richer for their contribution.'

The head dropped again. 'Perhaps so, perhaps not.' Fulton begrudged. 'But you also let the slaves and children do it too! Shocking! What if the slaves expect now to have a say in everything? How will we control them? We'll have nothing but trouble from now on!'

Thomas nodded. 'I understand your worry, but this matter was about people's souls. You own your slave's bodies. You don't, and never will own their souls. Everyone has responsibility for their own soul. All I did was let them have the power to exercise that responsibility.'

The man said nothing.

Thomas shrugged his shoulders. 'Well, I am sorry you are so vexed. Perhaps you could grant me the same time you granted Cuthbert, to see if I will measure up to your expectations in other ways? And if not, I have given you your remedy. You can leave anytime you like. I'll make the arrangements to swap you with someone from another manor somewhere.'

The answer snapped back instantly, catching Thomas by surprise. 'I accept! When can we make it happen?'

'Well,' said Thomas, thinking quickly, 'does anyone else want to join you? I need to know the numbers involved before I start talking to other manor owners, so as to guarantee you a livelihood and a home. But,' he paused for effect, 'if you are so vexed that you don't want to wait for that, you have my permission to leave immediately. I won't stand in your way. You're a free man after all. I just ask that you tell me the day before you leave that you are doing so. Then I can give your house to someone who wants it.'

'Ha!' spat Fulton. 'I can't afford that and you know it! I'd never be able to get another home. I'd have to sell myself into slavery, and what good would that do me?'

Thomas looked up at the cross face. He was tired of looking at cross faces. It seemed like he'd been looking at cross faces since he arrived in this world, and he'd had enough. He looked around at the others. He put his hand in his pocket and brought out a handful of coins. 'Here's enough money for a year's worth of food. Pack your things and go.'

He put the coins into the man's unprotesting hands.

The man made no move.

'Well? Off you go. You'll want as much daylight as possible I imagine.'

He addressed the others. 'Anyone else want to accept the same offer?' He held out another handful of coins.

They all shook their heads vigorously.

Fulton still stood there bemused, staring at more money than he'd ever had in his life. Thomas patted him gently on the arm. 'Well, your time is your own now my friend. I guess you can do what you want with it. Just be out of the manor by tonight. There's probably someone else who can make good use of your hut.'

He turned to go, but Fulton had found his voice again.

'Your Highness? May I change my mind?' his face was creased with worry, as the reality of being alone in the world with a year's worth of money but no friends came crashing in on him.

'I'll think about it.' Thomas called back over his shoulder. 'Come and talk to me again around mid-afternoon and tell me what you want to do.'

And off he walked towards the rest of the village, who were laughing and chattering. Within a couple of minutes he'd brushed the belligerents from his mind.

Said belligerents themselves started to mingle with everyone else. Slowly they began to thaw, and seven of them were soon laughing along with everyone else.

Only Fulton stayed on the periphery. He felt on the outer because he'd asked to leave and not only had he been allowed to, but he was actually being paid to go. Did the money mean he was worth that much a year? Or did it mean the Prince thought it was worth that amount of money just to be rid of him? Most worrying of all, the Prince hadn't even tried to convince him to stay.

Sadly he turned away from the throng, and made his way back to his hut, where he began to pack his few possessions. It didn't take long because he didn't own very much. He came out of his door just as Hengist, Alfred and Cuthbert were coming past.

'What's up Fulton?' asked Hengist.

Fulton explained.

Cuthbert perked up at once. 'Put your things on the cart my friend, and we'll go and see the Archbishop together.'

With a weak smile Fulton did as he had been asked, and found himself pushing Cuthbert's handcart up the road, while the priest walked along unencumbered. A few minutes saw the pair of them out of the village and on their way. The priest had found his beast of burden after all.

Thomas and Wulfstan watched them go.

'That does however give me a problem.' said Thomas.

'Surely you'll have no trouble getting another priest?' asked Wulfstan.

'The Archbishop may try and make trouble over that, but that isn't the issue. The problem is, the only person in the manor who can read, write, and use numbers is now me! I need people who can read and write, but I also need to be out finding the rest of the girls and training them. I don't see how I can do both.' His brow furrowed in concern.

'I thought you could do anything?' muttered Wulfstan sarcastically.

'Not all at once I can't!' shot back Thomas. 'I'm going to need to find some help, and be quite creative about it I think.'

That night a huge party was held in the hall, with plenty of beer, and enough food to make everyone happy.

Alfred sat by the Prince's left hand, and Thomas made a point of talking with him at length, to show to the whole of the manor that Alfred had his trust and respect.

Ashlin was at a table close by, with his wife Maeve looking radiant. The stress of the last two months under Cuthbert's baleful watch was still evident on her face, but the relief of his departure, and the Prince himself begging her not to worry about the future, because it would all be sorted out, had washed most of it away. In fact she was washing a bit more of it away right now, drinking some of the beer that Thomas himself had put into her hands.

Wulfstan was once more doing duty on guard. He'd followed Cuthbert and Fulton a few miles down the road, marvelling at how far his thin cord let him go. He still hadn't found a point where he couldn't go on if he wanted to.

During the day he'd watched the preparations being made for the evening feast. And at Thomas's request, he'd spent a bit of time around the seven malcontents, to see how things sat with them.

Thomas had placed them at a good table, not far from his own, and throughout the evening he made a point of going over to drink toasts with them. By the end of the evening, they were going to be very merry, in every sense of the word.

Just before the feast had started, Wulfstan had done a complete search around the manor, this time out to a three mile radius. He'd done it on the far side of the river too, just to make sure. Halfway through the feast he was out there doing another check.

Job done, he swooped up high into the sky. It was a fine night, a gibbous moon, plenty of stars, and just the odd scattered cloud about. He delighted in the river, a silvery ribbon winding its way through the landscape.

He flew around and through a little cloud. Surprised at how cold it was, he was out again quickly, and soon warming himself in the hall.

Humming happily to herself, Sherelda was once more tending the fire, a trencher of good food at her side, and a goblet of fine beer sheltering from the heat of the blaze behind a large stone. A smile of peace and tranquillity sat permanently on her face, the kind of smile found only on those who have suffered deeply, and know that they are now safe and loved.

She looked over at the Prince, and Wulfstan could swear he could see a very slight golden glow around her as she did so. There was something about the quality of its light that reminded him of something, but he couldn't think what.

9 NEW WAYS AND MEANS

The next four days were very busy for Thomas.

Religion being as important as it was at that time, getting a temporary priest had to be the top of his agenda if he was to avoid having a rebellion on his hands. He sent Hengist to the next manor up the river to arrange things, while he tackled the blacksmith.

The smithy was on the eastern side of the peninsula, with a water wheel to drive the bellows, something that really impressed Thomas. Between it, the stables and the barn, was a large animal enclosure. Theoretically this kept everything close enough to work easily, but far enough apart to manage the fire risk from the forge. However, there were two huts right next to it, running up the side of the animal enclosure towards the hall, which did somewhat make a mockery of that idea.

The first thing he checked out was the smelting process used to extract iron from bog ore. It was the normal way of the age, although this blacksmith was unusual in doing it himself. A mixture of charcoal was burned in a primitive kiln, the required temperature being achieved by air being blasted into it by leather bellows driven by the water wheel.

Smashed up pieces of iron ore fished out of the bogs were dropped into the blaze, and heated as hot as the fire could go. Even with the water wheel bellows, it was nowhere near enough to melt the iron into liquid form, but after many hours of work, and a huge amount of charcoal, he got a bloom, a small lump of iron still full of impurities and useless for anything. The smith had to reheat it in the forge again until it was red hot, then smack it with hammers to drive out as many of those impurities as possible. Then he did it again, and again, and again for as long as he had to. The sparks from the hammer blows showed his progress in knocking out the slag and impurities, but with every blow the bloom got smaller. The process did eventually produce iron, but very little for the time and energy spent, and the quality ranged from okay to dreadful. Thomas wanted high quality steel for swords, and iron for ploughs and other implements. This simply would not do.

With wooden roof shingles serving as paper, and charcoal as his pencil, Thomas sketched out a design for a small blast furnace lined with clay. It would be sealed at the top to trap in far more heat than the smith's existing design, but the clay itself was just as critical. It would reflect the heat off the furnace walls, back into the furnace instead of losing it through the bricks.

He also designed some clay crucibles to hold the iron ore separate, away from the charcoal. With trial and error, and a bit of luck, he hoped they could make crucible steel. If they were successful, it would give him an edge in every possible sense.

Smith, for that was his name, at once saw the principle of the thing. He and his apprentice Buck began at once to collect the required materials to build the new furnace. Thomas swore them to secrecy on all aspects of their work, stressing that it would make them all rich within five years. Every smith was used to keeping their little secrets, such as the right colours to look for when working with the hot metal. There would be no problem there.

Next he met with Ashlin to find out what skills the man had. As a peasant farmer, Ashlin could turn his hand to most work, but he seemed to have a real flair for wood. Thomas was hugely impressed with the quality of the tools and furniture that Ashlin had made for himself.

He'd also found that there was nobody in the village who could make a really good bow. Oh there were the usual cheap and nasty home made hunting bows around the place, but nothing like what he was after.

'I need a short but powerful bow, so my warriors can use them on horseback.' he told Ashlin.

'It can't be done.' said the man. 'A Welsh bow is too long to use easily on a horse, and a short one will break when you pull it.'

'Ah.' said Thomas. 'I have a trick to show you!'

They worked together to choose a piece of wood which was short and strong, but already curved.

'If it is already bent, it will be too weak.' observed Ashlin.'

'No it won't.' said Thomas. 'We bend it the other way, against the curve.'

'Then it will break.' said Ashlin quietly.

'Normally yes,' said Thomas, 'but we're going to stick plates of animal horn on the front of the bow, the part facing the archer. They will resist the compression as the bow curves, and stop the wood on the inside from being crushed. We're also going to stick animal tendons on the back of the bow, the bit facing the target. They're a lot more stretchy than the wood and so will add more power, while stopping the wood from being torn apart. It's a composite bow, made of three different things, each material bringing its own kind of strength to support the others. It will be short enough, and strong enough to use on horseback.'

Ashlin pursed his lips in doubt. 'I don't know Your Highness. It sounds good, but whether or not it will work…'

Thomas knew full well it would work, as this was exactly the kind of bow the Mongol Horde would use when they swept out of Asia in the centuries to come.

'Well,' he said, 'we're going to give it a try. The key will be finding the right glue, and we'll have to play around with that. Don't use any of the best materials until you and I have agreed which glue we'll use. Play around with the lower grade wood, horn and sinew. If we can make the idea work with that, it'll work with the top quality stuff too.'

Secrecy was once more imperative, so Thomas moved Ashlin and his family from their house at the western end of the village, into the hall. He partitioned off the right rear corner for them to live and work in until the hall could be extended to include a proper home for them.

That left Thomas with three more big items to address. The productivity of the farm, public health, and administration. At the moment, almost everybody's time was spent either getting food or staying warm. He couldn't do anything with them until he'd freed up some of their time, and knew how much he had to play with. But none of that was worth anything if people were constantly getting sick and dying.

Sewage borne diseases like cholera were a huge killer in the dark ages, and they worried Thomas greatly. Fortunately, he got the perfect opportunity to tackle them the day after Cuthbert's departure.

Pee wasn't a problem because it was already collected for the tanner and the cloth fullers. However, the other, shall we say, more solid matter, was of great concern. His opening to discuss it came while he, Hengist, Alfred, and two other influential men were inspecting the river bank upstream. One of the peasant farmers walked out of the wood and down to the water's edge. There he dropped his pants, squatted down and did his business into the shallow flowing water.

This was perfectly normal behaviour so Hengist and the others didn't bat an eyelid.

Thomas pointed to the fishermen tending their baskets just thirty yards downstream. All this did was generate four blank stares, so Thomas walked upstream, picked up a flat lump of wood and fished out the man's leavings so they were perched on the end of it. Then he got a fresh fish from the fishermen, and opening its mouth dropped the man's business down its throat. Smiling broadly, he offered it to Alfred, who wrinkled his nose in disgust.

'Dinner for you and your lovely wife tonight!'

Alfred recoiled. 'Your Highness? I can't eat that with what's now inside it! Surely you don't really mean for us to actually eat that?' he pleaded.

'But Alfred,' smiled Thomas sweetly, 'what's the difference between this and any other fish you eat except that your eyes know what is inside this one? Surely every fish in the river has somebody's business inside it if people are allowed to use the river as their toilet? It's just that you don't see it, so you don't worry about it, but it's there in every single mouthful. No wonder so many of you die of sickness!'

Alfred had to admit that it seemed a fair point, but asked the obvious question. 'But if we are not to use the river, what are we to use? We can't just do it on the side of the road, or in the fields! The river takes it away for us.'

So Thomas taught them how to make a twin pit, pour flush toilet. Being people of the land, they understood it very quickly. They also understood him to be deadly serious when he said that anyone found using the river as a toilet from that day on was to be given a fish for their dinner like the one Thomas had handed Alfred.

Alfred promised that the first of the toilets would be completed within a week. In the meantime, people were instructed to collect their waste and deposit it in a hole dug into a depression on a piece of scrubby land on the edge of the forest, well away from the houses.

There were some grumbles about this, but the threat of a stuffed fish supper was enough to ensure they obeyed. One thing they were certain of, the Prince followed through on any threats he made. Nobody wanted him to follow through after they themselves had followed through. So they didn't.

Next he got them to wonder what flies had been walking on before they landed on their breakfast. The idea of a fly going from poo to bread was enough on its own for the village to start a fly eradication program. It also made it a lot easier to get them to start washing their hands, which made almost as big an impact as the new toilets.

He followed that by tackling malaria, the biggest killer of them all, by showing them how many eggs a single mosquito could lay, and asking them how often they were bitten. Without him even asking, they started to fill in all the puddles, and actively hunt out and destroy the larvae. He never even mentioned malaria, knowing they'd never believe him, because they believed disease was caused by bad smells. After all, the word malaria itself meant bad air, and it would be a hard slog to get them to change their minds on that.

So, with good progress being made against disease, he turned his attentions to the farm itself. He introduced the idea of four crop rotation to increase food production and supply enough fodder to keep the animals over winter. The extra cows would give milk, butter and cheese throughout the dark months to keep the villagers healthy, and would kick start the following year.

It would all take time to work of course, and the right types of turnips from the land of the Franks, but the farmers could see the sense of it. Thomas started his own land on the system, and let the other farmers decide what they wanted to do themselves. In the meantime, he'd have to order extra supplies from the palace market to be delivered, so they'd have enough food to see the animals through the first winter. Thank heavens the last year's harvest had been excellent, and thank goodness too for the King's money!

He kept silent about his future plans for new ploughs, seed drills and harvesters, all to be pulled by horses instead of oxen. Then he'd really make hay, but he was aware that all of these would be perceived as taking away the villagers' jobs, and their ability to feed themselves. With that would come rage and rebellion, so he had to make sure he created more appealing jobs for everyone before the machines were introduced. That would take some thinking through.

Wulfstan had watched all this with growing fascination. Thomas had answered every question he'd asked, and even a few that he hadn't asked, which was disconcerting!

But Wulfstan had been useful too. He'd flown out and found the right kind of clay for the smith's furnace, which saved Thomas weeks of searching. He'd managed to search out useful fields for demonstrating the ideas behind crop rotation, and of course he regularly flew reconnaissance circuits around the manor to check for bandits and other raiders.

Rowena and Berthilda spent a lot of this time practicing their archery and their riding.

Sherelda went along to watch them ride, helped out during archery practise by collecting the arrows, but took on a much more active role when it came to practicing with the swords. Thomas hadn't suggested that she become one of his warriors, but something he'd said had resonated deep within her.

"Teach her how to use a blade too. She may need it if she ever sees Cuthbert again."

She replayed his words again and again in her mind, and determined that the next time she saw Cuthbert, she'd be prepared. Every free moment she had, was spent practicing with a sword, slashing and stabbing into bundles of straw, building her muscles, quickening her reactions.

The villagers tried to get on with their normal day to day chores, but novelty was not a normal part of life for these people, and there had been plenty of novelty! The whole populous was chattering and gossiping from dawn to dusk, and almost all of it was happy, cheerful, and optimistic.

That was good news for Thomas, but he knew these were the easy times, the honeymoon. Things were bound to hit the odd rough patch, and then the resistance which for now had gone to ground, would come back into their hearts and minds. Lots of on going little benefits were the answer. That, and the promise of opportunities they had never dreamed of having.

Which was where administration came in.

Almost the only people who could read and write in this age were in the Church. That had come about after the fall of the Roman Empire, when most educated people reverted to simply struggling to survive, or died. Pretty soon the only places where reading and writing survived, were within the protecting walls of the monasteries. So when rulers needed administrative expertise, the only place they could turn to was the Church.

It would become the lynch pin of the Church's temporal power in Europe. Already hierarchical in nature and well organised, the Church was perfectly poised to influence every royal house on the continent. They had a place at every head table, and knew the financial, political, and all the other kinds of affairs going on in each kingdom.

Thomas by now had worked out that the year was probably 781. He also knew that Offa's relationship with the Archbishop of Canterbury was already tense, and that if this history followed his own, that relationship was soon going to get very nasty indeed when Offa pushed for a third archbishopric in a few years time.

Across the English Channel he knew that Leo the third would become Pope in 795 and that he would set out to make the Church the single greatest power across the whole of Europe. Leo's goal would not just be spiritual dominance, but to have control over every aspect of life in Europe. Everyone from kings to slaves would be under his influence. Perhaps for Leo it really was done with the best of intentions, or perhaps it was simply a lust for power. Only Leo himself knew for certain, but either way, Thomas knew what it would lead to in the future. In the near term it would seriously get in the way of what he wanted to achieve himself.

More immediately, Wulfstan had declined Jaenberht's offer to join the Church, and despite the Archbishop's grace in accepting his refusal, Thomas knew it would have irritated the cleric. He also suspected that future, less easy to decline invitations were already being worked on.

Plus of course, he had just ejected his own priest, and not just any priest, but one the Archbishop himself had foisted upon the manor. So not only did Thomas not have anyone to do the accounts, the Church might place unpalatable conditions on any replacement.

Oh sure, he could do the admin himself for the manor, but he had bigger dreams. He needed another way. And he needed it to be independent of the Church. He would have to create his own school.

His mind went out to Oscar, Gundy, Grimhild and the rest of that family.

'What do you think of Oscar and his family?' he asked Wulfstan.

'They're nice enough,' said Wulfstan thoughtfully. 'clever, and very loyal. They'd do anything for you I think.'

So Thomas invited them all to breakfast. Over three hours he questioned, probed, and tested their minds. In the end he couldn't believe his luck.

Sighard had a natural talent for numbers, and a quick mind to find applications for what he learned. He had listened to Thomas's dinner lesson on the uses of knotted string, and the very next day he'd used that knowledge to square up the door and doorway into their hut. It let in a lot fewer draughts now.

Lynette had a lovely voice, and when Thomas started to talk about music, she really lit up. Music in 781 was just single notes, with sometimes another background note underlying it, like the drone on a set of bagpipes. When he showed her how different notes could be sung by different people at the same time, to create a gorgeous rich chord, she was beyond speech.

For a nine year old, Grimhild had a simply astonishing ability to come up with verse. Even more useful, she had an excellent memory for words and phrases, and could quote back almost complete conversations when she'd been paying attention. Thomas remembered that this wasn't as exceptional as it appeared. In the times before printing, peoples' memories tended to be much better than they were in his own time. They had to remember, because there was no alternative.

Gundy and Oscar not only had their father's talent for numbers, they loved them, played with them, and were already beginning to discover things on their own.

Sigeberht and Oswin were more like normal boys, and at first weren't really interested in words or numbers. But they did like building things, so when Thomas showed them how being able to measure things allowed them to make better toy bridges, and then real bridges, they really perked up. Then he showed them how a measured drawing could be used to allow them to collaborate better and to share their ideas, and they became very interested indeed.

So Thomas had his students, and once he'd curtained an area off at the west corner of the hall, a temporary place to teach them until a proper school could be built. The problem was that he was the only possible teacher, and he had to be out and about in a few days, searching for the rest of his coterie, as he had begun to call them.

He spent three hours each morning for the next four days, closeted alone with the family. No interruption from outside was permitted. Hengist had been delegated all decision making power, and told to defer any decision he didn't think he could make, until the afternoon, when Thomas finished his lessons.

During day one Thomas drilled the family in counting and writing zero through to ten, then from ten to twenty, and from twenty to thirty. From there it was easy to teach them how to get to one hundred.

Thomas used Grimhild's brilliant memory for words, and her mother's love of music to teach them all the Hundred song by Flanders and Swann. The whole family sang the song, but whenever there was a dispute about the order or name of the words, Grimhild's word was law. Even over her father, which was a bit of a shock to him until he worked out that she never, ever made a mistake. And he did…

On day two he taught them all the eight note musical scale, and musical notation. He locked that in using the old Sound of Music classic, doe-ray-me-far-sew-la-tea, although he did have a little trouble with the tea part, tea being only available in China at that moment and completely unknown to Anglo Saxons. In the end he had changed it to we, and amended the rest of the words to cope.

With that base established, he did the times tables on day three, right up to ten times ten. Again he made it a musical experience, with each of the ten tables having a slightly different song. And once more Lynette and Grimhild between them locked it in, so it could be repeated time and again. It was rote learning, set to music, that they could practise by themselves when he wasn't around.

Day four was all about engineering basics using a weighing balance. He used a simple plank of wood with evenly marked lines that cut across the top surface, resting on a strip of wood about an inch thick.

He placed the strip of wood underneath the middle point of the plank, and showed that the two halves were roughly the same weight because both ends stayed off the floor. Boyish shrugs indicated a "So what?" response.

The previous day he had asked each of the five children to go down to the river and bring back ten stones each, ranging from heavy to light, preferably with at least one flattish side each, so they didn't roll around.

By placing a stone at each of the furthest out mark of both ends of the plank, they were able to find a pair of rocks that were the same weight. Using that pair, they continued to search for other matching rocks, including going back to the river for more, until they had ten rocks of the same weight.

A bit impressed, the boys were really still in "So what?" mode.

Only when Thomas put one of the stones at the far end of the right hand end of the plank, and told them to take two stones together and see if there was a place on the left hand side that would restore the balance, did they become interested again.

When they had found it, Thomas asked them to count the scratched lines out from the middle of the plank and tell them the number. They couldn't. So Thomas asked Gundy and Oscar, and they correctly said "Five!" with more than a hint of smugness. They then correctly identified the line number at the right hand end as ten.

Absolute delight all round when it became obvious that two rocks at five equalled one rock at ten, which matched one of the times table entries.

From there they started to play with the numbers and positions themselves, proving that three stones at three equalled one stone at nine, and four stones at two equalled one stone at eight. Again the cross checking with the times table matched perfectly.

But that was almost trial and error play, so Thomas made them do it the other way around. He got Oscar to choose a times table line where the answer was ten or less. He chose two times two equals four, and Thomas got them to put the rocks out to see if it worked. When it did, Oswin was dancing with delight.

Thomas brought out a measuring plate he'd made the day before, and made nine evenly spaced marks between each pair of existing marks on the plank, but only half way across the plank. He taught them how to use the newly marked plank to represent up to one hundred on each side, and set them working at it again.

It wasn't so accurate this time because of the different sizes and shapes of the rocks, and because the gaps between the plank marks were now so much smaller. But they were convinced of the principle now, and could use it to practise the times table and have a load of fun at the same time.

With all this in place, Thomas left them with a set of tasks to complete in three weeks time when he expected to return, secure in the knowledge that between them, Grimhild and Lynette would keep everyone correct.

Lynette was told to write one simple tune a week using the scales and musical notation, and teach the others to sing it.

Grimhild was told to write verse to go with her mother's tunes, and to make sure everyone else was word perfect in their numbers. She was also the best with writing her numbers, so she was given the additional task of making hers the best she could, so the others could copy her work.

Sighard was told he would be expected to have all the times tables learned word perfect. He blanched a bit at this, but Thomas told him he believed he could do it. He was also told to use his knotted string knowledge to help lay out the floors and walls for the bow works and the school, and make sure they were properly squared up.

Oscar and Gundy were given the same goal, and to help their father. They just smiled happily. Being ordered to play with numbers instead of working in the fields, was paradise for these two.

Oswin and Sigeberht were given a different task. They were encouraged to learn their times tables too, but Thomas used the plank to explain the idea of a counterweight that could be used to balance a long piece of wood stuck out into space. They talked about how that idea might be used for a crane that could rotate, and easily move a load from one place to another with little effort. Their job was to come up with the different combinations of lengths and weights that could balance a load of twenty pounds at the end of the crane, so that a little girl could easily move that load with a gentle push of her hand. Now that was the kind of maths a boy likes! You could do stuff with it!

With Hengist and Alfred fully informed about all this, Thomas made ready to depart for the slave markets. He needed his coterie as soon as possible. Hengist wanted to come of course, but Thomas needed him to run the manor and manage the temporary priest. He respected Alfred, but he knew that Hengist wouldn't allow any backsliding, whereas Alfred would probably ease back into the old ways, almost without noticing.

And so, on the seventh morning after he had arrived at the manor, Thomas, Rowena, Berthilda, Sherelda, and four armed men rode off down the road to market. Thomas was a bit worried about the small numbers, and the temptation of the extra horses they were bringing with them, but he didn't really have a choice. He just didn't have enough people yet to run the manor and take this trip with the security he wanted.

Wulfstan of course made things a whole lot safer than they would have been otherwise. He'd skirted out a three mile radius of the manor, and gone high so he could see a lot further than that. There were no raiders or armed bands to be seen, so the manor would be safe from disturbance for at least a day.

On the ride itself, he ran scouting missions ahead to clear the way. He hadn't been back in the body since they'd arrived in the village, but it didn't bother him a jot.

All was going well.

10 A NATURAL FIT

The first day of the journey retraced their steps back to Tamworth because it was a market town even when the court was not there. Thomas was disappointed that he'd missed by just over a week the best of the slaves sold there, as the traders had all been set up ready to go for when the court arrived. So before he'd left for the manor, Thomas had taken care to check when the next major sale was likely to be on, and it was this week.

He planned on picking up at least some of his coterie at Tamworth, and if necessary, he'd travel all the way down to Bristol where there was an almost constant flow of slaves on their way out of the country. It was sobering to think that almost ten percent of the entire population was enslaved. With the never ending wars and feuds, there were more added every day.

Corbridge had been another slave trade option, but it was deep in Northumbria, and even though the two kingdoms were currently on good terms, he thought it not worth the risk with such a small party.

But Thomas had another avenue to explore. He was after people with some spirit and potential. Rowena and Berthilda had been easy to pick out. They hadn't been slaves for long, and their deep reserves of courage and determination had been on open display when he'd met them. That wasn't normal at all. He'd be unlikely to see that sort of thing at the market because the traders wouldn't tolerate behaviour that would lower the value of their wares.

Which was where Wulfstan came in. As well as scouting ahead for ambush, he was out in the fields, the hedgerows, the forests, the rivers, the marshes, and inside buildings, looking for possible candidates.

Mostly the female slaves were near, or in buildings. They tended to be used for drudgery tasks such as grinding corn, but some had more advanced tasks like weaving which kept them around the buildings.

It was in a manor almost exactly half way between Tamworth and Hengist's that Wulfstan made his first discovery. Under his guidance, Thomas brought his group off the road down a track that led to an assart in the forest. A small cluster of huts and one modest hall sat near a stream that ran through the open space of farmland and pasture that was bounded by trees. The smell of wood smoke, ever present at any centre of human habitation in this world, hung lightly in the summer air, but here the sharper scent of burnt charcoal got stronger and stronger, the closer they got.

Coming around the corner of the barn into the main yard they saw a brazier, charcoal coals glowing red hot. A man with a grimly determined expression checked the heat of a long handled glowing poker, then plunged it back into the coals. Behind him stood the rest of the village, jabbering and chattering.

Next to the brazier was a strongly built "A" shaped wooden frame, with a young woman bound to it, face in, standing up with her hands tied to the top of the "A". The new arrivals could see her equally determined face glaring at them through the framework.

It was a striking face. Elfin in structure, framed with straight mousey brown hair. Even more striking was a very similar face standing next to her.

'Identical twins!' thought Thomas.

'Good day to you my friend, from Prince Wulfstan of Mercia.' he said to the man at the brazier. 'What is happening here?'

'I know who you are Your Highness.' said the man bowing low. 'Welcome to my home.'

'Thank you.' said Thomas. 'And what home entertainments are you performing here?' indicating the bound girl.

'She is a thief! Or her sister is.' he said pointing to her unbound companion. 'We can't tell them apart, but we know one of them stole a whole roast goose last night! She was seen! But each blames the other.'

'So how do you know you are punishing the right one?' asked Thomas.

'We don't Your Highness. They are both slaves. They are jointly lying to avoid punishment, so we are going to make sure we can tell them apart in future. This one is going to be branded on her right shoulder.'

'Won't that affect her work?'

'Only for a week Your Highness. And if she's the one we think she is, she doesn't do very good work anyway, so we won't notice much difference.'

Thomas nodded. 'And their work is?'

'Weavers Your Highness. One does wonderful work, always laughing and smiling. The other, this one, does mediocre work, always being punished, always scowling.'

'And how do you know they don't swap roles all the time just to tease you?' laughed Thomas.

The man smirked. 'Well if they do that Your Highness, they are very good at keeping up the game! Anyway, this girl was the surly, rude one when questioned about the theft, so she's the one getting marked. If they are swapping roles, the branding will tell us that too!'

He turned back to the brazier, took out the poker and checked the colour. 'Not hot enough yet. Another couple of minutes I think.'

'Or perhaps I can offer you an alternative solution.' said Thomas. 'I am looking for slaves to take part in my battle with Lord Grimketil in a year's time, and these two might be suitable.'

The man raised his eyebrows. 'You want to buy them Your Highness?'

'Only if they want to come. They have to know what will be asked of them, what they are risking, and what will be the reward. I can pick only slaves, yet I will choose only volunteers. May I ask them?'

'Of course Your Highness!' replied the man, who recognised a good opportunity to get rid of a troublesome slave for good money when he saw it.

Thomas dismounted and went over to the frame, beckoning the other girl closer. Huddling together, there was much low voiced muttering. Thomas returned to the man, took out his money bag and counted out a more than fair value for the two girls. 'Would that meet with your approbation?'

The man beamed. 'Yes Your Highness! It's an honour doing business with you.'

Thomas laughed. 'You mean it's an honour getting more than you were expecting for them! In this matter I want you to feel you have been treated honourably, and that's part of the price I pay. I want no complaints later on.'

'There will be none from me Your Highness, I swear on my mother's grave.' said the man.

An old lady came up quietly behind him. 'May I remind you Egbert, that I am not yet dead.'

He grinned 'Just practising mother!'

Thomas laughed and waved to Rowena and Berthilda, who leapt from their horses, strode over to the frame and cut the girl free. Half an hour later Deana, the girl on the frame, and her sister Deena, were being taught by Berthilda how to get on a horse. The villagers' jabbering had reached a level where Thomas had to raise his voice to be heard above it. It was only once the group had reached the main road again that the endless chatter finally faded away.

The girls had clearly never ridden before, but they seemed relatively comfortable on horseback. Thomas looked back at them over his shoulder.

'Welcome aboard ladies. You'll have a lot of fun with us. A lot of work too, but mainly fun. And don't worry about the battle at the end of the year. I am certain we'll win, and you'll be free.'

They nodded, one smiling impishly, the other impassive.

'Deana?' he asked.

They both looked keenly at him.

He shook his head. 'Don't even think of playing that game with me. I like the fact you look the same. We might be able to use that to our advantage, but I won't have you playing silly beggars with me.'

He looked pointedly at the real Deana. 'I know you are Deana, and always will. You'll never catch me out, so don't even try!'

She stared back at him, giving nothing away.

'I mean it girls.' he said. 'This is deadly serious what we're doing, and I don't have time to muck about. You can play this game with anyone else you want, but don't play it with us or I'll sell you on to someone else.' and he turned back to the front.

What he didn't say was how he knew. Deana had a small scar, just above the right knee, on her inner thigh. He couldn't see it below her skirt. But Wulfstan could.

What Wulfstan didn't spot was Deena saying to her sister. 'How do you think he knew that?'

And Deana saying back 'Maybe he was bluffing?'

Nobody else in the troupe heard it either, because neither girl had made the slightest sound.

There was great curiosity in Tamworth. After all, everyone knew the story of Wulfstan and his bet with the King, and here he was already with three more followers than he'd had only a week ago. The news of his arrival spread ahead of him, and throngs of people flanked their route to the palace.

Thomas, Rowena and Berthilda took it all in their stride, but to Deana, Deena and Sherelda, it came as a bit of a shock. Whenever they had been the centre of attention in the past, it had meant something bad was happening. So they were naturally nervous about the whole thing.

Thomas gave the three of them an encouraging grin, and waved happily to the onlookers. Some of them waved back cheerfully, some were silent, and others laughed and joked and pointed. Just like any group of people anywhere really.

When they arrived at the palace, the first priority was looking after the horses. Only then did Thomas see to their own living arrangements.

In most manor houses of the time, everyone slept in a single room, the main hall, but the palace was different. It had multiple rooms, including the one which Thomas and Wulfstan had used after the accident, and there was a separate kitchen because the fire in the main hall couldn't cook enough food for a full banquet.

The four men accompanying them slept in the main hall, but Thomas took over the room he'd recovered in, as it was amply big enough for himself and the five women. It gave them privacy, a rare thing in this world.

The following morning, Berthilda took Thomas, Rowena, Sherelda, Deena and Deana out to the butts to give them an archery lesson.

Berthilda herself was exceptional. Ninety nine percent of her shots hit the bullseye.

Rowena had good strength, and was quite good at working out the range, but tended to shoot to the left. They were both doing instinctive shooting, without sights, simply looking down the arrow at the target. Berthilda spotted that Rowena was looking too much at the tip of the arrow and not the target, but once she got her sufficiently relaxed, Rowena's shots moved more to the centre.

Deena was nowhere near as strong as Rowena, and couldn't fully draw the bow.

'I can't do it!' she complained. 'It's too strong for me!'

'Don't worry about it.' said Berthilda. 'The strength will come with practice. Just pull it back as far as you can until your arms start to shake, then back off a little. We'll get you accurate first, and the power will come on its own later on.'

Deena tried again, but still tried too hard and the arrow went well wide of the entire target. Berthilda stood behind her, and rested a finger gently on Deena's right shoulder.

'Try again, but this time stop drawing the bow when I tell you to.'

The instant Berthilda felt Deena's muscles begin to quiver, she told her to stop pulling and focus on the target. To Deena's astonishment, the arrow hit the target this time.

'Well done!' said Berthilda. 'Okay, let's do it again.'

It took another five arrows before Berthilda could remove her telltale finger, but after that Deena hit the thirty yard target every time on her own. By the end, she was positively glowing with satisfaction.

Deana was next, and having listened carefully to her sister's lessons, didn't try to pull the string harder than she comfortably could. She took careful aim, and shot the arrow clean over the top of the target. The second missed it on the left, and the third on the right.

Berthilda soothed her nerves.

'Relax. You're not keeping your left arm straight, so you're having to use its muscles to keep the bow drawn while you aim. Lock your elbow next time, and look exactly at which bit of the target you want to hit.

This time the arrow was comfortably in the target, something she managed to repeat for most of her remaining shots.

'Not bad at all Deana, not bad at all for a first go.' said Berthilda. 'Prince Wulfstan, would you care to go next?'

Thomas had the problem that he was still a boy, with a boy's body. He had even less strength than Deena, but he paid attention, and managed to develop into quite an accurate shot by the end of his turn.

Thomas noted that in fact all of them had range issues compared with a fully trained male bowman. They would never be able to pull the top strength bows, so they'd never get the same combination of range and hitting power of an English longbow archer at Agincourt. So accuracy was really going to matter, as would the ability to close quickly to within their own range during a fight.

Sherelda was walking around, tidying up clothes, quivers, spilled arrows etc. but Thomas noticed her watching everything carefully, paying great attention to all the instructions and guidance being given.

She hadn't asked if she could be one of his warriors. She was happy just being where she was. Thomas hadn't asked her to be one either, because he couldn't see the strength of will in her that he knew would be required. Cuthbert had ground her down most thoroughly. Could she recover from that?

More out of politeness than anything else, and to bring her closer into the group, he asked if she would like to try her hand at a bow. Initially she demurred, but Rowena and Berthilda laughingly coaxed her into having a go.

She took the lowest power bow, as her body was still quite weak from Cuthbert's brutal regime. Holding it lightly in her left hand, she picked up an arrow and effortlessly nocked it, correctly, against the string. Nobody said a word as she drew the bow, rotating back her right shoulder and opening her chest as Thomas had taught the others to do in order to maximise the power in the bow. It was a quite different technique to the normal practice of the time, and Berthilda had immediately seen the benefits of it.

Sherelda sighted carefully at a target 20 yards away, and released the arrow. It missed the whole target, off to the left. There was light laughter from the others, especially the twins.

'Well, we all have to start somewhere!' called out Rowena.

A blush suffused Sherelda's shy smile, but she picked up another arrow, and nocked it as if she'd been doing it all her life. This time she was on line, but hit the very top of the target.

Calmly she picked up her third arrow, ignoring the gently ribald comments. She was dead in the centre of the bullseye. The others all cheered in delight, making her blush again.

Berthilda grinned, and offered her another arrow. 'See if you can do it twice!'

She could, and she did.

Berthilda, nodded, a bit bemused, and offered her another arrow. She indicated the thirty yard target.

Bullseye again.

Wordlessly another arrow was proffered, but this time the farthest target was pointed to, a full fifty yards away.

Five shots, five bullseyes, at all ranges.

Everyone was stunned, Sherelda included.

Berthilda was the first to rediscover her voice. 'Where did you learn to do that?' she asked.

'Just by watching, and listening to you and Prince Wulfstan.' said Sherelda.

'But that's not possible!' frowned Berthilda. 'Nobody can do that straight away! You have to have done this before, surely?' she asked, her eyes pleading for the truth.

Sherelda backed away, alarmed, and shot a fearful sidelong glance at the Prince. 'No! I swear! This is my very first time.' Tears began to flow. 'Please, I meant no offence. I only did as you asked me to. Please don't think I am lying. Please don't sell me again!' the last sentence rising to a wail.

Thomas stepped forward and gently rested his hand on her bow arm. 'Relax. Nobody thinks you are a liar. And,' he smiled, 'nobody is going to sell you, not now, not ever. You're home now. We are your family now. So relax.'

Some of the tension left her face, but it was still full of fear.

So Thomas went on. 'Berthilda is just surprised. In fact we're all surprised! What you have just done would be thought impossible for anyone to do. None of us could have done that with our first shots, not even Berthilda, and she's the best I've ever seen.'

He indicated the twins. 'What these two managed to do today on their first attempt was really, really good. Better than most people would do on their first attempt. I'm extremely pleased with them.'

At this the twins perked up a bit. They had been somewhat shocked at Sherelda's instant expertise, and had wondered if they were now a bit of a disappointment.

'You, are simply astonishing. Here try some more.' and he pointed to a new quiver of arrows.

She shot twenty more shots, ranging back and forth between the targets. All but two were right in the centre of the bullseye.

After this virtuoso display, they practised individually until another full hour had passed. Thomas called a halt, and took them to the armoury.

Each of them took out a wooden sword, and a real shield. As they were swinging their practice swords about the place, Wulfstan floated down to have a word.

'If you're going to practice sword play, you should ask Kelsey to train you all.'

'Who's Kelsey?' asked Thomas.

'He's the one Hengist was sparring with when he hit me. Kelsey's the best fighting mentor in the Kingdom, but father has pushed him to the side after the accident.'

'Where is he now then?'

'He's down by the water mill on guard duty, bored out of his mind.'

'Guarding the mill? But why? An invader would have to get past lots of other guards before they could get to the mill, surely?'

'Punishment duty. The King wanted him to be bored so he would have nothing to do but reflect on the accident.'

Thomas shook his head. 'Your father likes to hold a grudge, I can see that. Right. Let's go and get him.'

An hour later, a somewhat nervous Kelsey was up at the palace teaching them all how to use a sword.

One of the first things he stopped them doing was the kind of play all children engage in when they pretend to sword fight. They were all hitting each other's swords, but that's not the point. When you sword fight someone it's them you try to hit, not their weapon. If you hit their sword, all you do is carve great big notches into your own carefully sharpened blade. Not helpful at all!

Once he'd got that sorted out, Kelsey started to teach them the Anglo Saxon ways of sword fighting. These swords were more for slashing and hacking than anything else, and only the upper classes had one. Swords were very expensive, and you had to be either very well off yourself, or you had to be provided with one by someone who was very well off. For a group of slave women to have swords was unheard of. Come to that it was also illegal. Only access to Offa's bottomless coffers, opened to Thomas by the bet, was making it possible.

Kelsey had never taught a woman to swing a sword before, but it wasn't long before the penny dropped. This wasn't going to work.

To demonstrate his concern, Kelsey arranged for a pig carcass to be brought in, and had it suspended by chains from the rafters. One by one he got them all to take their hardest swing at the body, with their own real sword.

None of them made much of an impact, but worst of all was Thomas's pretty sword from the King. Kelsey was surprised, but Thomas wasn't. He'd always suspected that it was for show, not for use. So he brought out the one he'd bought from the market the day they had first left Tamworth. It was a lot better, but still didn't make that much of an impact.

Then Kelsey brought out his own sword, which Offa had let him keep. He swung it firmly, but clearly not at his hardest. The blade cut easily through the complete side of the carcass, through the spinal column, and came to rest half way through the rest of the body. All that kept it together was the remaining skin and muscle. If the body had been a man's, Kelsey would have cleaved it in two.

There was no way that any of them were going to be able to do that. They just didn't have the strength. They'd have to think again.

Which they did at dinner that night, serving themselves in their room, because Thomas had given the servants the night off. He wanted total privacy for the discussion he was going to have.

'There are two things to note ladies.' he began. 'First of all, none of us is going to be able to do what Kelsey did so easily this afternoon.' He looked around their worried faces. He took a deep breath and continued. 'Secondly, what Kelsey did to the dinner we are all enjoying right now, Grimketil and his men can do to us if they get a clear swing. Even if we carry shields, their great strength will simply sweep us away. A single blow and we're gone.'

Nobody disagreed. Nor was anyone eating. He carried on.

'Grimketil knows this already. He knew it the moment the King laid down the challenge. And so did I. So why you might well ask did I accept the challenge? And more importantly to you as individuals, why am I taking you all with me on what seems like a death ride?'

'That's what I've been wondering all along!' muttered Wulfstan in his ear.

Rowena spoke up. 'I don't believe you think it is a death ride. From the beginning you've said that you expect to win. I've never seen you tell a lie to anyone since I met you, and I don't believe you were lying about that either.'

Berthilda nodded her agreement.

The twins stayed mute, looking from face to face.

Sherelda, humming to herself once more, reached for another pork chop, and began to eat. She caught the Prince's eye and smiled softly at him.

'And what do you think Sherelda?' he asked.

She swallowed, and said 'I think we'll win. I think we'll win because you're going to change the game. You changed the game as soon as you arrived at the manor. You changed the way the decisions were made, and Cuthbert was gone. You changed the game with Rowena and Berthilda in this very hall, breaking all the rules, and you got away with it. I don't think you'll let us fight with swords the way we tried to today. You're planning something different.' She cocked her head on one side, looked carefully at him, and took another bite of pork.

Thomas laughed. 'Two things Sherelda. First of all, you are absolutely right. I am going to change the game, and we're not going to even try to fight like that. But we're going to practise as if we were, so Grimketil will continue to be smug. Secondly, you used the words "we'll win", not "you'll win". Does that mean you want to be one of my warrior women?'

Sherelda looked down shyly. 'I never thought I could be. Not until this afternoon with the bow. But I'd like to.' she looked up, anxiety flitting across her face again as she glanced around the table. 'If you'll all have me.' Then quickly she dropped her gaze to the floor again.

'After what you did today?!?' cried Rowena. 'How could you not be one of us?' Then startled, she clapped her hand over her mouth. 'Oh! Forgive me Your Highness! I didn't mean to speak out of turn!'

Thomas laughed again. 'No need to apologise. I know I want her. It's even better if you all do too. Are we agreed?'

There were nods all around the table.

Thomas stood up, raised his goblet and said 'A toast then, to the first five.'

When the chatter and laughing subsided, he held up his hand for calm. 'Now, let me tell you how we are going to win this fight.'

As they talked, Wulfstan floated around, keeping one ear on the conversation, a nose on the lovely smells of dinner, looking at everything, but always, always, his gaze was drawn back to Sherelda.

That slight golden glow was back again. A little stronger than before. What was it that it reminded him of?

11 WHEN ALL AT ONCE

At breakfast the next day, Thomas wanted to get to know Sherelda and the twins a bit better.

'We got caught down in Kent about a year ago.' said Deena.

'It was a Mercian war band.' added Deana reproachfully.

'Sorry about that.' said Thomas truthfully. 'I can honestly say it was nothing to do with me.'

The twins looked at him thoughtfully for a moment before Deena continued. 'We were sold directly to the manor where you bought us. They found out we were skilled weavers, which is how we earned our living before.'

Deana laughed. 'But we made sure they had to work for what we made. We pretended that one of us was great and the other rubbish, but constantly swapped around so they couldn't tell who was who. We learned to steal food because we never got enough to eat ourselves.'

'So you were free before the war band came?' asked Rowena.

'Oh yes. We worked with our parents. They'd gone to the market when the war band arrived, so it was just us that got caught. About half the men in the village were killed because they fought back. Only a few of the women managed to get away. We saw them looking out at us from the edge of the woods as we were marched off.'

'A nasty business.' said Thomas. 'I hate slavery. I really, really hate it. I'd set you free right now if I could, but I can't. The best I can do is to promise you freedom when we win.'

The twins nodded.

'That's a lot better than where we were!' said Deana.

'So how about you Sherelda?' asked Berthilda.

Sherelda looked sad. 'My father sold me a year ago.'

'Could he not afford to keep you?' asked Rowena.

'Oh yes.' said Sherelda. 'But he said girls were a waste of food and he no longer wanted to keep me, so he sold me to a trader, who sold me to Cuthbert.'

Thomas reeled in shock. He hadn't considered the possibility of someone being sold into slavery by their family, except where famine or poverty forced them to do it. For a father to do it on a whim staggered him.

'You're joking?!' he said softly.

She sadly shook her head.

'He even tossed the coins from one hand to the other and grinned as the slaver walked me away.' She burst into tears. 'Then Cuthbert bought me, and life became unbearable. I really don't want to talk about it. I even hate my own name because it reminds me of my father.'

Thomas replied instantly. 'Well that's at least one thing I can fix. You can have any name you want.'

'What do you want it to be Your Highness?' she asked through her tears.

'That wasn't what I said.' he replied, his voice soft and gentle. 'I said you could have any name that you want, meaning that you can choose it yourself. A free woman, with a free choice about what she wants to be called.'

She stared at him. 'Really? Any name I want?'

'Anything at all.'

She thought for a moment, then a happy expression came over her face. 'I'd like to be called Melody.'

Rowena laughed. 'That's appropriate, the way you hum and sing all the time!'

Thomas joined in the laughter, grinning happily. "Right. Melody it is! New family, new name.'

He clapped his hands. 'Normally something like that requires a toast, but we'll do that at dinner. For now, I'd like you five to go and check out the horses, while I go and talk to the head of the guards about releasing Kelsey to me.'

In the guard house, the man had shaken his head and said he couldn't do it because it directly countered the King's instructions. However, Thomas persisted, and eventually won the argument by saying that Kelsey was vital to his bet with the King, and so came under the heading of essential equipment, which of course Offa had guaranteed. Equally of course, Thomas was the personal owner of the head which had been the cause of all the trouble, and he clearly wasn't holding a grudge!

Kelsey was overjoyed to be free from the boredom, and to be so visibly rehabilitated by the Prince.

Thomas was well pleased too, not just because of Kelsey's training skills, but also because having a big, strong, well trained warrior around was always helpful when difficult discussions were to be had! That was doubly important, as first thing this morning he'd heard rumours of a war band on the loose not far from the manor, and he'd made the decision to send his four male riders back to protect it.

At the palace, he set the women and Kelsey to work out a training regime for sword play. He only set down a few conditions.

1. The women were to learn the tactics of using an Anglo Saxon sword, and shield together. This was not to become expert themselves, but so they could learn what their opponent was up to, and likely to do next during combat.

2. They needed to learn how to deal with people fighting with hand axes and spears, as they were far more common than swords. There was a special need to learn how to deal with spear and shield, the most common combination of them all.

3. The programme was to build up their strength, especially their arms, but at the same time to enhance their speed.

4. They were to do this kind of training in public, for one very clear purpose. He wanted word to get back to Grimketil about how poor they looked, to keep the man confident and relaxed. If Thomas had been working with men, they would never have agreed to the consequent loss of face. The women could take the long view, and as slaves they were used to being scorned. Payback would be all the sweeter when it came.

As for himself, he sat down to really plan the weapons choice he believed would let them win the contest.

Wulfstan had the most important task of all. The first of the slavers were approaching the town, and Wulfstan's job was to seek out any possible candidates before they reached the marketplace, so Thomas could check them out before anyone else.

He drifted straight up above the palace, gently rising higher and higher, scanning 360 degrees as he went. At about five hundred feet he spotted the first of the slave groups bumbling their way towards Tamworth, currently about a mile away to the west. There was another group two miles behind them, and a third a mile beyond that. He swooped over to scout things out.

It was a beautiful day, warm and sunny with a light breeze, which was completely lost on the slaves in the first group. Misery and resignation showed on their faces as they walked along in their bonds. The slavers didn't need to do anything other than walk alongside. The slaves couldn't get away, and there was no point in hitting them for fun, as bruises would only mark the price down in the marketplace.

Wulfstan watched the slavers themselves. The leader appeared emotionally detached, just a businessman with cattle for the market. Money was what interested him, and the shuffling mass behind him was simply today's method of getting it.

A couple of his armed assistants were less detached, their grins and nasty comments revealing humanity's dark underbelly, the part that delights in the suffering of others. They clearly enjoyed what they were doing, getting both amusement and satisfaction from the misery they were inflicting.

For the most part, the slaves made no response to the verbal abuse. What was the point? They couldn't do anything to stop it, and to retaliate would only result in the abuse turning physical. So they walked on in silence, the dust clouding around their shoes.

Wulfstan took his time, carefully scanning the faces and body language of each and every one for that spark that might indicate the right spirit. Nothing.

He flew on down the road, skipping past the all male second group to the third. He wasn't very hopeful after the first two groups, so he was paying more attention to the wind shifts as he changed his altitude. This aspect of the air still fascinated him intensely, and Thomas's likening them to the currents in a river to explain what was happening, only partly assuaged his curiosity.

He was so intensely focused on the interplay between a higher and lower layer, trying to find and ride the exact boundary, that he almost missed the excitement breaking out beneath him.

Roughly in the middle of the column was a group of five women. There was nothing to mark them out from their fellows, at least not at first glance. But to someone really looking, there was an alertness that should have warned the slavers that something was up.

They all wore the same kinds of wooden stocks, two long pieces of wood joined by a hinge behind the neck, then a large hole that clamped around the throat, followed by a smaller hole that held the left wrist and another ahead of that for the right. At the far end, out of reach for the hands, was a simple clasp to hold the whole thing locked together.

A rope linked the back of each slave's stock to the front of the stock of the person behind them so the slaves were effectively shackled in strings of five. The stocks alone made it almost impossible for the slaves to escape, and even if one did, she couldn't even feed herself. Being roped together meant they couldn't run either, as they'd jerk each other around and would almost certainly fall within a few strides.

As they came level with a path that crossed from one side of the road to the other, the women made their move. Without a word, the one in front jerked her hands and the stocks flew apart. Within a second the other four had done the same, and all five were bolting down the path to the right, wordlessly fleeing into the forest.

The speed and silence of the break caught the slavers completely by surprise, and the women were a good fifty feet down the path before the one closest to them raised the alarm.

The guard kept his position and flung his axe about, screaming at the remaining slaves to sit down where they were. Cowed, they immediately tumbled to the ground, the slavers angrily waving their spears and axes around them.

Only two of the slavers were mounted, and these shot off down the path in hot pursuit, the grin of the chase etched on their faces. It would be a short run. There was no way a woman could outrun a horse. The only question was whether to recapture or kill them.

Wulfstan swooped down to get a closer look, but had to stay at tree top height to keep his ribbon from winding through the branches.

The tight and twisting nature of the trail allowed the women to increase their lead before they got to a bend in the track where a low branch came down to shoulder height. Their leader raised her hand, and they skittered to a halt.

'Here! Pull this branch back around the corner so they can't see it.' she said in an urgent yet quiet voice.

Their feet scrabbled for grip in the dirt, and their whole bodies strained to keep it pulled back as far as possible.

Wulfstan floated down through the branches to get a closer look.

The leading woman picked up a stone that she could hold in her right hand, which she held behind her. 'I'll go out as a dummy. Don't let go until you're certain you'll hit him!'

She stepped out onto the path at the corner so she could just be seen.

The lead horseman cantered into view, ducking his head out of the way of the lower branches. He gave a cry of triumph as he saw her, and urged his horse forward.

The woman stood stock still as he approached, her face frozen in a mask of terror. Then suddenly she turned and ran.

Another glad cry echoed from the horseman as he focused on her disappearing skirt and flying hair, but it never completed. The released branch caught him completely unawares, knocking the wind out of him and sweeping him off his horse.

He hit the deck face down and travelling feet first. The pain from the branch was forgotten as the rocks and roots on the path tore at his lips and nostrils. He'd have screamed if he'd been able to breathe.

Finally he came to a halt, pain hitting him from all directions. By god, he'd make that girl pay when he caught her!!! It was a thought both clear, and powerful.

It was also his last.

The woman dropped her blood stained stone next to the head she'd just smashed with it. She paid the bleeding corpse no attention at all, and grabbed the man's spear just in time to duck out of the view of the second mounted man as he came down the path in pursuit of his friend.

When he rounded the corner he saw one of the escapees falling to her knees next to his fallen friend as if to steal his purse. He howled with rage and raised his spear above his head as he rode towards her. He never saw the other woman's spear thrusting up from his left.

It entered his side below the ribcage, but in an upwards manner, slicing through his lungs and other organs. He gasped, and blood bubbled and oozed out of his mouth. A snarl twisted his face as he brought his own spear around his body and into the woman who had struck him.

But she was no longer there. She'd ducked under his horse and out of reach.

Uncoordinated, and struggling to breathe, the man had lunged too far, and had to struggle to sit back upright on his horse. It was a wasted effort. The rock claimed its second victim, thrown straight into his face by the purse stealer.

He toppled backwards off his horse and onto the ground, dropping his spear as he went. Like his friend he too fell on his face. Fury took hold, and the adrenaline shooting through his veins allowed him to raise himself on his arms, but that was as far as he got before the purse stealer plunged his own spear into his back. He felt the blow, but there was no real pain as he slumped once more to the ground. There was only the blood filling his lungs, even faster than before, stopping him from taking a proper breath. A horrible glubbing accompanied the bright red bubbles frothing from his gaping mouth.

A tenth of a lungful was all he managed to take. Dizziness began to take hold. In desperation he rolled onto his side, shifting his weight to snatch another tenth of a lungful.

In front of him, two other women were calming the horses. The one who'd stabbed him first, was watching back up the path in case of further pursuit, his own blood trickling over her right hand as she held the spear. The purse stealer and another woman were now searching the body of his friend, stripping it of anything they could use. One chuckled when she pulled out his purse, felt the satisfying weight, and heard the lovely jingle of coin.

The woman on watch turned to look at him. To his surprise there was no hatred on her face. In fact there was no emotion at all. She simply registered that he was still alive, turned and walked towards him, moving the spear into a two handed grip.

His vision blurred and began to fade. His chest heaved again and again, trying to get air into the fluid filled lungs. He barely felt the spear entering his chest, rupturing his heart. It made no real difference. Hypoxia took its last steps, and he drifted painlessly out of the world.

'Finally!' she muttered, as she pulled the blade free.

'Quickly girls.' she said, 'Strip them of anything we can use. We'll have to ride two on one horse and the three smallest of us on the other. I don't know how far the poor beasts will be able to take us like that, but it will put more distance quicker between us and the slavers.'

Wulfstan had been staggered at the quiet efficiency of the operation. They had shown a sense of calm, and acted cleverly under the ultimate pressure. The two who'd used the spears, had arms and shoulders with a bit more muscle than the average female frame, but the other three looked normal enough. Well that was a puzzle that would have to wait. These five were going to be just perfect.

He shot back up to tree top height where he was able to see a gang of 5 slavers running grimly down the forest path, axes held loosely in their hands. The girls were cantering away, and Wulfstan estimated that they would have about a half mile lead by the time this new lot reached the bodies of their friends. He took note of their heading and shot off as fast as he could back to Tamworth.

Just a minute later he was pouring the story into Thomas's ear.

Thomas jumped to his feet. 'Ladies! Kelsey!' he called. 'Grab your swords, bows and arrows. We're going on a ride!' and ran off towards the stables, calling out to get the horses ready as soon as possible.

He himself put the bridle on his jet black horse. He'd decided to call him Obsidian after the volcanic glass, because of the sheen on the animal's coat, and the hard muscles underneath it. He was a beautiful specimen, powerful, yet docile in the boy's hands. Thomas stroked the side of Obsidian's nose, gently but firmly, and murmured affectionately into his ear.

Rowena glanced over at him, and called out 'What are we doing?'

Thomas grinned. 'Practising! We have to be ready for anything that Grimketil might throw at us, so we're going to pretend that we're after a group of raiders.'

Deena and Deana looked at each other. Deena shook her head slowly and whispered to her sister 'Boys!'

Wulfstan, hovering nearby laughed to himself. 'Girl, are you in for a surprise!'

Fifteen minutes later Thomas and his troop were cantering easily down the road, the spare horses in tow. They slowed to a trot as they went past the first two slaver columns, then back up to the canter until they hit the third. Thomas would have preferred a gallop, but a canter is easy for a new rider to stay with, and a galop is not. He couldn't afford any of the girls to fall off now.

Rowena and Berthilda sat easily, moving as one with their mounts. Deena and Deana were clinging on tight with their legs, working hard to stay on board. Riding between these two pairs, the newly named Melody was having the most trouble, anxiety etched on her face, and her left hand gripping her horse's mane tightly.

Wulfstan dropped a word to Thomas who turned his head back to look at her. 'Try to relax Melody!' he called. 'Embers is a good horse, and she'll take care of you if you let her!'

Melody was too tense to reply, but she did try to relax her grip on the horse's mane a little. Embers ran easily and effortlessly behind Blade, Rowena's pure white horse. Melody had called the horse Embers because of the reddish undertones amongst its brown coat, and the warmth of its nature. Right now though, she felt that perhaps Raging Inferno might have been a better name, as the tree branches on the side of the road seemed to lunge out to try and sweep her off her saddle.

With Wulfstan scouting ahead, they hit the third group at speed.

'Stay tight in behind me girls!' cried Thomas, and following Wulfstan's directions he flicked left through the startled slavers onto the forest path. They slowed to a trot now and then, to manage the tree branches encroaching along the path, but Wulfstan's scouting skills were really sharp these days, and he enabled Thomas to maintain a high pace.

Ten minutes later they burst out of the forest into a grassy meadow that was surrounded on one side by the trees they'd just left, and on the others by the river which bent around it. The current here was both fast and deep.

The five women had their backs to it, faces determined, spears, knives and rocks held at the ready. They had nowhere left to run, but were determined to go down fighting. They had tasted slavery for a short time, and preferred death to a lifetime of misery.

The five slavers were moving warily towards them, axes held lightly in their hands. The death of their fellows had hardened their mood, and they had no interest in taking the women alive. There was no playfulness in their faces, just cold intent.

The thunder of hooves caused both parties to turn and look. The slavers were bemused, not recognising the riders but understanding the wealth and power that the quality of horses implied. The women's shoulders slumped a little, as what little odds they thought they might have had, now seemed to have slipped to zero.

Thomas cantered past the slavers, paying them just a nod as he passed, and rode on towards the slaves. The two women with spears raised them, as if preparing to throw.

'Hold hard ladies!!' he cried. 'We're on your side!'

He twisted in his saddle and called back 'Melody! Deena! Deana! Over to the women's left flank, dismount and ready your bows! Rowena and Berthilda secure their right flank! Kelsey, stay mounted and mind the horses on the left flank! Be ready with your sword if we need it!'

The escaped slaves operated as a unit once more. The two on either side rotated their stance to face the new arrivals, while their leader stared impassively at Thomas, spear held warily in her right hand.

Thomas gave her a nod before walking his horse slowly over to the slavers. 'I am Prince Wulfstan of Mercia. Which of you is the leader here?'

A man with a red hat raised his hand. 'Our leader is back on the road, but I am Wada, the senior man amongst us here. We are trying to recapture our property.' He indicated the women.

'I may be able to help you there.' smiled Thomas. 'I might be keen to buy.'

Wada shook his head. 'They are no longer for sale. Their escape would have incurred severe enough punishment, but they have killed two of our friends, and stolen two horses. They are to be put to death, here and now.'

The lead woman shook her spear angrily. 'They killed my father and his brother, and stole us as slaves! They got what they deserved, a life for a life!'

The slavers stiffened, ready for battle.

Thomas smiled. 'It sounds as if they may have a point. Did you do what she has accused you of?'

Wada snarled. 'They are Northumbrians! They are fair game. The men resisted and paid the price. It is their own fault they are dead! We would have sold them unharmed.'

'And your men attacked us when they could have left us alone!' cried the woman. Then she mimicked him cruelly 'It is their own fault they are dead!' and spat nastily onto the ground.

Wada started to run towards her, the muscles in his axe arm tense and ready to strike.

Kelsey drew his sword.

All five girls drew their bows, each picking a different target.

Wada stopped and turned angrily to Thomas. 'They are ours! We have the right to do what we will with them. Why are you interfering Your Highness?'

Thomas smiled gently. 'Come my friend, you cannot win this fight. They might be lightly built girls but you'll each have an arrow in you before you get another five steps.'

He straightened up on his horse, watching the man's axe hand clench white. 'Surely it's better to come to terms? I'll pay well you know.'

The man shook his head. 'I cannot agree terms. My master would not allow it. You would have to speak to him, and he is back on the road.'

Thomas nodded. 'Understood. So send one or two of the others back to get him. We'll wait.' He indicated to the women to relax their bows.

The man hesitated.

Thomas raised the stakes. 'I tell you what. Perhaps your master would prefer it if I took possession of them now, and he can meet me in the palace at Tamworth to discuss terms?'

The man's jaw dropped. 'My master would want them killed. He will certainly not want them taken away!'

'Then we are agreed I think. You will send one or two of your men here to fetch your master. The rest of us will wait and chat amongst ourselves until he gets here. We are agreed, are we not?' he asked, cocking his head the side, his trademark gentle smile in place.

Wada stammered and blustered for a bit, but eventually waved off two of his men back up the path.

Thomas walked his horse over to the women, dismounted, and offered his hand to the leader. He gave them his now well used spiel.

One of them objected that they were not slaves but free women who had been kidnapped.

Thomas countered with a description of their circumstances at that moment, but offered them safe passage with his party regardless of their choice. 'You can make your minds up tomorrow morning, after you've had a good meal, and a chance to chat with the others.'

An hour later the slave master walked out of the forest with five men. He scanned Thomas's group, assessing their strength.

'There are four archers moving into position on our left, just at the edge of the forest.' reported Wulfstan.

Thomas had a brief chat with Melody, then mounted and rode over to the slave master.

The man assessed him coolly. 'I am Polhard, the owner of these slaves. Is it not dangerous for a young prince to be out on his own in the forest?'

'I am not alone.' said Thomas, indicating his troop.

The slave master waved his hand. 'Children. Apart from that one of course.' he indicated Kelsey. 'But there are enough of us to take him down easily enough.'

Thomas drilled him with his gaze. 'So you think that twelve of you are enough to take us?'

'Twelve my Lord?' smiled Polhard smoothly. 'We are only eight. But yes, even eight would be enough.'

'If you are indeed only eight, then it should be alright for my friends to do a bit of target practice.' snapped Thomas. 'I think there may be some game over there in the forest.' he said, pointing to where Polhard's archers lay in wait.

The slave master looked at him, his face unreadable. 'We are only eight.' he insisted.

Thomas returned the stare for a full minute, then shrugged his shoulders. 'As you wish.' He caught Melody's eye and nodded.

She swiftly drew her bow, took aim and let fly. The arrow sped across the grass and into the trees, where there was a soft thud, followed by a rustle of shrubbery. A second arrow was on its way only seconds later, followed by a third. On each occasion there was the same soft thud and the shimmer of leaves.

The rustling exploded into the loud crashing of underbrush being smashed out of the way by a panicked animal, getting rapidly fainter as the one surviving archer ran for his life.

'You are indeed eight.' said Thomas with a straight face. 'As you said, and as you wished. My apologies for ever having doubted you.'

Polhard had gone very pale.

Thomas leaned down to put his face closer to his and murmured 'I prefer straight forward and transparent dealings.' his double meaning very clear. 'What if I pay you double what you'd get at the market for them? Then we can all get back to our lives.'

The slave master smiled anxiously. 'That's all very well Your Highness, but I have two dead men and two stolen horses to recover as well.'

'They tell me that the horses belonged to their families before you kidnapped them. That means they have simply retrieved their property, so you're owed no compensation there. The two dead men are wergild for that woman's father and brother. No compensation there either. Do you accept double their value? Yes or no?'

The man gulped, bemused by this very strange and frightening child. Finally, he nodded his assent, and Thomas handed over the cash. Thomas also asked for a receipt which offended the slave master, but he sullenly wrote one out regardless.

The men left the clearing, one of them casting curious looks at where the shrubbery noises had come from, but Polhard shot him a look of such antipathy that he quickly looked straight ahead again.

Thomas watched them go, then quietly turned his horse, and trotted back to the group by the river.

12 DOUBLE DIGITS

Thomas did the introductions from his side.

'I'm Freawaru.' said the leader, a strongly built blonde.

Thomas laughed. 'That means peaceful hearth, doesn't it? Well, I can certainly see the fire!'

She shot him a look. 'And this is my sister Storm. We're blacksmiths.'

The look continued, daring him to say anything.

He nodded. 'That explains the strength and the skill. Most impressive.'

Still guarded, she introduced the others. 'These are my cousins, Topaz, Scarlett and Jade.'

'And what do they do?' asked Thomas.

'Sometimes they help out at the forge, but Scarlett can read and write, so she kept the business books. Topaz and Jade are polishers and sharpeners for the knives we make.'

Thomas bowed. 'It's very unusual to meet any female blacksmiths at all, let alone two of them together. Throw in two polishers and sharpeners and it's unheard of!'

Freawaru glared at him defensively. 'Our father had no sons. He wanted Storm and me to marry so he'd have people who could take over the business when he got too old.'

Storm laughed, tossing her long ash blonde hair across her powerful shoulders. 'But we didn't think anyone in the village was worth marrying, so we put him off all the time!'

Freawaru nodded. 'So Storm and I insisted he teach us ourselves, and after a lot of arguing, he did. We're good too! Not as strong as the men perhaps, but we can do pretty much everything they can except the really heavy stuff, and some things we do better than them.'

'I don't doubt that for a moment.' Thomas replied. He knew that there had indeed been female blacksmiths through the ages, despite many people thinking it was a male only craft. 'So was that why he let Topaz and Jade try out the polishing and sharpening? Because you two turned out so good as blacksmiths?'

Topaz broke in. 'No. We did that ourselves. Our father, Freawaru's father's brother, sharpened the village tools. We stole two of the old worn out polishing stones and learned with them. When the old man saw what we could do with stones he thought fit only for the midden, he let us get on with it properly. It doesn't take strength. It just takes a good eye, and good skill.'

'People always wanted our knives if they had a choice.' added Jade.

Thomas nodded. 'I know just how much skill is involved to polish and sharpen a blade. So that leaves you.' he said, turning to Scarlett.

She blushed. 'Our fathers had a clerk in the early days who diddled them by cooking the books. They vowed to keep it in the family after that, so father forced the priest to teach me.'

Thomas laughed. 'How did he manage to do that?'

Freawaru said 'Easy. Father refused to fix his sickle until he agreed!'

Thomas laughed again. 'Excellent. I'd liked to have met your fathers.'

All five burst into tears.

Thomas winced. 'I'm so sorry. That was thoughtless of me.'

While all this had been going on, Berthilda had been checking out the two horses the women had used for their escape. She pronounced them a bit tired and sore after their runs with heavy loads, so Thomas insisted that all five rode the spare horses they'd brought with them.

Melody had asked if they should strip the archers in the trees of their weapons, but Thomas forbad it. In fact he didn't want his folk within touching distance, and he definitely didn't want them bringing back anything that might be used as evidence. He hadn't been sure of his legal rights when he'd ordered Melody to shoot, and in fact still wasn't sure. He didn't feel guilty though. When dealing with a slaver who sets hidden armed men at a negotiation, he felt there were no real rules. And that went double when said slaver made veiled threats.

So instead, they rode off in a column, two abreast back along the path they had come.

Thomas rode with Melody at the front, followed by Freawaru and Rowena, then Berthilda and Storm, Scarlett and Deana, Deena and Topaz, Kelsey and Jade, and lastly the girls' lame horses on lead ropes.

The intermingling was a deliberate ploy by Thomas, to allow everyone to get to know each other. When Freawaru's band made their decision later that evening, they'd have at least some experience of the others. He'd paired with Melody to take himself out of the discussions.

After a time, Melody, looking straight ahead, asked Thomas. 'How did you know the archers were hiding in the forest? I myself could only just make them out, and only because you told me where to look and what to look for.'

Thomas made no reply.

Melody turned her head towards him. 'And come to that, how did we chance upon the girls just where and when they needed our help the most? It was as if you knew from the moment you told us to get the horses ready.'

Rowena was having her own conversation with Freawaru, but she had excellent hearing, and her ears pricked up, hungry for Thomas's reply.

Thomas smiled his usual smile, and said. 'Coincidence. That's all. I felt we ought to inject a bit of realism to our training, and give the horses a bit of exercise. After that I just followed my nose. As for spotting the archers, I just have very good eyes and ears. I heard them moving into position, and after that I spotted them quite easily. So partly luck, partly paying attention.'

Melody continued to gaze at him. The constant state of fear she had been in with the priest, was nowhere to be seen. She knew it was safe to ask the Prince direct questions. 'And we brought all the spare horses.' she said. 'One for each of them. Was that just good luck too?'

Thomas kept his smile, but it was a bit fixed now. He'd overplayed his hand, and been spotted. 'All the horses needed exercise. Sometimes things work out, that's all.' he said lamely.

'It looked for all the world as if someone told you where to come, and even told you about those archers in the trees.' said Melody, before facing ahead once more. 'Good luck indeed. she murmured.

Understandably, the conversation died off for a bit after that.

Rowena continued her chat with Freawaru, but was mulling over what she'd just heard. She thought back over the events that had happened since she'd met the Prince. There were some things that had puzzled her at the time. For instance, how had he known about the beer? How did he know so many things?

Further back in the column the conversations were warmer, as the women chatted, laughed, and got to know each other.

When they got to the bend in the track where the slavers had been killed, all that was left was the blood stained earth and red splashes on the grass. It looked as if the slavers had carried the bodies away with them, but Wulfstan told Thomas that they'd simply tossed them into the river, and they were lying under the surface a bit downstream. Not a lot of loyalty or compassion amongst slavers it seemed.

Thomas desperately wanted to ask Freawaru how she and the others had been able to execute their escape in total silence, and then with so little talking, manage to execute the attack that killed the two men. But of course it had been Wulfstan who'd witnessed everything, not him. With Melody already on the qui vive, he could hardly risk a question like that. He'd need to wait for another opportunity.

Wulfstan was doing his now customary scouting, but he spent quite a bit of time flitting back and forth along the column.

Most of all though, he watched Melody. That golden glow she'd had around her by the fire that night, was definitely back. And it seemed to him to be a lot stronger this time. Melody may be having questions around her Prince, but increasingly, there seemed to be questions around Melody herself. Wulfstan said nothing of this to Thomas. For now, it was his own little secret.

When they hit the main road, Thomas felt he needed to reopen the conversation with Melody. 'That was excellent shooting today, just as good as you were in practice. The one does not always follow the other, and I was very impressed.'

Melody smiled. 'Knowing they were there to possibly either kill or kidnap us, it wasn't hard to do. I just pictured Cuthbert's face on each of them, and it was easy.'

'Well, it certainly worked. A word of advice though, try not to hate Cuthbert. Hate is very bad for your own soul, and it does him no damage at all. It only hurts yourself.'

She shook her head strongly. 'I can't not hate him. Not after all he did to me.'

Thomas nodded. 'Understood. But what does it feel like in your body when the hate builds up?'

She thought for a moment. 'My chest tightens. my face frowns or scowls, my shoulders tense up, my hands clench, and my stomach does back flips inside.'

'And does that feel nice?' he asked.

'No. I feel like I'm not me anymore.'

He nodded again, and looking straight ahead said 'Next time, try taking a deep breath, then breathe out slowly while relaxing your shoulders and making yourself smile.'

She shot him a look. 'How can I smile when I feel so angry?!?'

'I didn't say to feel happy. I just said smile. Fake it.'

She frowned at him.

He grinned. 'Right now you're a little cross with me. Right? You think I'm asking you to do something impossible. True?'

She gave just a flicker of a nod.

'So try it now. Take a deep breath. Seriously, take a deep breath.'

She did.

'Now hold it in. Feel the tension in your chest and face. Now, relax your shoulders, slowly breathe out, and force your face to smile.'

She slumped her shoulders in an exaggerated way, pouted at him, then slowly breathed out.

He laughed at her expression. 'What a lovely face!'

Enjoying that she'd made him laugh, Melody broke her pout and laughed properly herself. This caused him to laugh all the more, so she laughed harder again. Together they laughed for a full minute. Each time one of them almost stopped, a glance at the other would set them off again, until eventually the laughter died away.

Thomas wiped a tear from his eye. 'Now how do you feel?'

'Fantastic!' she said.

'And the great thing is, it always works.' he said. 'A laugh or a smile will always make you feel better, even if you're faking it. It releases things inside that make you feel good, and that helps you deal with whatever is going on at the time. You can be crying, but force a smile onto your face and it will help you to feel better.'

Melody turned her face upwards, allowing the sun to soak into her skin, further relaxing her muscles. Turning to him once more she said softly, 'Well I certainly feel good now!'

He extended his right hand towards her, which she took in her left. He gave it a gentle squeeze, and together they rode down the road together, hand in hand, the warmth of their expressions matching the warmth of the sun on their faces.

Freawaru, watching from behind, jerked her head towards the hands and murmured to Rowena. 'I've never seen a man of rank treat his people like that. Not even a boy of rank. He's not normal.'

'True enough. He's not, and thank God for it.' said the redhead.

'And if he faced a choice between your life and his, which way would he jump?'

Rowena cast an affectionate glance at the back of the Prince's head. 'He's already stood in harm's way for me. He's physically protected Melody, and put his reputation on the line for her at the manor. And together he, Berthilda and me have stood side by side in a marketplace to face off five armed and angry men, including the thegn he told you about.'

'So,' she said, turning to Freawaru, 'he would jump to my side. And I would jump to his. We all would.'

'And in a year, you will all face this thegn once more in a fight to the death? And you expect to win?' The woman's voice was sceptical.

'You don't know him yet. The world seems to change around him. So yes, I expect to win. But even if I didn't believe that, I would still be with him.'

'And why is that?' frowned Freawaru.

Rowena took her own deep satisfying breath of the warm summer air, and following the advice she had overheard, gently shook the residual tension out of her shoulders. 'Because a year of freedom with such as he, is worth more than a lifetime of servitude under a cur with a whip, even if death lies at the end of it.'

She took her left hand and gently stroked Blade's neck. 'And death does not lie at the end of it. Only life, or freedom, or both.' She smiled. "And you and your friends have the choice. He has to take slaves as part of the bet with his father the King, but he only wants those who choose to be at his side. So he means it when he says you have the choice to stay or go. You really do get to choose.'

'And why would he not sell us at the slave market if we say no? We do not really have that much of a choice!' Freawaru growled under her breath.

Rowena shook her head. 'He would not do that. He has paid for you, and would probably keep you in a position you could use to earn your freedom. You would be well cared for and allowed to prosper, and to be happy. But you would never be forced to be one of us. If you don't want to be with us, he won't want you either.'

'So why not just set us free?'

'I'm sure if your people can pay him back what he paid for your freedom, he'd be happy to.'

'And where is the justice in that?'

'It is not his fault you were enslaved. Nor was it his fault that any of us were enslaved. What he offers is a way out, if you want it. That alone is a miracle. You cannot expect him to find the money to buy the freedom of every slave in the Kingdom. Perhaps it would be wise not to ask God for too much, or you may get nothing at all.'

Freawaru stared ahead for a few moments, thinking. And then nodded her head slowly in agreement.

The column walked on peacefully to Tamworth.

In the stables, the Freawaru family's two horses were seen to by the grooms. They'd confirmed Berthilda's diagnosis that apart from being a little stiff and sore from their exertions, there was little else wrong with them.

Thomas watched with great interest as the five newcomers set about fettling the horses. As in the fight, they worked with very little noise, and little conversation. Topaz's head rose, glanced at Storm who nodded in reply and passed over a brush. Just past her, Jade pulled taut part of a horse's mane so Scarlett could more easily spot the biddy bid that was eluding her brush.

Freawaru watched Thomas watching them.

'Amazing how working in a loud place like a smithy can make you able to pick up the visual cues as to what others need.' he observed.

Obsidian turned his head, and gave Thomas a none too gentle nudge in the back, causing the boy to stumble forward.

'Hoy! Have a care!' he cried.

Obsidian looked at him, swung his head around to his hay net, then back to Thomas, who laughed. 'Yeah, yeah, I know. But you'll have to wait a minute.' He stroked the horse's nose softly.

Thomas thought for a second, then asked 'How much work did you do in steel as opposed to iron?'

'Making good steel is almost impossible.' said Freawaru. 'We can't get the forge hot enough to make it properly, so we only get little pieces here and there.' She shrugged her shoulders. 'And that makes it hard to do anything good with it, because each little bit is different, and even the best always has slag left in it, and that makes it weaker than it should be. So yes, we put around the edges of our blades, but it's not as good as we'd like.'

'Would you like to work with really good quality steel?'

She looked at him cynically. 'Do you have some?'

He laughed. 'Not yet, but in a matter of weeks we will. The smithy is being built to my specifications as we speak, and yes, we will have steel. More to the point we will be able to make different kinds of steel at will, which means…'

She cut him off. 'It means you'll have better weapons than the thegn's men.'

Thomas just smiled.

'But,' she frowned, 'that's still no good if your people are too weak to use them. Do you really think a group of young women can go hand to hand against a body of men who do nothing but fight?'

'Who said anything about a normal fight?' he asked.

'But…'

'The bet was that I couldn't get a bunch of slave girls to beat the men in a fight. Nobody said anything about how the fight is to be run. Oh everyone expects we'll fight in the way our people have always fought, in a shield wall with spears, shields, axes, and for the very rich few, a sword. But,' he paused for effect, 'we aren't going to do that.'

Freawaru stuttered uncertainly. 'But how?'

'If you decide to join us, you'll learn. If not, you'll have to wait and see like everyone else. But in your case, there may be an extra motivation to join us, and that's being able to work with really good steel. You can join my smith if you like.'

She shook her head. 'We need to talk it through, the five of us. And what happens to the other three of us, and what happens if we say no?'

'Are you kidding? A polisher and a sharpener are incredibly valuable to me, so no issues with Topaz and Jade. I'm trying to teach some people to read and write myself, so Scarlett is incredibly valuable to me, even more valuable than you in some ways. I'm not just about sharp edges you know.'

He smiled again. 'As for you saying no, you can all work in the roles we've just discussed. You just won't be my warriors. You can earn a good living, save up, and in a few years you can buy your freedom back and return to Northumbria. The catch for you is that although you will have learned to work with steel, you won't have learned how to make it. In fact, you won't know how to make it for a while yet either way.'

'We get to work with the steel, whichever we choose?' she asked.

Thomas nodded. 'Uhuh. But you won't learn how to make it unless you're one of my warriors. I can't afford that knowledge to get out of Mercia and back to Northumbria. If you choose the warrior path, you choose to be a Mercian. For life.'

'You're asking me to be a traitor!' she cried.

'No.' he replied gently. 'I'm just putting a condition on you learning one particular skill. Your own king wouldn't even think of letting you work with the stuff. I'm offering you a chance you'll never get any other way, but I'm not forcing any of you to do anything you don't want to do.'

They left it at that.

Thomas gave Obsidian his hay, and made a fuss of him.

Freawaru and her kin went off for a walk on their own down to the river. There they sat, and for the next four hours talked, and walked, and talked, and walked, trying to come to a decision.

Every hour or so Thomas sent down a couple of serving girls with some food and drink.

Occasionally Freawaru would come up and ask him a question.

Just before the evening meal was due to be served, they all arrived back in the palace to meet with the Prince.

Thomas cocked his head questioningly.

Five grins shot back at him.

'Welcome aboard.' laughed Thomas. 'Lowena!!! Five more for dinner please!!'

13 STEELING THEMSELVES

They spent the next four days in an extended shopping expedition, throughout the palace market and beyond.

Berthilda took on the responsibility of equipping the five newcomers with bows, and also bought a lot more arrows for the entire troop.

With the court away, there were no swords to be had in the market, but there were scramseaxes. The biggest of these very large knives was close to 75 cm long, a bit over two feet, but with just the one sharp edge. They weren't particularly well balanced, being a bit point heavy like the swords, so Thomas took care they each got one they felt they could deal with. Kelsey got them to do a few exercises, just to double check.

Then came the standard equipment, two large iron headed spears, three leather covered, iron bound, lime wood shields, an axe and two throwing axes for each person.

The girls looked askance at the ever growing pile of equipment, and it didn't even include any armour or helmets yet. Even Berthilda and Freawaru were concerned about being able to carry it all.

Thomas just said not to worry. They wouldn't ever have to carry all of it at once. To make his point he hired two carts, to which he promptly added twelve large purchases of cloth, two pairs of leather shoes each, leather belts and straps, and three complete tanned cow hides.

Knowing the manor's own stocks would not be able to cater for the additional mouths and horses, especially once winter hit, he placed orders with a number of merchants for foodstuffs, particularly oats and barley. He wanted far more than the market currently held, and so arranged for it to be delivered to the manor later. Wulfstan was a huge help here, as he'd been able to spy on the merchants earlier in the day to separate the honest from the scoundrels.

Thomas also placed orders with three different merchants for the turnips and beets he wanted from the land of the Franks for the four crop rotation. To try and make sure they got him the right ones, he gave them drawings and descriptions of both the plants and their seeds, asking them to send out their agents that very day.

This year he'd be making a huge loss in the manor's accounts, and only the King's gold was enabling him to do what he was doing, but he was hopeful of making something "magical" that might bring him back into profit. To that end he bought one hundred pounds of copper, twenty pounds of tin, several pints of mercury, and a hundred pounds of lead. With that little lot he ought to be able to make something!

He also visited all the blacksmiths in Tamworth, and bought half the iron they had in stock. This too was expensive, but he needed raw materials pretty much instantly back at the manor, and couldn't afford the time to go through the smelting process from scratch.

To work it, Freawaru and Storm acquired a complete set of tools for their own smithy, including an anvil each. All this additional metal meant Thomas had to add another two carts to his shopping list.

Topaz and Jade were particularly thrilled at being given free reign to select whatever polishing and sharpening stones they wanted. It being Tamworth, the range and quality was quite unlike anything they'd ever come across before. Thomas then got them to choose a range of stones the others could use to help, because sharpening and polishing swords was a lengthy business. He'd need all hands on deck doing the donkey work to make them quickly enough.

The King was going to go ballistic at all the expense of course, but by the time he found out, it would be too late. Thomas was hoping his "magic" items would make it alright again.

They all spent the afternoon practising in public with their new blades, shields and spears, under Kelsey's direction. Their struggles caused much mirth amongst the population, especially the slavers. Deena and Deana in particular were having difficulties with the scramseaxes, their own light builds struggling to deal with the heavy, badly balanced blades. It looked more as if the scramseaxes were thrown around the place, rather than the other way around.

Polhard was paying particularly close attention, which pleased Thomas no end. He was certain that the slaver would be running off to Earl Grimketil, to try and exchange information for cash, and that suited Thomas just fine.

Rowena and Berthilda were of course the best at this stage, dancing around each other, feinting, striking, parrying. Good friends they may have been, but boy they were competitive too! Thomas had to buy another six shields for them as they'd each worn one out by dinner time.

The next day after a leisurely trip at cart speed, they arrived back at the manor. Thomas was pleased to find out that the watch system was working well, as there was a welcoming committee half a mile before the village.

The children came running towards them, hair flying, eyes sparkling with excitement.

'You're back so soon!' gasped Grimhild.

'Yes!' shouted Gundy. 'Only seven days! Why are you back so soon?'

Thomas laughed. 'We were incredibly lucky. Meet Deena and Deana, who we chanced upon on the way to Tamworth, just down the road from here in fact.'

The little girls goggled at the twins.

'But they're the same!!' gasped Gundy.

'Yes they are!' laughed Thomas. 'There's no fooling you is there?!'

The twins each nodded to the girls.

'This is Gundy, a magician with numbers, and Grimhild, who's fantastic with words. Two fine minds.' said Thomas, before the twins asked him.

Deena and Deana raised their left eyebrows in harmony with each other.

'And these,' Thomas went on, 'are Oscar, Oswin and Sigeberht, each with their own special talents.'

He turned in his saddle to introduce the others. 'These five ladies we met on a forest ride. Freawaru and Storm are blacksmiths, Topaz and Jade are polishers, and Scarlett can read and write.'

Gundy and Grimhild goggled again. 'Blacksmiths?' they cried. 'Girl blacksmiths?'

Freawaru frowned in annoyance.

'Yep.' replied Thomas. 'None of my doing either!'

'And someone else who can read and write?' shouted the children again.

Scarlett waved shyly.

'And that,' he pointed to the rear of their column, 'is Kelsey. A really good man to have on your side, and a great friend of Hengist. He completes our company.'

Oscar sidled up to Obsidian's flank, and stroked his neck before looking up, his face filled with worry. 'So will you be leaving soon to fight Thegn Grimketil?'

Thomas shook his head. 'No Oscar. We have a lot of things to do before that happens. You'll have to put up with us for a year yet.'

'Hurrah!' shouted Sigeberht.

'Hurrah!' shouted the others, their faces filled with relief.

So it was a happy company that entered the village a little later, but nothing compared to the joy of Hengist and Kelsey as they embraced for the first time since the King's anger.

Thomas spent the rest of the day directing the unloading of the carts, making sure the carters were looked after for the night, and ensuring the horses' welfare. He was helped assiduously by the five children, who were desperate to show him how they had progressed on the tasks he had left them only a week before.

Sigeberht and Oswin boasted that they had designed their crane, in their heads at least. They were certain it would work perfectly, but they hadn't actually built any of it yet.

Gundy just smiled at this, but carefully, so the boys didn't see her do it.

Oscar told of how he, Gundy and their father had already managed to square off the floors of the new bowyery and school extensions to the hall. They were trying to work out how they could square up the walls without having to rebuild the outer walls of the hall itself.

Grimhild sang him the words for the song that Lynette had written. Twice.

By then the horses had been seen to, the carts unloaded and their contents stored in the appropriate places, and it was time for dinner.

The following morning, Thomas hit the ground running. He sent the coterie off to do archery practice under Berthilda's instruction, except for Scarlett who he took to school. He needed to know where her skills lay compared to the rest.

She turned out to be a confident woman, secure in her knowledge of letters and numbers, but Gundy rocked her back on her heels right from the start, when she counted up to a hundred by starting from zero.

'But what is zero?' asked Scarlett.

Thomas applauded Oscar's explanation, then told them to take Scarlett through all of the homework he'd set them before he'd left for Tamworth. After that he left them to it, while he visited the smithy.

'Welcome back Prince Wulfstan! We have something to show you!' cried Smith over Buck's hammering.

He walked over to the forge, pulled out a roughly cylindrical lump of red hot metal from its coals and placed it on the anvil. A loud clang rang out as Buck gave it a relatively gentle tap with his hammer, and to Thomas's delight there were almost no sparks.

'Excellent!' he breathed. 'Oh very well done my friends! Pure iron, and so soon!'

'It worked perfectly, just as you said. We put bits of old iron into the crucible with some white sand and a little bit of broken glass, sealed it, then cooked it in the furnace as hot as we could make it, and this is what we got. Pure iron!' said Smith, grinning broadly.

Thomas nodded enthusiastically. 'Just the one?' he asked.

'We did one in the first firing, then five in the second. Each billet has more than enough metal to make a sword, just like you said.' Smith pointed to four more metal cylinders, and one that was broken into three parts.

'This one,' he said, picking up the three bits, 'was the first. We put it into the forge so we could work it, but it broke at the first blow. So we've learned to hit it more gently now.'

Thomas nodded. He knew the chemistry involved, and why the iron was so brittle and reluctant to change shape, but without a microscope he wasn't going to be able to explain it to them. What he could explain though, was the next step in the process, and not just to the smiths.

Wulfstan sat on his shoulder throughout, paying attention to everything that was happening. Partly it was so he'd be able to pick things up if there was another body swap, but mainly because he was genuinely interested. He was however, beginning to wonder if he'd ever return to his own body! It had been a long time since he'd been the one in control.

Using a simple balance scale, Thomas weighed each "sword billet", then measured out enough pure charcoal dust to make just over 1% of the billet's weight. That was added to the billet in a new crucible, with more sand and glass. The carbon in the charcoal would alloy with the iron to make the steel, while the sand and glass would attract away any remaining impurities, as well as act as a flux to reduce the overall temperature required to melt the steel. If all went well, each crucible would produce a billet of uniform, high carbon steel.

There were just two things that concerned him about this approach. Firstly, in an ideal world he should be adding other carefully measured things to the mix such as manganese, chromium, nickel, molybdenum, vanadium etc. to get exactly the right mix, but this wasn't an ideal world and it simply wasn't possible.

The second concern was a bit more of a worry, and that was that he didn't have any idea about how much carbon was already in the iron. Ideally they'd get rid of it all in the smelting process, but that really required air to be bubbled through the metal in the crucible, and that too was beyond him for now. So he'd just have to trust to luck and assume it was low after the first crucible melt had taken out most of the slag.

He knew that by adding a large amount of carbon, and 1% was a very large amount indeed, he'd get a blade that would take on a lovely edge and be easy to sharpen, but it would also be brittle and prone to breaking. On the other hand, if he went for something like 0.45% carbon, then the sword would be a lot more flexible and less prone to snapping, but the edge wouldn't be as good.

Of course he could use different types of steel for different bits of the blade, lower carbon steel for the core to provide the flexibility, and higher carbon steel strips welded to it for the edges, getting the best of both worlds. That would do well enough, but Thomas wanted to use a single billet if he could.

The trick to making it work with his high carbon steel was to forge it at a lower than expected temperature, and once the blade had been finalised and quenched, to retemper it back down until the core achieved a more usable level of hardness. This was how the famous Ulfberht swords had been made, and Thomas knew they'd been far and away better than anything else for hundreds of years.

Which all sounded easy enough, but knowing how something was done and actually doing it were two completely different things, as anyone faced with walking a high wire fifty feet above the ground could tell you!

Team work was also a big deal, so he went and brought all the women to meet Smith and Buck. There was a degree of professional reserve between the local smiths and the Freawaru family, but that was only to be expected. He dealt with this by having them work together to set up the two huts next to the smithy as additional forges for the newcomers. As it rapidly became clear that both sides knew their stuff, mutual respect grew, and the cooperation improved.

To keep the villagers sweet, Thomas made sure those hut's original families went into much nicer huts nearer the quay, where they'd have a quieter life away from all the banging!

By the time the team was putting the finishing touches to the new forges, Polhard had reached Grimketil's manor and was sitting down to a nice horn of beer.

'News of the King's bet has spread across the land my Lord, and I have information for sale that may interest you.' he said smoothly.

Grimketil looked at him impassively. 'I wasn't aware that I wished to buy any information.'

Polhard nodded. 'Your prowess is as well known as the King's bet, but you may find it easier to win that bet if you know what your opponents are up to. I can help you there.'

'I don't need your help master slaver.' said Grimketil.

'Fair enough. I apologise for my mistake and shall trouble you no further my Lord.' Polhard replied, rising to his feet and draining his horn 'I wish you good luck, and thank you for the beer.'

Grimketil raised his hand. 'Wait. What exactly is it that you are proposing?'

Polhard remained standing. 'I can tell you how many of his girls Wulfstan now has, and what they look like under arms.'

Grimketil stared at him impassively. 'And your price?'

Polhard doubled the figure originally in his head, and then wished he'd doubled it again when Grimketil nodded his agreement without haggling further.

'He has all ten –'

'What? Already?' gasped Grimketil. 'Is he taking just any old thing that comes across his path?'

'Quite the contrary my Lord. Five of them he took from my own stock. They'd escaped, killing two of my best men and stealing their horses. The rest of my men then cornered and were about to kill them when Prince Wulfstan rode up with his other five, plus a mounted man at arms. I arrived to negotiate, placing some men in the trees,' he smiled, 'in case negotiations didn't go in the way I wished them to.'

'Very wise.' said Grimketil.

'But not wise enough my Lord. The Prince somehow saw them getting into position, and instructed one of the women to shoot her arrows into the forest, ostensibly after game. She killed three of them in half a minute.'

Grimketil's eyebrows shot up. 'One woman?'

'One woman, three arrows, three kills, in less than thirty seconds.'

'And you say the five escaping slaves killed two on their own? How?' asked Grimketil.

Polhard shrugged. 'We're not entirely sure. Both bodies had bloodied heads, probably hit with rocks, but the fatal wounds came from their own spears.'

Grimketil gasped again. 'Their own spears! And these men of yours, were they skilled?'

Polhard nodded. 'Not to the level of you or your men my Lord, but yes they were skilled, and strong.'

Grimketil stroked his chin. 'So they must have been surprised.'

'Quite, my Lord. They didn't have the required information…' Polhard's smile was positively catlike now.

Grimketil pursed his lips. 'Anything else?'

'Yes my Lord. The Prince then bought many goods in the Tamworth market, iron, copper, lead, knives, shields, spears, cloth, shoes, and leather.'

'Horses?'

'He had those already my Lord, top quality too.'

Grimketil considered this for a moment. 'And can they ride?'

'It varies my Lord. One or two can ride extraordinarily well, three of them hardly at all, the others somewhere in between. I only saw them riding on the way into the forest, and on the way back to Tamworth. They weren't mounted when they practiced with their weapons on the meadow.'

'And how did they seem with the weapons?'

'They were mainly terrible my Lord. Two of them could hardly wield their scramseaxe knives at all, four were slow and cumbersome. Two of mine, blacksmiths and therefore strong, did much better, but they lacked any real skill.'

He paused.

'And the remaining two?'

'Ah, a redhead and a brunette, both well made women, very confident and strong. They set about each other with sword and shield. They couldn't threaten any of your men yet, but they knew what they were doing. A man called Kelsey was doing the teaching.'

Grimketil frowned. 'He's good. A friend of Hengist. Knows his stuff. That's a pity. The redhead will be Rowena, and the brunette Berthilda. I'm not surprised they performed well.'

Then he came to a decision. 'You were quite right to come to me with this information. It is indeed worth your price, and if in the future you come across any more, please bring it to me.'

As Polhard was taken away by a minion to be paid, Grimketil turned to Ward, his right hand man. 'That boy's doing better than I expected him to. The question is, what do we do about it?'

Ward bent down and whispered into his ear. Grimketil's face resolved itself happily into the nastiest of grins.

Once the new forges were up and running, Thomas had Freawaru create a set of iron dumbbells ranging in weight from one to three pounds.

He and the women took it in turns to find the heaviest one they could each comfortably handle to mimic sword movements, and not get exhausted. Speed and stamina were going to be more important than hitting hard.

'This is all very well,' noted Storm part way through, 'but these are nothing like the real thing. Here the weight is balanced in the palm of the hand, but a sword's weight lies out near the end of the blade, and that changes everything!'

'Stage two!' said Thomas. 'Go and make yourself a rough iron sword blank with a longer tang, half a pound lighter than that weight you're playing with now.'

When the blank was ready, Thomas placed in on the scales and added some smaller pieces of iron until it reached Storm's ideal weight. Then he carefully tied them in place one at time up and down the tang until the "sword's" centre of gravity lay just two inches above the guard.

'Okay, try that.' he said.

Storm held the mock up with care, and began to thrust and slash. She found she could spin the blade very quickly, with perfect control over her thrusts and parries. Equally important, she could withdraw, or change a thrust's direction far quicker than with a normal blade.

She shook her head in appreciation. 'I see what you've done now. It's much faster than any other blade I've ever handled.'

Then she frowned. 'But it's not going to be much use slashing into a mail shirt. You need weight to smash the bones underneath, and this won't have it.'

Thomas nodded. 'Absolutely right, but we know we're not strong enough to wield a blade like that anyway, so there's no point even trying. We need to be fast, to be able to lunge, hit exactly what we're aiming for, then withdraw before they can strike back. This will let us do that.'

Rowena broke in. 'Blade against blade that's fine, but we'll be carrying shields and they'll slow us down, so what's the point?'

'Ah.' said Thomas. 'I have an answer to that too, but let's deal with the swords first.'

When the first of the steel billets arrived, Thomas got Freawaru's forge up to temperature, then gathered Smith, Buck, Freawaru, Storm, Topaz and Jade together for a lesson.

'Now you're the experts here, but when it comes to working this kind of steel, I know some things that you don't, things you need to know if you're going to be successful.' He paused, looking around at their faces. Seeing no dissent, he continued.

'Freawaru, please put the steel billet into the fire, but not in the absolute centre. Put it half way down the fire as you normally would, but slightly off to one side, and rotate it every thirty seconds or so. It's important that it doesn't get too hot too soon, or it will develop cracks. We need to warm it gently from cold.'

Freawaru followed his instructions until Thomas was satisfied it was hot enough to enter the heart of the coals. As the colour of the steel gradually changed, he continued his lesson.

'You mustn't try to work it when it's blue hot. It's still too cool, and hammer blows will almost certainly damage it. Continue heating it until you get a nice cherry red colour. If it turns orange, then you've gone too far and you need to cool it back down before attempting to forge it.'

Smith raised his hand. 'Your Highness, we often work metal hotter than that, even when it's white hot.'

Thomas nodded. 'Understood, but this steel is different. It mustn't be worked above cherry red or you'll damage it. Worse than that, you probably won't be able to see the damage you've done, but the sword will be weaker as a result, and break in battle.'

Once the billet had reached the required colour, Storm took it out and held it on the anvil for Freawaru to strike.

'Be gentle Freawaru.' warned Thomas. 'Smith found that the pure iron smashed easily if he hit it too hard, and this steel ingot is even more fragile. We really should have a piece of wood between the ingot and your hammer, but I trust you to be careful.'

Freawaru gave him a look that said volumes, but did as she was told. The blow made not the slightest visible change. She blinked in surprise, then hit it again with the same result. Annoyed now, she prepared to hit it harder but Thomas was watching her carefully.

'No. Gentle, always gentle, until we've made the bar.'

'But it's not doing anything!' she growled.

'That's because of its internal structure. It's formed crystals in there that are all locked together, and they resist the metal moving. It's okay, because those crystals will help to give us a sharp and sustainable edge once the sword is made, but for now we just have to nudge it into shape. If you go harder than what you've been doing, you'll simply break it into pieces and then we have to re-melt it and start from scratch. You really don't want to do that if you can help it!'

'How long will this nudging take?' asked Storm.

'About eight hours.'

'Eight hours!' came the startled chorus.

'And that's just to form it into a bar. Then comes all the work to make it into a blade.'

They looked at him in silent astonishment.

'I never said it would be easy.' he shrugged. 'I just said that it would be worth it for the end result.'

For the rest of the day Freawaru and Storm worked together on the ingot, teaching Topaz and Jade to work it in the fire, and hold it correctly on the anvil while it was being hit.

Then, after six hours work they learned a very hard lesson. Hot, tired, and frustrated with the slow progress, Freawaru hit a bit harder than usual and the ingot cracked. Aghast, she and Storm turned the ingot crack side up and tried to hammer it back together again, before Thomas stopped them.

'Sorry folks. That one's ruined. We'll need to give it back to Smith and Buck to re-melt. Start again with a new ingot.' he said.

Freawaru gave him a ferocious look. 'We can fix it! We can hammer it back together again! There's six hours of my life in that!'

Thomas shook his head. 'Nope. Even if you manage to make it look okay, it won't be. That crack will never really go away. It will kill the sword's owner. Start again.'

At dinner that evening the chastened team worked out a rota that would use the entire coterie to run both forges without anyone getting too tired and making another mistake. It worked well, but it still took some days before they had twelve sword blanks ready for the next stage.

'Okay, time to make proper blades.' said Thomas at the beginning of his next lesson. 'Ideally we'll continue to work with it between blue, and bright cherry red, the same as we've been doing.'

'But this gives us very little time to work it before it gets too cold!' complained Freawaru.

'True enough. but that's the way this steel needs to be worked. The good news is that you can hit it harder now you've got it to this point. However, I want you to make a new kind of sword, not the big double edged ones you're familiar with.'

'Really?' asked Storm, her tone highly dubious.

'Really. We know what weight each of us can handle, so step one is to chop off the excess steel to get each bar to the right weight. Then I want you to remember that the balance point of the sword is to be a couple of inches above the guard. We can use the weight of the pommel to help, and the guard will be bigger than you're used to, but if the pommel's too big the vibrations can be awful, so try and get the weight as right as you can with the blade and tang.'

'But that means the sword will be short! A man has longer arms than us to start with, give him a longer sword than us and we'll never get through!' complained Rowena.

Thomas nodded. 'Normally yes, but with this steel we can make a narrower blade, so you won't lose as much as you think you're going to. Also, this one is to be single edged, so it will be narrower and you'll get most of the length back.'

'But-!' started Berthilda.

'A single edge! It won't work! It can't work!' cried Topaz, cutting her off.

Thomas held up his hands. 'Remember that we're not going to be slashing away with it. Most of the time you'll be thrusting. The edge is important, but it'll do its damage on the way in and out, not just by slashing.'

They looked at him uncertainly.

'Also, the sword is just part of the equipment. You'll have something in the left hand to help.' he added.

'What exactly?' asked Storm.

'You'll have to wait and see. If I told you without being able to show you, you'd think I was crazy.'

Storm's expression indicated she had some doubts about his sanity already, but she didn't say so.

While work continued on the blades, Smith and Buck carried on producing more steel until Thomas felt they had enough, and switched them over to using it to make a new kind of shield. He drew them a picture on a roof shingle, with accurate measurements.

'But this is very small my Lord! I know the women are smaller than the men they'll be fighting, but all the same…' said Smith, looking shocked at a picture of a shield less than half the normal diameter.

'Against a hail of spears or arrows, it's not much use I'll grant you, but in one on one combat it has some advantages. It's called a buckler, and it won't be used like a normal shield.' said Thomas.

For the next two days Smith and Buck worked in parallel with the two sword teams, and they'd just created the final shape of the first one when Deena and Deana walked in to say hello.

'That's a cute little thing!' cried Deana. 'Is that for the children to play with?'

'It's yours!' laughed Buck.

'What?!' shouted Deena. 'No way!'

'Yep, especially built, just for you!' said Smith.

Once the twins were certain it wasn't a joke, they rushed off to tell the others, and it was a deeply unhappy coterie who greeted Thomas when he arrived to check progress later that day.

'We don't understand Your Highness. It seems like madness to have small bodies, skinny swords and now a tiny shield.' said Deana bluntly.

Thomas managed to keep his face straight. Now was not the time for flippancy, when they were genuinely worried about being hacked to pieces.

'Well, now you know why I didn't want to tell you before I could show you. A wise woman once said, "Fools and bairns shouldna see a thing half finished!" And she was absolutely right. Oh well, seeing as you all know, let's go and watch it being finished, so you can see the quality of what you're getting.'

He led them into Smith's smithy where the buckler was being heated slowly on top of the coals.

'Smith's taking it up very slowly through the colours to avoid heat shocking the steel.' explained Thomas.

When parts of it began to turn cherry red, Smith worked hard, moving it around above the coals to get it all cherry red as fast as possible.

'When the steel is cherry red, crystals are forming inside it.' explained Thomas. 'They form fast, and they grow. They make the steel look pretty, but big crystals will make it weak, so that's why he's working so quickly.'

Smith dunked it carefully into a barrel of cod liver oil to quench it, and left it there, despite the appalling smell. He was even more careful when he pulled it out again and rested it on the floor.

'He's quenching it in oil, because if we did it in water the steel could crack. In fact it's so hard, that if Smith dropped it at this point it would shatter.' said Thomas. 'We need to temper it to make it usable. Once it's cooled back to room temperature, Buck is going to polish it until it's nice and shiny, getting rid of that pretty marbling we can see, then we'll come back and do the actual tempering.'

They spent the rest of the day practicing, and it wasn't until evening that they reassembled in the smithy. Smith placed the tiny shield above the coals and carefully warmed it.

'Now watch the steel change colour.' said Thomas. 'It's going to go through pale yellow, bright yellow, straw yellow, dark straw yellow, brown, purple, violet, dark blue, bright blue and blue grey. If we were making a blade, the colour we stop at depends on what the blade is for. An everyday knife needs bright yellow, a fighting knife or a normal sword needs dark straw or brown, but our buckler here, and our special swords need to be done in the blue range. That's because they both need to be springy to do their job.'

'For the buckler,' he went on, 'we're looking for a nice dark blue, over as much of the steel as possible. Smith has to take care not to go beyond that colour.' said Thomas. 'There we go! That's it! Quench it now Smith, like I told you!'

Smith picked the buckler up in his tongs and plunged it back into the barrel of oil for just five seconds before pulling it out again.

'And that ladies, is that!' said a very pleased Thomas. 'That shield is now the toughest shield anyone on Earth has ever seen, but on its own that isn't enough. You need to know how to use it in combination with the swords you're making.'

Once the buckler had cooled enough to handle, the coterie clustered around to look at their new toy. They were astonished at its lightness, and how hard it was when they knocked it with their knuckles.

'That's amazing...' murmured Topaz. 'It's so light and strong!'

'So it's like the swords.' added Melody. 'Everything's light so we can move much more quickly than anyone else.'

'But it's too small!' cried Deena. 'How can anything that size keep a sword or a spear off us, let alone an arrow shower?'

'You must have patience grasshopper.' said Thomas, making an allusion they hadn't a hope of understanding.

'And a whole lot of luck!' whispered Wulfstan, who like Deena, didn't believe what he was seeing.

The following day, Thomas took them through the hardening and tempering of the first completed blade. It was hardened just like the buckler, the sword being plunged vertically, point first into the oil and held there. When it came to the tempering though, Thomas had another trick up his sleeve.

'We're just going to drop the back of the blade into the heat, not the edge. We'll slowly take it up past brown to blue, then quench it. That will make the back of the blade flexible, but keep the cutting edge nice and hard and sharp.' He said. 'If we do that three times, re-polishing it between each heat cycle, we'll end up with a blade that's the best of both worlds. A really flexible creature, with a sharp edge.'

As soon as it was finished, Freawaru used it to take out her frustrations. She didn't trust this overly fragile thing a bit and thrust it into a shield with every ounce of strength she had, trying her hardest to break it. There was a collective gasp as it bent two inches out of shape before snapping back straight and true.

'That's miraculous…' murmured Storm.

'Which means you're all miracle workers!' laughed Thomas. 'Okay, we know it's flexible, now it's time to get edgy.'

14 THE GAME'S AFOOT

If you'd asked Fulton to name a creature that was highly flexible with a sharp edge, he would almost certainly have said 'Cuthbert!'

The priest had been careful to avoid having to push the handcart any more than he absolutely had to, which worked out to be about one mile in every twenty. He was also wilfully blind about sharing out the food and comfort whenever they stopped to refresh themselves. Cuthbert made sure he got the pick of whatever was on offer, while Fulton got the leftovers, if he was lucky. Fulton had lost quite a bit of weight on the journey, while Cuthbert looked if anything, a little plumper than when they'd left.

The one thing Fulton felt happy about, was that he'd managed to keep Wulfstan's money a secret. He was quite certain that Cuthbert would have found a way to trick him out of it. In fact, over the many days and miles, listening to the priest's endless rants and complaints, and watching his inhumanity to practically every life form he came across, Fulton had come to appreciate Prince Wulfstan's stance on Cuthbert. He was also thinking fondly of his old home, and wondering if the Prince would have him back. It was in this happy state of mind that he pushed the hand cart into sight of Canterbury.

Cuthbert's smile had never seemed so full of cunning as he took off his shoes and hid them deep at the bottom of the cart.

'It's time for revenge my friend. Bring the cart.' he said to Fulton, and strode off down the road, feet twitching as the sharp stones bit into his tender flesh. By the time they actually entered the town,

Cuthbert's feet were bleeding freely over the ground, and he was genuinely hobbling, leaning on his staff.

'Well Fulton, this is where our journey together ends.' he said. 'I'll take the handcart from here. Remove your things and we can go our separate ways.'

Fulton looked at him in astonishment. 'What do you mean? Aren't you going to at least give me a meal and a bed after I've pushed it all this way for you?' he asked.

Cuthbert just smiled, and handed Fulton his small bundle of goods. 'God has told me that our paths diverge from now on. Only he knows where you are to go, but separate we must. I am sad of course, but we must obey.' he said. Then without so much as a backwards glance, he hobbled away, silent but grimacing for all he was worth, trying to drum up sympathy from any onlookers.

Abandoned in a strange town, many miles from home, Fulton had no idea what to do, and found himself shuffling after Cuthbert. Perhaps there would be a market near the cathedral where he could at least buy something to eat.

Cuthbert went into full performance mode as he staggered up the road towards a group of priests chatting by the cathedral doors. One of them rushed inside to spread the news of his arrival, while the others ran over to help their limping colleague.

As Cuthbert was sat down on the steps and offered a bowl of water, Fulton edged closer, close enough to hear the conversation when the Archbishop himself came out of the cathedral to see what the fuss was about.

'Cuthbert!' cried Jaenberht. 'What are you doing so far away from your manor?'

'My Lord, I have been sorely wronged.' sighed Cuthbert. 'The Prince threw me out with no good reason, denying me both servant and beast. I have had to push my own handcart all the way here. My shoes fell apart some days ago, but with God's help I have managed to reach you.'

Jaenberht looked down at Cuthbert's bloody feet, then back to his pain etched face. 'This is appalling!' he said. 'I must speak to the King, and see that justice is done! We will force the Prince to take you back, and to humble himself in sorrow. Come into the cathedral and we can pray together while they bring the herbalist to see to you!'

Even after days of close exposure to Cuthbert, Fulton was still staggered by the audacity of the man. How could he believe in God and still tell such barefaced lies, knowing the day of judgement was coming?

It was at this point that he was accosted by a nobleman on a horse.

'It's Fulton isn't it?'

Fulton looked up into the rider's face, and recognised Earl Marwig, one of the Queen's closest advisors.

'Yes my Lord. That's me, Fulton.'

'I remember you took extra good care of my lame horse the last time I was visiting Hengist. He recovered completely thanks to you, when we might well have lost him. I was most impressed! What brings you to Canterbury?'

Fulton dropped his head.

'I am no longer at the manor my Lord. I am a free man in search of a home.'

Marwig's eyebrows rose markedly. He hadn't been at Tamworth when Hengist fell from grace, but he knew all about it, and about the Prince's rejection of Jaenberht's offer to join the Church. There might well be something worth learning from this peasant.

'It sounds as if you have a story to tell, and I would welcome a beer and a tale. Come, there's a tavern around the corner, and I owe you a drink!' he said.

An hour later, Fulton's appetite had been sated, and Marwig's decidedly piqued.

'So he let the whole village decide, slaves and all? Well, well, well. Remarkable...'

'He was right to do it, and I was wrong to object.' said Fulton sadly. 'He saw instantly what kind of man Cuthbert was. I needed days on the road to see the same thing. I wish I'd never left. I don't know what to do now.'

Marwig nodded. 'We all make mistakes. Sometimes we get lucky, and sometimes we don't. Today you got lucky.'

Fulton looked up at him hopefully.

'I think the Queen should hear what you have to say. The King too come to that. I think there's going to be real trouble with the Archbishop, and they need to be warned.'

Fulton's face filled with fear, but Marwig held up his hand soothingly.

'Relax! You've done nothing wrong. They won't do anything to you, but they will want to hear your story. Then we'll see about finding you a home. In the meantime, you can join my retinue and we'll go to Court together.'

For the next five days, Topaz and Jade focussed completely on polishing and sharpening the finished sword, while Rowena and Berthilda took over their forge duties to make the remaining blades. The coterie members not on forge duty, watched and learned the art of polishing in order to be able to finish the swords as fast as possible.

Thomas spent some of his time in the school, and some of it with Ashlin. The bow maker was getting very frustrated.

'I have found all the wood I need my Lord, and I've got the hang of cutting the horn, and hammering out the tendons, but the glue…'

'Well, I did warn you that's where the trouble would lie. What specific issues are you getting?' asked Thomas.

'Two. Some of the glues just aren't strong enough, and the bow… what was the word you taught me? Delaminates? Yes, that was it, it delaminates, falls apart. I have made up some glues that are strong enough, at least up until they get wet. Then the glue breaks down and the bow delaminates again. It's maddening!'

'What glues have worked, at least until they get wet?'

'Fish glue my Lord. It's fabulous. The only downside is that the smell is threatening my marriage. Maeve says it's almost as vile as Cuthbert!'

Thomas laughed heartily.

'Okay,' he said when he got his breath back, 'fish glue it is. If we can't get a waterproof glue, we'll just have to waterproof the bow somehow.'

By the end of the sixth day, the sword was complete, and fitted with hilt and guard. Thomas held it in his hand, revelling in its lightness and perfect balance, then walked over to where a fresh pig carcass was hanging and addressed the whole group, including Smith, Buck, Hengist and Kelsey.

'Fantastic effort everyone, I'm really pleased! It's beautifully balanced, and we know it's springy. The question now is, will it cut? Will it thrust?'

Fifteen faces looked back at him, their feelings writ large in their expressions. Deena, Deana and Scarlett looked doubtful. Freawaru, Storm, Smith and Buck were serious, as would be anyone with their reputations on the line. Rowena, Berthilda and Melody were hopeful out of loyalty to their Prince, but Topaz and Jade looked completely confident because they knew exactly what kind of an edge they'd managed to create, and couldn't wait to see it in action. Hengist and Kelsey looked serious, aware that what they were about to see could change everything they knew.

Thomas stood stock still in front of the pig, and just using his arm, thrust the sword into the carcass. The blade slid in smoothly, burying itself up to the hilt. When he withdrew it, he pushed the edge into the flesh which it sliced like a razor, leaving a gaping wound.

The group erupted into cheering and applause.

'And that was just your arm!' cried Rowena. 'You didn't even have to swing it, or use your body!'

Thomas just grinned, and handed her the sword. 'Your turn I think.'

Rowena took a fighter's stance, and thrust the blade into the rear haunch, using her upper body to deliver a much harder blow than Thomas. The tip of the blade appeared almost instantly on the other side of the leg, and when she withdrew it, she was able to slice the blade clean out through the flesh as if it was being butchered. She looked at it in awe.

'My turn please.' said Berthilda. 'I want to try something.'

She took her stance, and like Rowena, struck hard into the back leg, but aiming for the bone. The carcass jolted and the blade bent under the force of the blow, but crucially it sprang back into shape and didn't break.

'Hurrah!' shouted Smith. 'That's a real blade for you!'

'May I try?' came a soft male voice from the back.

'Of course Kelsey.' smiled Berthilda. 'We all want to see what you can do with it!'

Kelsey took his own stance, and struck hard and fast into the chest. The blade sliced effortlessly through, and out the other side, breaking a rib as it went. He withdrew it thoughtfully, then swung it in a slash across the belly. It didn't penetrate anywhere near as far as his own sword would have done, but it went far enough in to inflict a fatal wound on a man. Then he flicked the sword around in his hand, feinting and striking, trying out multiple attacks, and in the end declared himself impressed.

'In a one on one fight, this would be a dangerous weapon to come across.' he said. 'Against a shield wall though, I think it would struggle. And having just a single edge is not so good I think.'

This was the thing that worried them the most. To make the blade as long as possible, Thomas had taken one of the normal two edges away, repurposing the metal to lengthen and stiffen the blade. It was very much like a sword from the nineteenth century, if they had but known it.

Thomas nodded. 'You're absolutely right. That's why the blade is only part of the answer. We need to change the fight itself. The new guard is part of that change.'

He ran his fingers over the curving basket that spread out beneath the quillons.

'It has the same cross guard quillons that your normal swords have, but the basket will protect the top of your hand from your opponent's blade, and its curve down to the pommel will protect your fingers.'

Hengist raised his hand. 'I was going to ask about that Your Highness. Will it not force us to fight with one hand?'

Thomas nodded. 'Yes it will, but with the buckler in your other hand, you won't have much choice anyway. Come, pick up a wooden mock sword and I'll demonstrate.'

Hengist retrieved the training tool and took up position opposite Thomas.

'Okay, don't hit me too hard please, but try and get through my guard.' said Thomas, carefully positioning the little metal shield well out in front of himself.

Hengist moved his weight easily from foot to foot, impressed at just how much of Thomas was obscured when the buckler was held that far out. Then he lunged his blade underneath it towards Thomas's thigh. The Prince easily deflected it downwards with the Buckler and flicked the back of his own blade lightly against the right hand side of Hengist's throat.

'One nil.' said Thomas quietly.

Somewhat chastened, Hengist took up position again. This time he feinted a slash to the left side of Thomas's head, intending his real strike to be the following backstroke but he never had the chance.

Thomas simply deflected Hengist's "blade" upward, and came in to rest the tip of his own sword against Hengist's chest.

'Two nil. This time try and hit me hard. Go on. You're allowed to this time!'

Hengist began to circle his prey. He was a good man, but he had his pride like anyone else, and didn't much like being made to look a fool by a ten year old boy. He launched a sudden attack, the flurry of powerful blows forcing Thomas to retreat, but every slash and thrust was deflected by either the sword or the buckler, allowing the Prince to dodge the "blade".

Then, as Hengist swung what he thought was going to be a killer vertical strike from his elbow, Thomas stepped forward, caught Hengist's blade on his own, pushing it out and down, allowing him to swing the edge of the buckler over the top in a haymaker, just brushing Hengist's face.

Hengist looked at the boy in amazement.

'The trick for us little ones, and for those not so strong as you, is to use the buckler to deflect your blows, not to block them. If we try and block a hard blow, you'd just break our arm, or worse. But because I can change the position and angle of the buckler so quickly, as long as I see you coming, I can always deflect or punch your blade away no matter what you do. And, if the blow isn't so strong, I can choose to block if I want to, or I can catch it on my own blade and use the buckler to hit you with. If I'm really smart, I'll use your own strength against you, so you throw yourself off balance, or open yourself up as your sword goes past where you meant it to.'

'Why did you fight with it pushed out so far away from your body?' asked Berthilda. 'Surely your arm is weak if you hold it like that.'

Thomas turned to face her, and held the buckler close to his chest.

'Well there are lots of other ways to use it, but this is a nice introductory technique. See when it's held so close, how little of me it protects? It really doesn't do that much as a static shield, but,' he said pushing the buckler out towards her, 'when it's out here you can see a lot less of me, and I don't have to move it far to counter your blade.'

Then he grinned and brought his sword in behind the buckler, elbow back, and the tip of his blade nestling in behind the shield. 'And if I do this, you have no idea at all what I'm going to do with my sword. I can attack in all sorts of ways and you get no warning until the tip of my blade is well on its way.'

Thomas demonstrated a number of different strikes, all hidden by the buckler, until Berthilda expressed herself convinced.

'Like I said, there are many other ways in which we can use these two weapons. This is just one of them.' said Thomas.

'How will it cope with a spear?' asked Kelsey.

Thomas nodded. 'The same way it does with a sword.'

'And what if your opponent has a shield as well as a spear or a sword?' continued Kelsey, coming back to his point about the shield wall.

'Ah.' said Thomas. 'That does make life more difficult to be sure. Let's try one on one.'

Kelsey stepped up, taking Hengist's "blade" and a large lime wood shield. With no warning he rushed at Thomas, trying to push him off balance with the shield, to open up an opportunity for his sword. Thomas saw what he was up to and threw himself to the ground, rolling right, under the shield as it swept over him, and flicking up the blunt side of his own blade into the back of Kelsey's knee, before bouncing to his feet again.

'The lightness and size of my weapons allow me a wider range of options than you, and I'm faster.' he explained to a startled Kelsey. 'Come, try again.'

Kelsey moved in more carefully this time, positioning his sword behind his shield much as Thomas was doing with his buckler. Time and again Kelsey's "blade" flicked out at Thomas, but every time it was batted effortlessly away.

Thomas in turn was looking for an opportunity, but Kelsey was an expert, and always made sure that he opened up his shield no further than he needed to in order to make his strikes. If Thomas had been a grown man, he'd have had more options, but in the end he decided to go low again.

He waited until Kelsey had just recovered himself from a failed strike, then threw his buckler arm up as if to strike towards Kelsey's face, which Kelsey caught easily on his shield, but opened a small gap below, allowing Thomas to gently strike him on the shin.

'Hardly a killing blow.' said Kelsey dismissively.

'No, but it would slow you down! If I was an adult, I'd have more options. Hengist, why don't you take over from me.'

A few minutes later, Hengist and Kelsey circled each other warily. The first three points went to Kelsey, largely because Hengist was fighting the same way he'd always fought, as if he had a larger shield. It took him a while, and a lot of encouragement from Thomas before he started to adapt, but once he had, the speed of his weapons allowed him to beat Kelsey every time from then on.

At Kelsey's insistence, they swapped weapons, and repeated the duel with the same results. A few losses as Kelsey learned the hard way, and from then on the new sword and Buckler won every point.

Both men agreed that the combination had real strengths, but Kelsey returned to what he considered the killer argument against it.

'The problem is my Lord, that you won't be fighting one on one. You'll be fighting ten against ten, and they'll almost certainly use the shield wall, at least to start with. Their heavier slashing swords will break you down, and you won't be able to dodge away. Your speed will be useless.' he said.

'I completely agree Kelsey, which is why we won't fight them like that. We'll have to either take out their shields or force them to split up.' replied Thomas.

'And how do you mean to do that?' asked Hengist.

'Oh there are ways and means!' laughed Thomas. 'Let's learn this first, and I'll take you through how we'll deal with the shield wall later on. Okay everyone, time for you all to have a go, but for the love of heaven, be careful if you're the one with the new sword! If you draw blood with it, you'll be on bread and water for a week!'

'Arrrgggghhhh!' hissed a highly frustrated Wulfstan in his ear. 'I want a go too!!! It's my body after all, and it's been simply ages since we swapped!'

'Over to you Fulton, please tell their majesties what you told me in Canterbury.' said Marwig.

He and Fulton had finally caught up with the travelling court, and Marwig had straight away asked for an audience with the King and Queen. Standing there in front of the two most powerful people in the Kingdom, Fulton froze, unable to speak, his eyes fixed at the King's feet.

'Come on Fulton, don't waste their time please, there's a good chap. You're not in any trouble. They just need to hear your story.' coaxed Marwig.

Still the man stood there, rigid in fear.

'Marwig tells me that you have news of my son Fulton. I would much like to hear it.' said the Queen softly.

His terror softened a little by her gentleness, Fulton at last managed to find his voice. 'When Prince Wulfstan arrived in the village, he came across Cuthbert the priest chasing and beating one of the villagers, which he stopped. When he found out it was because the man had lost almost all his goods, and was no longer able to pay his tithe, the Prince grew very angry and sent Cuthbert away to think about what he had done.'

He paused to look up at the Queen, whose smile encouraged him to go on.

'Then the priest tried to kill his slave, chasing her into the great hall where in her terror to get away, she accidentally knocked the Prince to the ground, but the Prince's servants saved her. She told the Prince that in her hearing, Cuthbert had threatened to kill the Prince, and that he wanted to kill her to silence her tongue. Cuthbert grew angry and accused her of lies, but the Prince believed her, and insisted on buying her to save her life.'

He glanced at Offa who was looking stern. Fulton swallowed in fear but continued on. 'So the next day, the Prince gathered the entire village together, including all the slaves, to decide whether Cuthbert should stay or go. Prince Wulfstan spoke his arguments, and allowed the priest to state his, then everyone including the slaves, got to drop a coloured stone in a barrel, dark to go, light to stay. When the Prince counted them, there were many more dark than light, so he ordered Cuthbert to go.'

Offa held up a hand. 'The Prince counted the stones? On his own?'

'Yes Your Majesty.' said Fulton.

Offa turned to Cynethryth. 'Is this ability to count another piece of magic from that thump on the head, or is there something you've not been telling me?' he asked.

'It's news to me too.' she replied, pursing her lips in thought. 'Carry on Fulton.'

'Some of us were upset that the slaves had been allowed the same say as we freemen, and we complained when he came to ask us why we seemed vexed. He offered me the chance to be exchanged with someone in another village if I wanted, and like a fool I said yes. I was then even more foolish and asked for it to happen as soon as possible, and he gave me what he said was a year's income in coin, so I could leave and start a new life. I went back to my hut, but when I came out again with my possessions, I ran into Cuthbert and his handcart as he was being escorted out of the village. He bade me join him, and even though I had decided to ask the Prince if I might be allowed to stay after all, I was too frightened of the priest's anger to say so.'

Nobody said a word, so Fulton carried on. 'Cuthbert said he had a handcart because the Prince forbade him a slave or an animal as Cuthbert would be too cruel to either. So he used me instead. We walked to Canterbury, and along the way I learned how wise the Prince had been in his understanding of men. Cuthbert is an evil, selfish man, hurtful to others, and cunning beyond all measure. When we arrived at Canterbury, he had pushed the cart hardly at all, but then he took off and hid his shoes, told me to go away, and pushed the cart barefooted to the Cathedral. Not knowing what else to do, I followed, hoping to find food-'

'He abandoned you without even a meal?' interrupted the Queen.

Fulton nodded. 'I received nothing Your Majesty. No food, no bed, no coin, nothing.'

She frowned. 'Hm. Carry on.'

'When he arrived at the Cathedral, his feet were bleeding badly, and he was hobbling, but when the Archbishop came out, Cuthbert pretended that he had pushed the cart alone all the way from the manor, and had been walking barefoot for days. The Archbishop got very angry, and said he would make the King and Queen force the Prince to take Cuthbert back, and to beg his pardon for so wronging him. Then I was fortunate enough to be recognised by Earl Marwig who brought me to you, and that is my story Your Majesties.'

Offa looked at him thoughtfully. 'Thank you Fulton. Earl Marwig was correct. We did indeed need to hear your story. My servants will now take you to the kitchens, and give you the meal that Cuthbert should have given you.'

'Wait!' said the Queen. 'What are your plans now Fulton?'

'I have none Your Majesty. I am seeking a home.' said Futon, looking very sad indeed.

'Would you like to return to the manor?' she asked.

He looked up into her face. 'More than anything else in the world. I have learnt the folly of my ways, and long to be the Prince's man, but I fear he would not have me back, or that my hut has been given to another.'

Cynethryth smiled at Marwig.

'Perhaps you might like to pay a visit to my son Earl Marwig, taking Fulton along with you? I'd like to know how he's getting on, and Fulton could go with you to find out if the Prince is as forgiving in his nature, as he seems to be wise.'

Marwig nodded. 'It would be my pleasure Your Majesty.'

'Then that's settled.' said the King. 'Fulton, go off and get your meal, then rejoin Marwig's people. Marwig, you stay please. We three have to decide how to respond to this piece of news about our troublesome priest!'

15 A VISITATION

Wulfstan's frustration at being locked out of his body, finally ended a week later when Marwig, Fulton and three men at arms arrived in the village. He was out doing his patrols as normal when the riders were spotted, but it wasn't until they arrived in the village itself that the event took place.

'I bring greetings from the King and Queen to their beloved son.' was all it took from Marwig before Wulfstan was instantly back in the body, and busy in conversation.

Thomas found it a bit of a relief if he was honest with himself. Playing the ventriloquist's dummy was awfully hard work, and it was much better if Wulfstan could speak for himself. However, this conversation mattered, so he couldn't just swan off and go for a relaxing flight as he wanted to. He needed to listen to this.

Wulfstan saw his guests settled in the two guest houses, and their horses seen to, before they gathered in the hall for a proper discussion where he heard all about Fulton's adventures, and Cuthbert's games.

After the tale was over, Fulton clasped his hands in front of him and fell to his knees. 'I beg you Your Highness to take me back. I was foolish beyond words when I asked you to let me go. I want nothing more than to return to the village, and to be your man. I have learned your worth and wisdom the hard way, and will never forget it. I will be your loyal servant forevermore.' he pleaded.

Wulfstan looked thoughtfully down at him.

'Well?' asked Thomas.

'Well what?' replied Wulfstan.

'Do you want him back or don't you? He seems perfectly sincere to me. You might find that degree of loyalty useful.'

Wulfstan nodded. 'Of course Fulton. We'd love to have you back. Mind you, it would be nice to have the money too!'

Instantly Fulton produced the bag of coins from inside his tunic. 'It's all there Your Highness. Every bit of it. Please, take it with my thanks!'

Wulfstan opened the purse, and waited while Thomas counted out the coins for him. Finally, Wulfstan looked up and smiled at the still anxious Fulton.

'Excellent. Well, wisdom and honesty deserve their own reward, so here's a third of it back, so you can get your life started again. I'm afraid we've given your old hut to someone else, so you'll have to stay in the guest accommodation for now, but we're building a number of new huts between the smithy and the quay, and you can have one of those when it's ready.'

'Thank you Your Highness!' gushed Fulton, bowing as deeply as he could, without actually hitting his head on the ground.

'You're most welcome Fulton. Now, I know you're a horse expert, so I suggest you go off to the stables, and familiarise yourself with our herd, and introduce yourself to their riders. They could do with another skilled hand.'

'Yes Your Highness! Thank you Your Highness!' said Fulton, and removed himself as fast as he decently could. The tension that had dwelt in his shoulders for so many days, finally began to ease, as hope for the future returned. It would be all right now, he thought.

'Well, do I need to return to court do you think?' Wulfstan asked Marwig.

'Not if you don't want to Your Highness.' replied Marwig. 'The King and Queen have things well under control for now, but you may wish to prepare your... arguments... for when you meet with the Archbishop. He'll come out fighting, your word against Cuthbert's, and talking about the honesty of priests to strengthen his case.'

Wulfstan frowned. 'I've seen all I need to as regards the honesty and decency of the clergy. They're not quite mutually exclusive, but you could be forgiven for wondering. Tell their majesties not to worry. I'll be prepared.'

Marwig looked at him closely, wondering about Wulfstan's choice of words. He wasn't to know that the Prince's vocabulary had increased in leaps and bounds through spending so much time with Thomas.

'I believe you will my Prince. I believe you will… How are your other preparations going, those for your battle with Thegn Grimketil?' he asked, changing the subject.

Wulfstan laughed. 'Oh quite well I think. I have all my warriors now, their training is coming along nicely, and they'll be properly equipped a few weeks from now. That gives us the winter to practice, and prepare for the fight to come. Father will be pleased. I'm not going to be spending much more of his money!'

Marwig's expression gave nothing away. 'I imagine that will please him greatly. He has been, impressed, at the bills you have generated. Indeed, he has commented about them at some length.'

Wulfstan grinned. 'I'll bet he has! Well, he can't blame me for doing what needs to be done, not when it's all of his own making!'

'I couldn't possibly comment.' said the ever diplomatic Marwig.

'What? Not even after a good dinner and lots of beer?' asked Wulfstan.

'Not even then.' said Marwig, wearing the gentlest of smiles on his face.

'We shall see my friend, we shall see!' laughed Wulfstan, but Marwig was as good as his word, maintaining his diplomatic poise throughout the entire evening.

The following morning, Wulfstan introduced Marwig to the coterie, but kept their new weaponry out of sight, and made no mention of it either. Instead he had the women demonstrate their archery skills, which impressed the earl greatly.

'That's ten bullseyes today Deana!' cried Berthilda. 'Well done that girl, well done!'

Her words gave Marwig the opportunity to introduce a subject of great interest to the King and Queen. 'Prince Wulfstan, Fulton said that you counted the voting stones yourself. The King and Queen were somewhat surprised at that. They didn't know you could count.'

In an instant Wulfstan found himself outside the body once more, and Thomas was back in control.

'Oh well.' he said to Thomas. 'Short but sweet, and I enjoyed the food, but when it comes to talking about the school, I'm happy it's all yours again! I'm off for a scout around.'

'Have fun!' called Thomas after him, before addressing himself to Marwig.

'Ah yes,' he murmured, 'the King thought I was just playing childish games, yet all the time I was learning, just as I told him. Perhaps my parents just weren't as observant as they thought they were.'

Marwig inclined his head diplomatically. 'Learning to count is not usually done as a game Your Highness. Generally speaking, children learn it from an adult, and it looks anything but a game to me. It looks downright unpleasant!'

Thomas laughed.

'I have some people I think you should meet.' he said, and led Marwig to the new schoolroom. Somewhat to his surprise, there was no one there, but he quickly snapped his fingers in realisation. 'I know where they are! They'll be down by the quay.'

Sure enough, the children and their parents were on the wooden pier, clustered around Oswin and Sigeberht's new crane, which had just been erected.

Its base was a squared off oak tree trunk, trimmed of bark, about two feet thick and two feet high, mounted on its side onto a solid platform, that had itself been secured tightly to the pier's structural timbers. On top of the trunk was a wrought iron plate attached to the top of the bottom trunk, and a second plate attached to another worked oak trunk above that.

Mounted halfway through this second trunk was a cutout containing a long ash pole, with a stout iron rod through it that allowed it to rotate up and down. Most of the pole stuck out one side, with a hook at its far end, while the shorter side had a series of notches cut into its top at regular intervals.

'Well, well!' said Thomas, clapping his hands in appreciation. 'You finally did it! Well, come on then, show me how it works!'

Sigeberht pointed to the hook at the far end. 'We dip the pole down into the boat, and the boatman,' he said, indicating a cheerful man in the boat by the quay, 'hooks one of his sacks onto the end there like he's just done.'

'Then we hang these iron weights into the notches on this end, until the sack lifts out of the boat.' added Oswin, proceeding to demonstrate just that.

The sack lifted easily, and ignoring the slightly unpleasant noise of the two iron plates grinding against each other, despite the grease between them, Gundy was able to push the weighted end of the pole around with just one hand, until the sack was above a hand cart on the pier.

'It works!' cried Oscar. 'It works!'

Gundy looked up proudly.

'And, we know how much the sack weighs too!' she said. 'We just need to read off the iron weights and where they are on this side of the pole.'

She quickly did the maths in her head, and proudly declared that particular sack to be forty pounds, a figure confirmed by the boatman.

Marwig broke his silence.

'That's most ingenious. Who built it?'

Thomas laughed.

'You're looking at them! Oswin and Sigeberht designed the structure and did the basic calculations. Oscar and Gundy here, checked and refined those calculations to make sure it would work, before they started to build it, and Grimhild wrote it all up with chalk on these slates so they'd have accurate information to refer to during the build. Smith helped by making the iron plates and the rods that hold it all together. Sighard and Lynette, their parents, helped them with the build. And that's the whole team.'

Marwig finally lost his diplomatic cool. 'But they're just children! That's not possible! And they're peasants to boot!'

Thomas just smiled. 'I don't care what class someone is. I care about who they are as people, their attitude to life, and their potential. Class doesn't come into it. This family is amazing, and they were an easy choice for my school.'

'Your school?' asked Marwig hollowly. 'Not the priest's school?'

Gundy stuck out her bottom lip. 'That mean old priest wouldn't teach anybody anything! He just wanted to keep it all to himself! Prince Wulfstan taught us everything, not the priest!'

Marwig knelt down so his face was at the same level as hers. 'And how old are you Gundy?'

'I'm eight!' she said proudly.

'And the Prince taught you how to use numbers to be able to do all that?'

'Yes.' she smiled bashfully. 'It's not really difficult you know. It's just fun!'

'Fun?' asked Marwig weakly.

'Fun!' chorused the rest of the family.

After that experience, Marwig needed a walk to settle his mind, but he was about to get another shock. Alfred walked in front of them, and into a small building the size of a modern garden shed.

'What's he doing?' asked Marwig.

'Evacuating his bowels.'

Marwig stopped dead in his tracks. 'You have a building for that? In a village?'

'Actually, we have eight now.' said Thomas. 'They have to be convenient if people are going to use them.'

'But why do it at all?' asked a bemused Marwig.

Thomas laughed. 'Does this village smell the same as other villages, or does it smell sweeter?' he asked.

Marwig sniffed thoughtfully. 'Sweeter.' he said. 'Much sweeter indeed.'

'That's because nobody does their business anywhere but in one of these four toilets, even you and your men. I had your chamber pots emptied for you this morning, in case you were wondering. But it's not just to keep the smell down. It stops disease.'

Marwig looked at him.

'Well, of course if you get rid of the smell, then it follows that the disease will go too.'

'It's not quite that simple Marwig, but certainly there's a correlation of sorts. Anyway, we haven't lost a single person to dysentery, cholera or any of the puke and poop diseases since these were built. Not even an infant.'

Marwig was staggered. Out of a village of close to two hundred souls, you'd expect to lose a significant number every year to disease, especially children.

'Good heavens! So you're already making good on your boasts to your father, that you could achieve a lower death rate than anywhere else in the kingdom?'

Thomas grinned broadly.

'Uhuh. And, we have a new arrangement for the fields which we're implementing right now. It will triple food and wool production within a year, something else I said to my father.'

'But how did you come to learn all of this?' asked Marwig. 'Or perhaps I should ask, how did you manage to keep the knowledge a secret until now?' his diplomatic skills coming back to him.

Thomas chose his words carefully. The last thing he needed was an accusation of witchcraft. 'As I said to the King that fateful evening, as a child I played, as I played I observed, as I observed I learned, and as I learned I thought, and imagined how things might be, with a little change here and there. None of it's a very big change you know. It's not magic, just common sense once you see things as they really are.'

Marwig looked at him thoughtfully. 'And the idea for the school? Why did you do that instead of relying on the Church?'

'Oh come on!' said Thomas, losing his cool for once. 'You know about Cuthbert? Well what kind of idiot knowingly puts himself at the mercy of that sort of creature? And then extend that thought. If the Church can wilfully appoint such a man to the rank of priest, what makes you think it will be any less fallible when it's appointing its Archbishops? If we end up with a corrupt Archbishop, where does that leave the kingdom if it's wholly dependent on the Church for all its reading, writing and accounting?'

Marwig stared at him, open mouthed.

'No.' Thomas continued. 'The kingdom needs its own supply of trained scribes and numbers people, independent of the Church, and for that we need a school! That's why I started my own here.'

'But the Church must have scribes to replicate the holy texts, and priests who can read them!' argued Marwig.

'Who's stopping them?' asked Thomas. 'My running a school doesn't stop the Church from running theirs. It just stops them from having as much power in the kingdom as they do now.'

He smiled thoughtfully. 'And you know what? The King will agree with me when he thinks about it properly! After all, who writes the history of our people at the moment? The Church, that's who! And if the King falls out with the Archbishop, which is always likely, what do you think they're going to write about him after he's dead? Will it be Offa the Great, or Offa the Awful? If the only people who can read or write are the clergy, then the King's memory is entirely in their hands. Will he want that do you suppose?'

'And it applies to you too!' he went on. 'Will it be Marwig the Magnificent, or Marwig the Malfeasant? How's your own relationship with the Church going to be after this Cuthbert business shakes out?'

For a minute or two they walked on in silence, as Marwig digested this new view of the world. 'I think,' he said, slowly stroking his beard, 'that you may well have a point.'

By the time Marwig slid into bed that evening, his head was buzzing. This young boy could be the greatest king Mercia had ever had. If he survived that is. And if he did survive, how would his older brother take to the idea of being supplanted? Marwig thought the future looked turbulent, but never expected it to break upon him quite as quickly as it did.

Wulfstan was enjoying his favourite night time pursuit of watching the owls hunting. He never tired of their silent flight, and unerring accuracy in locating their prey. Tonight, he was following a young female on the prowl for mice around the barn. The bird was sitting silently on the east gable, intent on a tiny rustle near the river, when it suddenly took fright and flew away.

Puzzled, Wulfstan looked around to see what might have disturbed her, and if he'd had a heart, it might have missed a beat. Two men were moving stealthily between the hall and the barn, heading for the stables. Then he looked again. There were more of them, flitting through the village paths, and they were armed.

Wulfstan shot back into his body.

'We're under attack!' he shouted at a startled Thomas. 'Get up there and tell me what they're doing!'

Then he bounced out of bed rousing the other sleepers in the hall. 'Everybody up! Seize your weapons! This is not a drill, we're under attack!' he yelled.

Rowena and Berthilda moved to grab regular swords but Wulfstan stopped them.

'No! Grab your new ones, and the bucklers. We can't keep them hidden now. Deena, Deana and Melody, you grab the other three new swords. Everybody else, you're stronger at present, so you grab the regular blades!'

Thomas swooped in to give a warning.

'There are two men outside the hall door, one each side, with axes.'

Wulfstan ran out through the door, dropping into a barrel roll as he went. The axeman on the left of the door was so startled that he did nothing, and the one on the right swung his axe into thin air.

Melody was the first girl out, plunging her sword into the startled axeman's chest, stopping his heart instantly.

The other one raised his axe to cut her down, but Freawaru was there, thrusting a shield into his face to block. He cursed loudly and stepped back, trying to give himself space, which he did, but Storm filled it, thrusting her blade up into his throat. With a horrible gurgle, he fell backwards out of the way, and the rest of the coterie burst out into the moonlight.

Thomas watch them go, and for the first time, he saw Melody's golden glow.

'I wonder…' he said to himself.

A group of four men with swords ran past the guest huts, yelling for all they were worth, intent on hacking the women to pieces. They didn't see Marwig and one of his men come out behind them.

Marwig swung his sword down hard from right to left, onto the right shoulder of one of them. It exited just above the man's left hip, cleaving him in two.

This alerted the other three, who spun to face this new line of attack. One engaged Marwig, while the other two went for his man at arms. Marwig's man managed to kill one, but as he was trying to withdraw his sword from his victim's groin, the second attacker took his head off with a finely judged blow.

Marwig had found himself facing a master swordsman, who could counter his every move, and now had to deal with the beheader as well. He flicked his sword point back and forth between the two, keeping them at bay.

'What ho Marwig!' came a childish voice from behind the master swordsman. 'Need a hand?'

Marwig's expert opponent spun around, and laughed when he saw Wulfstan, Deena and Deana.

'Oh good!' he cried. 'I could do with a snack or two. It's a pity the rest got cold feet though.' he said, watching the other girls running off into the night. Then he leapt towards Deana, leaving his colleague to deal with Marwig.

He swung his sword hard and fast from above his right shoulder, down at Deana's chest. There was a clash of iron on steel as Deana caught it on her buckler and deflected it into the ground.

Sparks flashed out as the tip of his blade bounced off a stone. He cursed, recovered his balance and struck again, a thrust this time, straight at her face.

Again, she caught it on her buckler, this time flicking his sword out past her left shoulder. That left him open, and she managed to strike him on the forehead with her own blade, its razor sharp edge slicing away the skin to reveal the white bone beneath.

Startled, the man drew back. These mice had claws after all!

Deena moved out to the side, trying to get around behind him, but he was wise to her intentions. He feinted, as if to attack Deana once more, but instead swung his sword horizontally at waist height towards Deena. She caught it between her sword and buckler, trapping the blade, but was lifted off her feet by the sheer force of the blow.

The man growled in frustration, forcing his blade up and around, tumbling her to the ground, face down. With a snarl of satisfaction, he prepared to bring his blade down across her back, but never got the chance. Wulfstan's sword pierced his belly and ran all the way up inside his ribcage into the heart.

The man twisted away to address his new attacker, opening his stomach on Wulfstan's withdrawing blade. Appalled, he watched his own intestines spilling onto the ground, then his knees gave way and he fell face first into his own gore.

'You need to send someone to the stables!' cried Thomas. 'There are six men there trying to steal the horses!'

Wulfstan told Deena and Deana to help Marwig deal with his remaining man, while he ran off towards the smithies, where he could see Rowena and Berthilda finishing off two more.

'Come with me!' he shouted as he ran past them. 'We need to protect the horses!'

The three ran around the corner to an awful sight. Scarlett lay motionless by the stable door, Fulton astride her, back to the wall, determinedly wielding a pitchfork, trying to keep six men at bay.

'Gerrofoutofit!!' he yelled in a voice quite different to normal. 'Ye'll not have her, or the horses ye evil mongrels!'

'We'll have whatever we want.' said one of the men calmly. 'and what we want right now is you, dead. So that's what we're going to have. Boys? Get him!'

Just at that moment, Storm, Jade and Topaz came running down past the barn towards them, the moonlight glinting off their swords.

'Drop your weapons!' commanded Wulfstan.

The leader spat onto the ground.

'I don't think so. Not on the orders of a little runt like you! You three take the women, Alcott, you take the peasant, Nash, you and I will take the brat and his trollops!'

The six split up as directed, to face their respective foes, but at that very moment two horsemen burst past Wulfstan heading towards the stable door.

Wulfstan gasped. There was nobody left to stop them stealing the horses!

Then suddenly there was a high pitched cry.

'Leave them alone you bad man!'

Gundy!

'Yeah! Get out here!' came another child's voice.

Oscar!

The two children stood bravely in the doorway, each holding a spear that was far too big for them, waving the points at the riders as best they could.

The riders' horses had shied to a halt at the sudden appearance of these strange little creatures, but now moved forward under the calm urgings of their riders, who were drawing their swords.

'No!' shouted Wulfstan. 'Oscar, Gundy! Get away! Now!'

The siblings ignored him, and stood their ground against the advancing horsemen.

Then all hell broke loose as the six footmen launched themselves into the attack.

Topaz, Storm and Jade caught the onslaught of axe, spear and scramseaxe on their shields. Jade's opponent fell instantly with a thrust through his eye, but Storm's managed to overwhelm her with his strength and speed, knocking her to the ground.

The man then ignored her, spinning to launch another powerful attack on Jade. The fury of his axe blows forced her back a couple of paces before Storm's sword swung low from behind, taking off his right leg at the knee.

He screamed as he fell, until the tip of Jade's sword smashed through his skull a few seconds later, silencing him forever.

Topaz grinned at her own opponent. 'That's two nil little man. You're all on your own now! Time to go!'

The man snarled in fury. 'I'm not running from a chit of a girl!'

Jade laughed from behind him. 'No. You're running from three of them!'

He looked over his shoulder, and realised he was surrounded. He flicked his spear around to protect himself, but it was hopeless. A spear might keep away two swords in front, but not three from all sides.

Seconds later he too was dead, all three blades slamming into his body, one after the other.

In the meantime, Nash had been despatched by Rowena, and Berthilda was withdrawing her blade from the leader's temple.

'I really think you should surrender.' said Wulfstan calmly to the remaining Alcott and the two riders.

The lead horseman quickly assessed the situation. 'I didn't come all this way for nothing. Let's grab those kids and go!' he ordered the other rider.

They threw their mounts forward, and swung their blades down hard at the two children.

'No!' screamed Wulfstan.

Gundy and Oscar's spears were swept aside and smashed in two by the blows, then they themselves were scooped up onto the horses, and dumped in front of the riders, who then charged straight past the Prince, and onto the main path south.

Alcott looked around him in dismay, waving his scramseaxe ineffectually, until Fulton plunged his pitchfork into his back so hard that the forks came out his chest. The man gave the most awful groan, and collapsed next to Scarlett.

Berthilda ran past him into the stables, cut the tether of her horse Thunder, leapt aboard, and tore off into the night after the two horsemen.

'Well that's torn it.' said Rowena, kneeling down to see to Scarlett.

'She'll be okay.' Jade said. 'She's just stunned thank heavens. Good job Fulton.'

'Yes. Thank you Fulton.' said Wulfstan, shaking his hand vigorously. 'I am more glad than ever that you came back to us!'

Fulton blushed, and said nothing, because he didn't know what to say.

Thomas streamed after Berthilda who was riding Thunder as hard as she could in pursuit of the two raiders. She rode as she normally did, with no equipment, using her weight, and pressures in her legs to tell the horse where to go.

She could smell by the dust kicked up by her quarry's hooves that she was slowly closing them down, and occasionally the light of the full moon allowed her to see them ahead of her through the woods and hedges. For twenty minutes they galloped on before the lead raider slowed them to a canter.

'We should be clear by now Radley!' he called back to his fellow. 'And we're almost at the meeting place! He won't be pleased, but at least we've got something to sell for our troubles.'

He looked down at the top of Gundy's head and laughed.

The thunder of their own horses' hooves meant they never heard Berthilda galloping up behind. She held her sword arm almost straight, slightly bent at the elbow, and aimed for the left side of Radley's neck. Straight and true, the blade plunged in just to the left of his spine, the edge cutting all the way out to the left of his neck, severing the jugular.

Blood poured out of the wound, triggering panic in Oscar as it cascaded onto his head. Radley screamed, and yanked his horse off the path to the right, where a tree branch thwacked into the remnants of his throat, sweeping him to the ground, with Oscar still in his arms.

Radley landed on his back, and Oscar landed on Radley, knocking out what little air was left in the man's lungs. The boy sprang to his feet and raced to hide behind the tree, leaving Radley to die on his own.

'Berthilda!' cried the leader, who'd brought his mount to a halt.

'Hello Ward.' she said. 'Is that what you're reduced to now, stealing children for your master?'

He shook his head sorrowfully. 'Grimketil was going to give you to me as a present. Did you know that? Why did you have to be so foolish as to join that stupid little boy?'

'Because that little boy is more of a man than any of you.' she replied. 'And so am I come to that!'

'No you're not.' said Ward. 'What you are now, is dead, either right this minute or when you meet Grimketil on the field of battle. Either way you're dead.'

'Ooh! Who's a big boy then?' she mocked.

Ward swung himself off his horse and tied it to a branch, before picking Gundy up and placing her on the ground.

'Now you listen to me girl.' he said fiercely. 'You stay right here, because if you don't, I'll cut you into tiny pieces once I've finished off your friend here! Understand?'

Gundy nodded fearfully.

'Good girl. Remember now!'

Ward stood up to face Berthilda, who had likewise dismounted. He unsheathed his sword and swung it effortlessly in highly practiced moves, demonstrating a great degree of skill in the moonlight.

'I'm looking forward to this you know. Not as much as I would have looked forward to our wedding night, but there we are. You've made your choice.'

Berthilda said nothing at all. She just stood quietly, her sword visible by her side, the buckler hidden behind her back. Ward spotted the sword.

'A new blade? It looks a bit puny to me, so thin, and only one edge to it. I suppose that's appropriate, a half edged sword from a half arsed Prince.' he laughed coarsely.

Then he took up his stance and began to move towards her. With no shield to carry, he held his sword in a two handed grip, flicking rapidly from one attack position to another. Berthilda knew just how quick and strong he could be like this, and watched him carefully.

Without warning, he swung an attack from his right to left at chest height, but it was a feint to position the sword for his real attack, flicking it back to thrust towards the right of her head.

She caught it effortlessly on her own blade, then swung the edge of her buckler into the bridge of his nose.

He reeled back in astonishment, tears streaming down his cheeks.

'You cow! You'll pay for that!' he growled.

'Maybe, maybe not.' she said softly, shuffling her stance to adjust to his own.

Ward's blade flickered again, a savage cut slashing downwards at her left hip. She caught it between sword and buckler, deflecting its energy towards the ground.

Ward backed off a little, looking at the miniature shield.

'Interesting little toy he's given you there. A tiny shield to go with a skinny sword, from a tiny brat. How sweet! Much good may it do you!'

She laughed.

'I once gave you something special, don't you remember?' she asked.

'And what was that, pray tell?'

'That fine beer Rowena and I gave you and Grimketil at the King's feast the night we left you. Did you two ever figure out what was special about it?'

'I remember it well, the finest beer I ever drank. I'm sorry I won't have the opportunity to drink it again.' he said nonchalantly. 'But I can live with that.'

'I can give you the recipe if you like.' offered Berthilda.

'That would be a most generous final gift. I'm almost sorry now that I have to kill you. Do tell.'

And she did.

He froze in astonishment, then swore at her loudly, his cursing rising in volume and nastiness as her laughter continued to echo in his ears, until his rage thrust him once more onto the attack.

He moved in quickly, not making any specific moves, just flicking his sword from position to position, hoping to catch her out. Berthilda danced out of reach, catching each feint on buckler or sword until in his fury he left a tiny opening.

Catching a thrust to her head on the buckler, she pushed his blade wide and stabbed her own at his face. He managed to flick his head to the side, but not quite quickly enough. There was a soft plopping sound as his left ear landed on the ground.

'First blood...' murmured Berthilda.

Ward put his hand up to where his ear had been. The endorphins and adrenalin were flowing strongly, and he felt no pain, just a sense of loss.

'It's the last blood that matters!' he snapped back.

Meanwhile, Gundy had slipped quietly away, and would have screamed if Oscar hadn't thought to clamp his hand over her mouth when he came up behind her.

'Shush!' he hissed. 'It's me. Oscar. Come this way, there's some bushes by the stream here that we can hide in until Berthilda kills him.'

'Clever kid.' thought Thomas, floating above.

Berthilda smiled sweetly at Ward behind her weapons.

'Incidentally, you've lost your prize.'

Ward glanced across to his horse. The girl had gone!

'I'll find her. I'll have all the time in the world once I've dealt with you!'

'Ah, but you saw she was brave enough to fend you off with a spear. What do you think she'll do with that scramseaxe you had on your saddle?'

Ward looked uncertainly back at his horse. The blade in question was stored on the other side of the horse where he couldn't see it. Could the little monster have taken it?

He was brought back to the here and now by a flash of light in his peripheral vision, and he blocked a sneaky thrust just in time, flicking it away and countering with a downwards slash to the head.

Berthilda caught it on the buckler and cried out. 'Now Gundy! Strike now!'

Ward danced away to his left, spinning as he went, looking for the little girl with the blade, while trying to fend off Berthilda's attacks. Spread too thin, he allowed her blade another bite, this time a deep cut to his right thigh.

'Argh!' he swore. 'It's sharp, I'll give you that!'

'Quick too!' she laughed, as he limped away to give himself some space to recover.

Ward knew he was in trouble now. He was losing a lot of blood, and beginning to get light headed. If he didn't finish her soon, he'd had it. He positioned himself so that the moon was behind him, using its light to disguise his movements. Then, as Berthilda moved left to try to circle round him, he matched her, keeping his shadow between them.

Seeing what he was up to, Berthilda kept moving left until he bounced up against a sapling with his sword arm. Momentarily distracted, he jerked himself free, but it was too late. Berthilda pushed his blade down with her buckler and ran her own straight through his chest.

When she withdrew it, she knew she hadn't hit his heart. He was still standing, and then he struck at her. It was hard and wild, and she blocked it easily, but got a hefty spatter of blood straight into her face as he coughed violently.

'Oh! That's not nice Ward!' she complained, dancing away. 'It's too late to want to be blood brothers you know. You should have asked earlier! We could have toasted that with a beer!'

Ward looked terrible. The blood streaming from where his ear should have been, was as nothing compared to the river flowing from his thigh, and his mouth, chin and neck were covered with the burbling, foaming mess that was sliming its way from his lungs up past his lips.

He lurched towards her, clumsily swinging his sword, but she didn't even bother to block it. She just turned and walked away.

'Have a nice afterlife!' she called back over her shoulder. She didn't stop walking until she heard the thump of his body as he finally collapsed.

'Hurrah.' came two happy voices from the trees.

'Gundy! Oscar! You're alright!' she called back. 'Wonderful!'

The children ran out from their hiding place and threw themselves around her in the biggest hug they could give.

'Thank you, thank you, thank you for saving us!' sobbed Gundy.

Berthilda held them tightly in her arms.

'That's what friends do for each other, just the way you tried to save Thunder and the others.' she said.

She became aware of a horse and rider watching them from atop a small hill on the other side of the stream. The man was wearing a very distinctive helmet.

'Grimketil!' she spat.

'Where?' gasped Oscar, looking fearfully around.

'Up there.' she said pointing. The man stayed on the hill just long enough for the children to see him, before he rode down the other side and away.

'Are these bad men his?' asked Gundy.

'Yes. They're his.' Berthilda answered. 'In fact, this one was supposed to be my husband.' she said, nudging Ward's body with her foot.

'What are we going to do with them now?' asked Oscar.

16 MARWIG'S EDUCATION

Back at the manor, they were counting the cost.

Thomas had lost a total of four villagers, the newly married couples on either side of Sighard and Lynette's hut on the south eastern corner of the village. The men had heard the raiders, poked their heads out to look, and been killed on the spot, followed by their wives. Only the raiders' intent on silence during the initial stages of the attack had saved Sighard's family from being wiped out too.

On the western side, the raiders had had the misfortune to encounter Hengist and Kelsey who were taking advantage of being on guard together to have a quiet chat about old times. Two of the raiders were despatched even before they were aware they'd been spotted, two more in the immediate confusion after that, and the final two after a hard fight where teamwork between old friends made all the difference.

Marwig was distressed to discover that both his other men had been killed, as well as his own companion. They'd been taking their turn on guard and been surprised by an attack from within the village boundaries. Although they'd fought bravely, killing four of the raiders, they'd been cut down from behind by the two riders as they galloped into the village.

'I have paid a heavy price for my accommodation.' he sighed. 'They were good men.'

'I am so sorry this happened while you were our guest Marwig.' apologised Wulfstan. 'We've not had a raid before now, not according to Hengist anyway.'

Marwig looked sadly into the flames of the fire that was boiling the water for the wounded. Wulfstan was insistent that it be well boiled before any wound was washed. Thomas's lessons had plunged home on that point.

'What was that clear liquid you had people splash onto their wounds?' he asked. 'It hurts like hell!'

Wulfstan passed on exactly what Thomas had told him.

'It's like very, very strong beer, and it cleans wounds. We've had far fewer infections since we started doing it.'

They were interrupted by a frantic Lynette.

'Has anyone seen Gundy and Oscar?' she cried.

Wulfstan took her hands firmly in his own.

'I'm sorry Lynette. Somehow they got into the middle of the fight, and stood in the stable door with spears trying to hold off the raiders. Incredibly brave. They even ordered the raiders to go away! Astonishing really.'

'Unfortunately the raiders grabbed them and bolted on horseback. Berthilda has gone after them, and we don't know any more than that for the moment.'

Lynette dissolved into tears.

'Those two silly… Gundy said she'd heard something, and Sighard and I just told her to go back to sleep… she and Oscar must have sneaked out regardless… oh, if only we'd listened to her-'

'If you had, you'd all be dead like your neighbours.' consoled Wulfstan. 'It could have been a lot worse. We've got Rowena and Freawaru out looking for them, and everyone else is on guard, looking for any stragglers. I'm sure you'll have them back.' fibbed Wulfstan. In fact he was anything but confident of their safe return.

Sighard took his wife gently by the shoulders and led her back to their remaining children in the barn, where most of the women and children had gathered for safety until the all clear was given.

Marwig looked out into the night.

'A full moon is a double edged sword at times like these. Without it we could not have defended as we did, yet equally, they could not have attacked without it. Even so, they seemed to know exactly where they were going. I wonder how that came about?'

'I can answer that.' said Melody, who'd just come up to check if the water was ready for Scarlett. 'The man Fulton killed was Alcott, Cuthbert's other slave. He must have been working with the raiders and told them the layout of the place. Poor silly Alcott.' she said sadly. 'Always a gift for being in the wrong place at the wrong time…'

'Do we know if anyone knows any of the other raiders?' asked Wulfstan.

Melody shook her head. 'People are saying they were just an outlaw band.'

'Outlaw bands don't have horses of that quality, or if they do, they sell them quickly! Nor do they have that many swords. Perhaps they were an outlaw band, but I think they were working with someone else.' said Marwig.

'I agree.' said Wulfstan. 'In fact I'm sure I recognised the voice of the rider giving the orders, but I can't quite place it.'

Their deliberations were interrupted by loud cheering coming from the southern edge of the village.

'I think you'll want to see this.' said Thomas in his ear.

'Where the blazes have you been?' snapped Wulfstan. 'I needed you to chase the children and tell me what had happened to them!'

'Come and look for yourself.' laughed Thomas.

They ran down the southern path past the guest huts where they met Berthilda astride Thunder, with Gundy in front, and Oscar behind. Two horses with baggage slung over them followed on lead ropes, and Rowena and Freawaru brought up the rear. The villagers were crowding around them all, laughing and crying in excitement.

'Berthilda!' cried Wulfstan. 'Thank heavens you're back! And Gundy and Oscar too! How marvellous! How did you do it?'

Berthilda grinned happily. 'I just rode faster than they did!'

'You should have seen her!' said Gundy, bubbling in excitement.

'She knocked Radley clean off his horse to let me escape!' added Oscar.

'And then she fought the man that had me, and fought him, and fought him, and fought him till he was killed!' shouted Gundy, not to be outdone.

'Radley?' asked Marwig. 'Grimketil's man?'

'And the other one is Ward, Grimketil's right hand.' called out Rowena from the rear. 'We recognised him.'

'Are you sure?' asked Marwig. 'It's a big accusation to make, if we have to explain this at Court.'

Berthilda eased off her mount.

'You can check for yourself if you like. We brought the bodies back on their own horses.'

The men were draped across their mounts, head down on the right hand side. Berthilda grabbed the hair of the one in front and twisted its head to allow Marwig to see.

Marwig whistled softly. 'That's Ward alright. You three did well to take him. He's an expert swordsman.' he said looking at Rowena and Freawaru.

Freawaru shook her head. 'Nothing to do with Rowena and me. We just gave Berthilda a hand lifting the bodies onto the horses! She'd despatched the pair of them on her own before we got there.'

Marwig's jaw dropped in astonishment. 'You killed both of them? On your own?' he asked Berthilda.

Berthilda hung her head modestly.

'Radley hardly counts. I took him by surprise.'

Gundy couldn't restrain herself. 'But you fought my man face to face! He went to get you, and you beat him!'

'Gundy! Oscar! Where have you been?' Lynette rushed up to Thunder and threw her arms around her children. 'We've been worried sick!'

'We're fine mum.' explained Oscar. 'Berthilda saved us!'

'You shouldn't have been out at all!' chided his mother. 'You wait until your father gets hold of you!'

Berthilda laughed. 'They did really well Lynette. They stood up to these two creeps, and then escaped as soon as they had a chance. You should be proud of them!'

Lynette turned to Wulfstan in confusion.

'A bit of a fright to be sure Lynette, but Berthilda's right. You've even more reason to be proud of your children than you usually do.' he said. 'But it's a good idea to take them off to their father. You should all be together I think.'

Lynette scooped her children off Thunder, and ushered them away, their excited chatter continuing unabated until they passed out of sight behind the hall.

When the horses had been safely settled in their stable, and the humans were back around the fire, Marwig held out his hand to Berthilda.

'I wonder, most marvellous lady, if I might have a look at your blade?'

Berthilda looked to Wulfstan for confirmation.

'There's no point in trying to hide them now.' said Thomas. 'He saw them in action with Deena and Deana. The best we can do is try and get him to keep his mouth shut.'

Wulfstan nodded, and Berthilda reluctantly handed over her sword. Marwig touched the edge, immediately cutting himself.

'Ah!' he expostulated. 'Heavens that's sharp! What an edge!'

Then, holding it to catch the light from the flames he looked at the rest of the blade, and was astonished to find a complete absence of the beautiful markings he'd expected to find on a pattern welded weapon.

'It's a single piece of iron! And yet it must be incredibly brittle to hold an edge like that. How on earth do you fight with it and not break it?' he asked.

'Try a thrust into that fence post.' said Wulfstan.

Marwig stood up and gave a gentle thrust into the wood as he'd been asked. The blade flexed easily. A second more vigorous thrust followed, and then a third with all the force he could muster. The blade sprang back into shape undamaged.

'Hell's teeth.' murmured Marwig. 'What an astonishing blade! And so nimble and agile to use.' he said, flourishing it through a number of moves. 'Where did you get it?'

'We made it.' said Wulfstan simply.

Marwig lowered the weapon and rested the tip carefully on his boot.

'How?' he asked.

'Can you keep a secret?' replied Wulfstan.

'Yes.'

'So can I!' said Wulfstan, and the entire coterie burst into laughter.

Marwig the diplomat, nodded in understanding, and returned the sword to Berthilda.

'Thank you. I confess I do not want to hand it back! I have never encountered its equal, not even in the Kingdom of the Franks.'

'We would have you keep our secret too please Marwig, until after the fight with Grimketil. I want the element of surprise.' said Wulfstan. 'Will you do that for us?'

Marwig, a Queen's man to his core, nodded his agreement. 'Of course Your Highness. I shall tell no one.'

'Then you shall have a blade of your own after the battle, as a token of my thanks.' said Wulfstan.

'I am not asking anything for my silence.' said Marwig softly. 'I give it freely.'

Wulfstan rested his hand on Marwig's arm.

'That my friend, is why I am giving you the sword.'

Offa was holding court in London when the Archbishop made his appearance, with Cuthbert two steps behind him.

'Ah, Archbishop. What can I do for you today?' asked the King.

'I'm afraid I come on a most disturbing matter Your Majesty, concerning your youngest son.'

Offa lifted his right index finger slightly to indicate his acknowledgement.

'Indeed?'

'Yes Your Majesty. As you may remember, I personally selected the priest for Hengist's manor, young Cuthbert here.' said the Archbishop, indicating the offending article.

'I do remember.'

The Archbishop drew himself up to his full height. 'Prince Wulfstan saw fit to publicly humiliate his priest, the very moment he arrived in the village, and not content with that, had him thrown out the following day with only a handcart to carry his possessions. Even worse, he wilfully deprived the Church of the tithe of one of the villagers. These are grave offences against the Church, and must be put right.'

Offa steepled his fingers.

'A handcart you say? And Cuthbert pushed it all the way to London, unaided?'

Jaenberht nodded vigorously.

'All the way Your Majesty, not just to London but to Canterbury! Even further! On his own! He had to complete his journey in bare feet when his shoes collapsed some days before he reached me. I personally saw the blood and callouses on his feet.'

The King looked serious.

'Goodness me! I am astonished to see him walk in here so easily. He seems to have recovered remarkably swiftly from such a travail.'

Jaenberht played what he thought was to be his trump card.

'A miraculous recovery Your Majesty! Truly has God looked well upon this son of the Church, a sign no doubt of the virtue of his case.

I am afraid I must insist that Cuthbert is reinstated at the manor, and that the Prince be held to account, and forced to apologise in public for his actions!'

The hall had fallen completely silent, all eyes upon the two men. Offa made no sound or movement for over a minute, and then a thin smile crept onto his face.

'I wonder if you would consider it so miraculous, if a priest had walked no further than from the edge of town to the cathedral?'

Jaenberht maintained his stony face. 'But that is not the case here Your Majesty.'

Offa's smile deepened slightly.

'You and I have received our news from different sources. My source tells me that Cuthbert had a servant, in all but name at least, who pushed the cart more than nine miles in every ten while Cuthbert walked unencumbered.'

The Archbishop's mouth opened and he began to remonstrate. Offa raised a hand.

'To quote my son, I am not finished yet Archbishop. My source also tells me that Cuthbert wore his shoes all the way to the edge of Canterbury, where he removed them, hid them amongst his belongings, and then abandoned his servant in all but name, and made great play of piteously pushing his handcart barefoot to the cathedral, where he told you his tale.'

Jaenberht was spluttering now.

'Your Majesty! I do not know who your source is, but a priest's word is the word of God and must be taken as such. You should not listen to the lies of men who denigrate the Church!'

Offa carefully maintained his smile.

'I am also told that Cuthbert was not denied the tithe. The villager in question had apparently lost all his grain, and most of his land in a flood, and so no longer had the tithe to give. Really, he should have been asked for no more than a tenth of what remained, or rather offered some poor relief from the Church. In any case, the Prince offered that the manor pay the man's share if it could be proven that the obligation still stood. So the Church lost nothing.'

The Archbishop's face was creased with anger.

'Your Majesty. I have known Cuthbert for some time now, and have no reason to doubt his word.'

'And I have no reason to doubt my own source.' replied the King.
'Oh. I'm sorry. I meant sources.'

Jaenberht looked his sternest.

'Your Majesty, the word of a priest should always be taken over the word of a layman.'

'Oh? Pray why?' asked the King.

'Because he does not just represent God, he must have been chosen by God, and therefore he is always in the right!'

Offa steepled his fingers again.

'Did you not have a case two months ago, where two of your priests had been fighting? Over a woman, gossip tells us, but that is neither here nor there to my argument. The point is that those two… gentlemen… of the Church, gave differing accounts as to the facts of the case.'

His smile was positively angelic now.

'They can't both be right Archbishop. Therefore, we cannot say that whatever a priest says is the correct view of the world, because we have the example of your own people to prove that it is not. Priests can clearly lie, or at least be mistaken just as much as normal men. Don't you agree?'

A blush suffused Jaenberht's face, but he had no counter. Offa looked past him to a visibly alarmed Cuthbert.

'You do not appear to be quite so sure of yourself master priest, as you were when you first walked in. Why is that?'

Cuthbert gasped.

'I told the truth Your Majesty! I have only ever done my duty.'

Offa steepled his fingers yet again, much to the Archbishop's annoyance.

'Well, your duty as you yourself saw it perhaps. I have enquired into this matter since it came to my attention. I can indeed find golden commendations on your behalf.'

Cuthbert beamed.

'But only from the Archbishop and his minions.' continued the king. 'I cannot find a single lay person with a good word as to your character. Not one!' he said, his voice rising in false astonishment. 'Now, how do you account for that, master priest?'

Jaenberht intervened.

'Your Majesty, when a parent chastises his child, the child is not always grateful for his correction.'

'Point. Point.' acknowledged Offa. 'But if the entire family thinks the father is a monster, then the odds are that he actually is! However, we can resolve the dilemma as to your future, master priest. I have been made aware of a vacancy to the south east of Tamworth.'

Jaenberht stiffened.

'Your Majesty? Church appointments are my affair, not yours. With respect.'

Offa airily waved his hand.

'With respect, of course you meant with respect old friend. It's only a suggestion on my part of course, but Thegn Grimketil's village priest passed away from the bloody flux, as I believe the peasants call it, and he needs a replacement. Given the match between their characters, I would have thought Cuthbert would jump at the chance to join Grimketil?'

'But your son!' cried the exasperated Archbishop.

'Has so far been proved to have done nothing unwise nor illegal, and until such proofs have been furnished, there is nothing to be done. Good day Archbishop, I wish you well in your peregrinations.'

He waved his hand dismissively, and asked for the next supplicant to be brought in.

Jaenberht stormed out of the hall, only just in control of his temper. When they'd reached a semi-private place, he rounded on his hapless priest.

'Well?' he demanded.

Cuthbert held out his hands to the side, and looked agonised.

'I told you the truth my Lord, as God is my witness.'

Jaenberht glared at him.

'Do not forget Cuthbert, that he is exactly that!'

The following day, Marwig was still concerned about getting the King and Queen to believe that Grimketil had been involved in any way with the raid.

'Oh it's quite easy.' said Wulfstan. 'We'l hack the heads off and stick them in buckets to take to Court with us.'

Marwig grimaced. 'They probably won't be all that recognisable when we get them there, and the smell in the meantime will be intolerable!'

'Ah.' said Wulfstan. 'That's where the alcohol comes back in. Come with me.'

Wulfstan led Marwig to a hut just west of the kitchen, where a large horizontal copper pipe came out of the wall, before dropping down into a big water butt.

'Come and look Marwig and I'll explain how it works.'

Inside the hut was an almost spherical copper cauldron, about four feet in diameter, with the copper pipe coming out of it and through the wall. Below the cauldron a fire was burning gently.

Thomas put on a pair of gloves and pulled off a circular lid part way up the upper slopes of the cauldron and gestured Marwig to look inside.

'We put beer in there, and gently raise the temperature. The steam comes out the top, goes through the chimney and into a copper tube that curls around the water butt outside. That turns the steam back into liquid again, and we get alcohol instead of beer.'

'So you can drink it?' asked a dubious Marwig.

'Absolutely not!' said Thomas emphatically into Wulfstan's ear.

'Not this stuff no.' said Wulfstan. 'It would kill you, or make you blind. Not a good idea.'

Marwig stepped slightly away and looked at the boy suspiciously.

'How do you know all this stuff? It looks like witchery to me!'

In a flash Thomas was back in the body.

'Thank heavens for that.' sighed Wulfstan in relief. 'I was getting well out of my depth!'

Thomas remembered something. 'Speaking of which, Melody has a golden glow around her-'

'I know.' said Wulfstan. 'I was going to surprise you!'

'Well you did! Do you know what it is yet?'

'Nope. So far it's just a glow.'

'Okay.' said Thomas, and picked up the conversation again with Marwig.

'It's not witchery! It's what I told you before. It's watching, and learning!'

'What do you mean?'

Thomas picked up a cup and dipped it into a bucket of beer that was waiting to go into the still, and took a sip before offering it to Marwig.

'Go on. It won't hurt you.' he said.

Marwig took a cautious swallow and handed it back.

Thomas then took another cup and filled it with some fresh water.

'Now try that. It's just water.'

When Marwig had sampled it, Thomas added the water to the remaining beer in the cup.

'Okay, now drink it and tell me what the difference is between the first lot and this.'

Marwig took another careful sip.

'It's watery.'

'Why?' asked Thomas.

Marwig frowned.

'Because you've just added water to it!'

'So beer and water are two different liquids correct? And you can tell if someone has been watering the beer, can't you? Now what would happen if you were able to remove some water from the beer, instead of adding it. What would it taste like then?'

'More beery?' suggested Marwig.

'More beery. Exactly! Well that's basically all we're doing here. We're leaving the water behind and taking out the beery bit and collecting it out there under the water butt.'

Marwig shook his head, trying to get his head around things.

'So why can't you drink it if it's still beer?'

'Ah.' said Thomas. 'You will be able to, once I've made some refinements, but right now we're getting a mix that's great for cleaning wounds, or drains come to that, but lethal to people if they drink it. Promise me you won't try it until I tell you it's okay? I don't want you hurting yourself.'

'I won't make a promise I can't keep.' said Marwig laughing.

Thomas pursed his lips.

'Hm. Okay, well a single sip won't hurt you, so come on. You can have one.'

They went outside where Thomas scooped a tiny quantity of the collected liquor into a wooden spoon and handed it to Marwig, who sniffed it gingerly.

'Woah!' he gasped, his eyes watering. 'That's strong stuff!'

Then he put it in his mouth, and swilled it around. Horror was the first emotion to appear on his face, followed quickly by revulsion as he spat the liquid out onto the grass.

'Ye cats and little kittens!' he gasped. 'That's horrendous! First of all it sets your mouth on fire, and then the taste hits you! Nobody in their right mind would drink that!'

'Good!' said Thomas. 'That's just the way I want it then!'

'So why did you make the stuff?' asked Marwig, desperately flushing his mouth with water.

Thomas thought carefully.

'Well, you know when puke and poop diseases appear? Have you ever noticed that people who drink beer tend not to get sick as much as those who drink water? No? Well, I did. And I thought that maybe there was something in the beer that stopped disease, and that if I could get hold of it somehow, it might be able to stop other diseases. Simple really.'

'And it works?'

Thomas grinned. 'Lowest death rate from injuries in living memory. And it's a great preservative too. We just need to hack those two heads off, drop them into a barrel of this stuff and they'll not only still look like themselves in a year's time, they won't smell bad either. How great is that?'

17 MAKING GOOD

Marwig stayed a few days more, watching Thomas mobilise the villagers to dig a curving ditch across the south end of the village, mounding up the soil on the village side to make an embankment, ready for a wooden palisade.

'We'll dig open the two ends once we're finished,' said Thomas, 'and allow the river to flow through it to create a moat. No more surprises after that!'

'What about in times of flood? It might sweep away the bridge, and then the village could be cut off.' suggested Marwig.

'Initially we'll have a droppable sluice gate at both ends so we can stop a flood from entering.' said Thomas. 'Later on, when I have lots of money, I'll replace the regular bridge with a drawbridge.'

Marwig squinted at him.

'A what?'

Thomas recollected where, or rather when he was, and reminded himself to be a bit more careful.

'I've designed, in my head for now, a bridge that can be withdrawn into the village. A draw bridge. That means it will be out of the way of any flood, and won't be available for any attacker to cross over.'

Marwig gave him a long hard look.

'Your father made his bet to try and force you to become a warrior. I think you have already become far more than that. I also think there may be few limits as to what you could achieve as a son of the house of Offa.'

Thomas smiled at the delicacy of the diplomat's words, but cut straight to the chase in his own response.

'Not quite. My father has already decided on his successor, my older brother. He's a good man. I am happy to serve whichever is King.'

Marwig gave him just the hint of a smile, and almost imperceptibly raised one eyebrow.

'You may choose not to put yourself forward, but if you carry on as you are, it is inevitable that others will suggest it, and then the tensions and politics will commence between the three of you, and the Queen. There is no way to avoid this. It will happen, whether you wish it to or not.'

Thomas watched a worker carrying a bucket of earth up to the top of what would become the eastern rampart.

'Then the royal family will need all the wise council it can get. I like my own advisors to tell me the truth, not what they think I want to hear. Just as you are doing now.'

'I am the Queen's man.' said Marwig softly.

'And I wouldn't dream of asking you to be anything else.' replied Thomas. 'Just keep telling me the truth, whether I like it or not. The more powerful a man grows, the more arrogant he becomes, shedding his wisdom as quickly as a tree sheds its leaves. I'm not asking you to take my side, only to share your honest opinions.'

Marwig pursed his lips.

'I think I can undertake to do that.' and then changed the subject.

'You said "when you have lots of money" you would build a drawbridge. How do you propose to get rich? At present you are relying on your father's wealth, and that won't last beyond the battle, even if we assume you're going to win.'

Thomas pointed behind him to some bags of seeds that had been delivered the day before.

'My turnip seeds have arrived from the Kingdom of the Franks. I now have everything I need from a plant and animal point of view to treble production on the farm in the next twelve months. Most of that extra production will be food, but we'll be able to run a lot more sheep, keep more of them alive throughout the winter, and so have more wool to sell. I have ideas about making that into cloth, rather than selling it as raw wool, so we'll get a much higher price.'

'Do you think you have enough people to do that, with the right skills?' asked Marwig.

'I will have.' said Thomas confidently. 'I will have. However, that's as nothing compared to what I'm going to create over the winter. I've designed a few things that have never been seen before. Father will receive two of each, one to keep as compensation for how much I've cost him, and one to sell or gift to someone else. I'll keep a number for myself, and sell some of them.'

'How much do you think these things will sell for?' asked Marwig.

'The big ones should fetch over two hundred pounds in silver, two hundred hides, or twenty four thousand acres. Each.'

Marwig gasped in astonishment.

'That's a fortune! What on earth are you making?'

Thomas tapped the side of his nose.

'All in good time my friend, all in good time. All I'll say is that you'll be astonished. No court in the world has such a thing, but they'll all want one once they hear of it. The King can buy them from me and gift them himself, or I'll sell them directly. Either way, they'll make me one of the richest men in the Kingdom.'

Grimketil on the other hand, was feeling nothing like so cheerful. Even with a full moon, he hadn't been able to see well enough to identify the man who'd killed Ward and Radley, but whoever it was, they were good.

'It must have been Kelsey my Lord.' said Sigwulf, Ward's replacement as Grimketil's number two. 'Hengist isn't skilled enough to have handled them both.'

Grimketil nodded slowly as he considered the idea, but there was another possibility. 'Or Marwig, the Queen's advisor. I know he was there with some of his men. He could have matched Ward, and those extra men might explain why the entire raiding party was wiped out. Ward's little adventure has turned out to be very costly indeed!' he said.

'Surely not that costly?' suggested Sigwulf soothingly. 'It was bad to lose Ward and Radley, but it was just two men. The others were just worthless outlaws.'

Grimketil glared at him. He was only too well aware that Sigwulf wasn't the sharpest arrow in the quiver compared to Ward, but found it depressing to be constantly reminded of it.

'Plus two extremely fine horses, two first class swords, and the rough ones we gave the outlaws in payment! That's the equivalent of four hides of land on their own. No, this was a very expensive indulgence! And we'll be two top men down in the battle next year. We must start training the new lads immediately. We'll need them!'

Too stupid to be abashed at the implied telling off, Sigwulf simply focussed on the here and now. 'What would you like them to start training with?' he asked. 'Bows?'

Grimketil shook his head decisively. ' No. Not bows. I know Wulfstan has at least one top flight archer, so I'm going to have a word with the King to have bows banned from our little encounter. After all, they're just not manly enough to meet the King's expectations, or at least that's what I'm going to suggest to him! No, we'll use the shield wall like real men, so get them started on spear and shield.'

After seeing Marwig off the following morning, Thomas walked into the stables to collect Obsidian for a ride. Fulton was standing in the doorway, watching the play of the sunlight on a small item in his hand.

'What's that Fulton?' he asked companionably.

Fulton started. 'Sorry Your Highness. I was just admiring a little trinket I found in the road on the journey home from London.' He held out his hand to reveal a beautiful glass bead, its colours warm as it sparkled in the sun.

'It's beautiful isn't it?' said Thomas.

Fulton nodded. 'It's the most beautiful thing I've ever had. I wish I knew how to make another.'

Thomas looked at him thoughtfully. 'Do you really mean that? If I taught you how, do you think you would be interested in doing it for your living?'

Fulton's eyes widened. 'What? Me become a glassmaker? Of course I would!'

'Well then,' said Thomas, 'let's give it a go. There's no guarantee you'll be any good of course. It's a tricky business, and you'll be learning your whole life long, but we can at least try. You can always come back to the horses if it doesn't work out, so you've nothing to lose.'

'Thank you Your Highness! Thank you very much indeed!' gushed Fulton, quite overcome.

Thomas patted him on the shoulder, and collected Obsidian. 'We'll start the planning when I come back from my ride.'

Thomas had been wanting a glass maker for some time, for reasons so secret he was reluctant to bring in a stranger to do it. With the now loyal Fulton, he would have no such fears, It was just a question of whether or not he was capable of acquiring enough skill without an experienced glassblower to help him.

Over the next two weeks, Thomas oversaw the construction of the glass making hut. It backed directly onto the smithy, so he could run another shaft off the smithy's waterwheel to drive the bellows for the glass furnace, which had temperature demands as tough as those of steel.

While it was being built, he addressed the small matter of the required ingredients. Fulton could do his learning using the sand to hand, but the glass would be coloured by its impurities. Clear glass required white sand, which he ordered via a merchant in Tamworth, to be delivered by boat up the river. It should arrive before winter set in, and if it didn't before the sailing season ended, they could always resort to crushed quartz.

The other things he knew he'd need, were potash to lower the sand's melting point so the furnace could liquefy it, and quicklime to stop the resulting glass from dissolving in water. Fortunately, both were easy to make.

The village already had a lime kiln, safely upstream away from the village, where limestone was loaded in alternating layers with wood or charcoal, and allowed to cook. The end product was quicklime, which just needed to be raked out the bottom of the kiln.

Potash was almost as easy. The wood ash from the hall fireplace was collected into buckets and soaked for a while in water. After skimming the muck off the top, the clear solution was then carefully decanted into a pot and simmered gently over another fire until it had boiled dry, leaving behind the sugar like white crystals, Thomas's potash.

As the autumn equinox approached, Thomas began work in earnest on his real money spinner. He was going to make a clock, a real clock, not just a timer. This one would not only run and run, it needed to be highly accurate too. If he wanted it accurate to the second, then first of all he had to be able to measure what a second was, and doing that from first principles was a lot harder than it sounded.

The key was knowing that a pendulum 0.994 metres long would take exactly one second to complete one swing, and that was close enough for Thomas. If he had something he could compare the swings of various pendulums against, he could find the right one.

So he set Smith, Buck and Ashlin to work, creating a number of copper basins in various sizes. He arranged three of these one above the other, filling the top two with rain water.

The middle of the three had a small tap in it which allowed water to drip into the bottom one, but the rate the water poured out would drop with the water level in the middle basin. The trick to getting a constant flow was to keep the middle one full, and that was done via a tap in the top basin which poured out just a little more water than the bottom one. The excess water in the middle basin flowed out a spout where it could be collected and returned to the top one if needed.

When the village sundial showed noon on the autumn equinox, Thomas opened both taps and let the water flow, until the sundial showed noon again the following day. That gave him twenty four hours worth of water in the bottom basin.

Using a balance beam and a set of identically weighted copper basins, he split the water from twenty four, down to twelve, to six, to three, and finally to one hour. A finer balance then split that into thirty, fifteen and finally five minute portions.

Ashlin then customised a small basin to hold exactly that amount of water, which Thomas swapped with the twenty four hour bucket at the bottom of the stack. Now when the taps were opened, he could measure exactly five minutes of water. It was then a simple matter of counting the number of swings for each test pendulum in that five minute period, until he found the one that did three hundred.

Thomas was ecstatic. For sure he could now measure a second easily, without all the palaver he'd just gone through, but his achievement was so much more than that. He also had a metre rule for distance measures, which he could use to make a container 10 cm by 10 cm by 10 cm, which when filled with water would give him a kilogram. From there he could derive every other unit of measure he'd need, making future technologies much easier to build.

To make sure he didn't lose all his hard work, he had ten more pendulums made of wrought iron, tested them all, and hid nine of them in various parts of the village as backups.

Now he could get on with building that clock.

It was about this time that Cuthbert was introducing himself to Grimketil at his manor. He carried a letter from the Archbishop recommending him to the thegn as a replacement priest for the one who'd died, but as nobody else in the manor could read or write, he had to read it out himself.

Grimketil accepted Cuthbert's version of its contents, with the internal satisfaction of knowing he could cut the man's head off if it was discovered later that he wasn't telling the truth.

Cuthbert got instantly to work, darkening the peasants' days as quickly as the changing seasons began to darken their nights.

Marwig by contrast, was bringing news to warm the Queen's heart.

'It's frankly astonishing Your Majesty! He's reorganised the farming process, and claims it will make the land three times more productive than it already is.' he said.

'And do you believe him?' she asked.

'I have no reason not to. He has already achieved a lower death rate than anywhere else in the Kingdom, just as he said he would. His people are loyal, not because they have no choice, but because they both love and trust him. Possibly most important of all to Your Majesty, is that the girls are already warriors and will only get stronger from now on.'

The Queen held up her hand to pause him.

'How can you tell if their practice fights will translate into winning a real one?' she asked.

Marwig's face turned grim.

'Because I saw them in action, in a real fight, to the death. The village suffered a night raid while I was there, all three of my companions being killed in the subsequent fight.'

The Queen's hand flew to her mouth in alarm.

'And my son?' she whispered.

'He acquitted himself extremely well, both as a fighter in his own right, and as a commander. He killed a man that I myself was struggling to deal with, then split his forces to both help me, and defend the stables. All the attackers were killed, except two mounted men who kidnapped a pair of village children and galloped off into the night.'

The Queen's face flashed with anger, and then sympathy.

'The poor things…'

Marwig smiled. 'Oh they're all right! One of Wulfstan's girls, and I stress the word one, leapt onto her horse and gave chase. She hunted them down, killed them both, and returned with the children.'

The Queen's jaw dropped, but Marwig wasn't finished yet.

'There's more Your Majesty. Those two men were Radley and Ward, Grimketil's right hands. Both were fine swordsmen in their own right, and she bested the pair of them, on her own.'

Cynethryth's excitement finally bubbled out of her.

'Really! Those two? You're certain? That's wonderful… if it's true.' she concluded, caution reasserting itself once more.

'It is true Your Majesty. I identified them myself, and their horses, and their swords. It was definitely them. So Grimketil is down two of his best men, two horses, and two fine blades, which I am sure your son will find a use for!'

A cold realisation struck Cynethryth.

'Then Grimketil ordered this raid! He struck at my son before he was ready, before the day of the bet! He must be brought to heel! I shall speak to the King about this!'

Marwig waited for her fury to abate.

'I fear Grimketil will dissemble, or, not to put too fine a point on it, lie. All he need do is to say that Ward acted on his own out of misplaced loyalty, and that will put an end to it.'

She glowered at him.

'So you suggest we do nothing about this at all?'

'Challenging Grimketil now will achieve nothing. I propose we let things lie. Your son was fortifying the village as I left. There is no hope of another attack succeeding. I believe the King asked him if he would be able to hold a manor against all comers? Well that tough fight has already delivered a resounding yes, and the fortifications will make it an absolute certainty in the future. It would need an army to take that village now.'

Cynethryth frowned.

'I'm not happy about letting this matter ride, but based on your confidence, I'll take your advice. I just hope you're right.'

Marwig grinned a most undiplomatic grin.

'I have never been more certain of anything Your Majesty!'

Thomas was constantly busy now, splitting his time between running the school, training with the coterie, teaching Hengist and Alfred about the four crop rotation, building his clocks, and developing more equipment for the glass blowing enterprise.

Wulfstan followed along for most of it. The moat and ramparts had significantly reduced the need for him to do frequent patrols, so he was able to focus more on what Thomas was doing. Of course he'd occasionally get frustrated that he wasn't able to be more actively involved, but a quick flight into the countryside, or to the bottom of the river usually reminded him of what he'd gained in exchange. But there was so much to learn, he didn't have that much time for frustration!

The glassworks he found particularly interesting. Smith had built a different kind of furnace to Thomas's specifications. It was more accessible than the steel furnace, with a small door which could be opened and closed at will so the glassblower could collect and replace the glass from the large crucible fixed in place at its centre.

When it was up and running, and the bellows connected to the water wheel, Thomas taught Fulton the core principles of glass making, and how to use the blowpipes which Smith had made for him, then left him to play and grow his skills through experience.

A few days later Wulfstan was watching Thomas cooking wood in a glorified kettle just outside the glass works. The smoke coming from the spout got less and less until it seemed to stop altogether, at which point Thomas connected a pipe to it that ran underneath a large upturned cast iron vessel sitting inside an even larger one.

Wulfstan had earlier watched in puzzlement as Thomas filled both of these containers to the brim with water, then stretched a piece of flexible leather across the top of the smaller one, secured it in place, and tipped the vessel upside down into the larger one.

'What on earth are you doing?' asked Wulfstan.

'Watch what happens now!' said Thomas, as he pulled the leather free.

The water rushed out from the upper vessel into the lower one, but nowhere near as much as Wulfstan was expecting.

'Where's the rest of the water?" he asked.

'It's still in the vessel. You can tell how far up if you gently tap on the side and listen.' Thomas demonstrated.

'So how did the air get in there? I didn't see or hear any bubbles?'

'There isn't any.' said Thomas.

'There must be! There can't be nothing!' complained Wulfstan.

'Why not? If it had water in it, and the water gets taken away, and air can't get in, what must be left is nothing. It's called a vacuum.' said Thomas.

Wulfstan was highly dubious about this idea, but was beginning to come around to it as he watched the kettle pumping its gas into the vessel. At first nothing much seemed to happen, but gradually, as more and more kettles of wood were cooked, the vessel began to rise off the bottom, and float higher and higher inside the larger vessel.

'We're collecting gas from the wood, and storing it in what I'm going to call a gasometer.' explained Thomas. 'We'll be able to burn it later, and don't ask why just yet. You'll see very shortly.'

The gasometer had a copper pipe and tap coming out of the top, to which Thomas affixed a finely made leather tube. It had been coated in pitch, a thick, gooey kind of tar collected from inside the bottom of the kettle after it had cooked the wood, and then been wrapped in another strip of leather in an attempt to make it as airtight as possible.

The tube ran all the way into the glass works hut onto a table where it was connected to another copper tap, which in turn was connected via another leather tube to an iron pipe set in a frame.

'This is a Bunsen burner.' explained Thomas. 'I just have to turn the gas taps on, bring in a flame on a stick from the furnace, and voila!'

A flickering yellow flame flashed into existence at the top of the iron pipe.

'It works!' cried Wulfstan. 'You burn the wood and you can burn it again! Magic!'

'Ah, but here's the really great thing about it. Watch this!' Thomas turned a sleeve sitting around the bottom of the iron pipe. It had a hole in it, and as the sleeve turned, that hole opened out across another hole in the iron tube itself. The more the two holes overlapped, the more air was allowed to rush into the tube, until the flame turned blue and began to roar.

'Now that my friend, is hot enough to melt glass! It's going to be very useful.'

He got down to demonstrating just how useful without delay. Following Thomas's instructions, Fulton used his blow pipe to pull a lump of glass, called a gather, out of the large crucible mounted inside the furnace, and set about the end of it with pliers.

He went right around the edge of the gather, making a series of bites, and then went around again, pulling each of those bites a little more out from the gather. Very quickly he created what looked a bit like a fluted glass with a hollow space in the middle of it. Then Thomas made him grab one side of the flute and pull the whole thing slowly away from the rest of the gather. Fulton gently worked the pliers and the blowpipe to allow the glass to flow more evenly, until the glass hardened too much to pull anymore. Once he'd broken off the two ends, he had a glass tube about an inch thick in diameter.

'But I can do this already with the blowpipe.' said Fulton.

'Agreed,' said Thomas, 'but now we're going to do it again.'

This time he had Fulton pull the flute away from the gather much more rapidly, and a very fine tube resulted, less than a millimetre wide inside.

'Oh wow!' exclaimed Fulton.

'Try doing that with a blow pipe!' laughed Thomas. 'Now, bring it over to the table here and I'll show you what we can do with the Bunsen burner.

He lit it, and set it to the hot blue flame setting.

'Now, put one end of the tube into the very tip of that blue flame, and rotate it slowly, making sure it gets an even heat all the way around. See the sharp broken ends are softening, and rounding off in shape? If you look really carefully, you can see the hole at the end of the tube slowly closing up.'

Once it was completely closed, Thomas had him stick the end of the tube back into the flame until the whole end became visibly soft. Then Fulton blew gently into the other, still cool, open end, and a graceful bulb shape formed in the hot part of the glass.

'That's beautiful!' whispered Wulfstan in awe.

'Fabulous!' said Fulton. 'But how do we put anything into such a small hole to fill it?'

'Ah.' said Thomas. 'With a tube this size, we have to be a bit sneaky. Let's make another one.'

This time, when Fulton was melting the end, Thomas stopped him just before the hole closed completely. It was small enough to allow Fulton to build sufficient pressure to blow a bulb in the end, and just large enough to allow liquid in and out.

'Now it's still open at both ends, so we can drop it into a liquid, bulb end down, the liquid will enter the tube, and the air can escape out the other end.' said Thomas.

He walked to the far corner of the glass works and brought back a glass vessel shaped like a candlestick holder, which Fulton had blown earlier. It had a broad circular base about six inches in diameter for stability, and a cylinder of glass roughly two inches thick up to a height of around eighteen inches. It was almost completely filled with mercury.

Very carefully, Thomas lowered the glass tube, bulb end first, into the silvery liquid, and held it there until it was completely filled except for the bit he was holding above the surface. Then he dipped his fingers into the mercury to allow the last bit to fill, placed his finger over the top, and withdrew it.

'Okay, the mercury can't fall out the bottom because I've got my finger over the top hole here. All we have to do is to heat the bulb in the Bunsen burner to melt closed that little hole, and this bit of the job is done, but before we do that, let's make sure we've got the best breeze we can get going through the glassworks. Mercury is dangerous stuff, especially in vapour form. We absolutely do not want to breath it in if we can help it.'

Two minutes later Thomas had his prototype thermometer. The only remaining problems were that it was still completely full of mercury, still open at one end, there was no scale, and it was made from a dark green glass which wasn't the easiest stuff to see through.

Clear glass models replaced the green when the white sand arrived at the end of October. Once Fulton had made ten new thermometers, Thomas filled them with mercury and set about making them usable.

For each one he gripped the centre of the thermometer with a pair of pliers, and carefully warmed the whole glass by moving it back and forth in the flame of the burner. As he brought the temperature up to what he estimated was about two hundred degrees Celsius the mercury expanded, the excess pouring out of the open top to be caught in a bowl below. The tricky bit was then maintaining it at that temperature, so the mercury still completely filled the tube while the open end was melted shut. Then, as the thermometer cooled, the mercury dropped back down the tube, leaving a vacuum at the top. One easy to read thermometer.

All it needed now was a scale, which was why Thomas was to be found down at the coast by the mouth of the Dee in mid December. He'd brought with him a pot of rain water from the manor, which had been left out the previous night so it was half frozen when he rested it on the beach.

Much to his travelling companions' displeasure, he allowed the thermometers to sit in the icy water for a full two hours, before using a file to grind a notch in the glass where the top of the mercury column was sitting. Zero degrees Celsius, the freezing point of pure water at sea level, was finally locked in.

From there it was an easy matter to put the pot on the fire by which they were warming themselves, bring it to boiling point and mark off the new mercury levels. That gave him one hundred degrees Celsius. All he needed to do now was to divide up the bits in between to get the right scale for each thermometer, mark it up from minus ten to two hundred, and it was job done.

Thomas was ready for market.

18 A LAST MEAL

Apart from Thomas's oddball trip to the seaside, the winter months saw much activity despite the sleet and snow.

Lynette really had the bit between her teeth musically speaking, and with no other live entertainment available, she had few problems enticing pretty much everyone in the village into the new sophisticated style of singing. As they got better and better, it gave Thomas an idea for the upcoming battle.

Entertainment aside, the villagers were having the warmest winter in their lives, thanks to three more of the Prince's ideas.

The first of these was the humble button. Everybody's clothes in the dark ages tended to be tubular, or at least loose fitting, and tied in place with laces or belts. The button changed all that, allowing a wide variety of shapes and styles, and most importantly of all, they kept out the drafts! A mini fashion industry was born as the womenfolk explored the possibilities.

The second was a lot less glamorous, but if anything, more important in the chill of winter. The string vest would never be anything other than utilitarian underwear, but wear it underneath something else, and by heavens it kept you warm! Just exactly how a bunch of holes was able to do that, kept the villagers chattering until spring.

The third was another fashion item, knitting. All the cloth in this world was woven, so turning half of that year's wool clip into yarn and teaching them how to knit, had created a whole world of new clothes, fabulous to look at, warm to wear, and fun to make. When they mixed the new buttons idea into the mix, it was probably the only time in history the cardigan was considered the acme of style!

There had been good news on the archery front too. The wood kettle that provided gas for the Bunsen burner in the glassworks, also provided pitch which was used to seal the gasometer's leather pipes to make them airtight. Ashlin and Thomas applied the same technique to create waterproof leather covers for the arms of the bows, which worked even when the bow was being shot.

'Good news team.' announced Thomas to the coterie. 'The first of the bows is ready for you to try out.'

'Excellent!' said Berthilda, who'd been looking forward to this moment for months. 'Where shall we try it?'

'In here, in the hall.' said Thomas. 'Not much of a range I'll admit, but that way we won't lose too many arrows in the snow while we get our eye in.'

Berthilda begrudgingly agreed, and was first up to try Ashlin's creation. She'd kept a close eye on his developments throughout the year, but she was still surprised at the bow's size when sat in her hand.

'It's so tiny!' mused Scarlett.

Berthilda drew back the string and let fly the first arrow. It landed on the extreme left of the target. She pursed her lips in displeasure, then loaded and shot again, this time high and to the right. It took her a full ten shots before she hit the bullseye.

She shook her head. 'Well, it's different! Either that or I've completely lost my touch! Here Melody, you have a go.'

Melody had been watching Berthilda carefully, and applied what she'd learnt to her own technique. Her first five arrows were all outside the bullseye, but after that she was consistently in the centre.

'It doesn't have the wide range of tension that our normal bows have. Its small length means I'm pulling it harder, and earlier than I'm used to and that's throwing me off. It's also more twitchy to aim. I think it'll be amazing when we've learnt to use it, but Berthilda's right. It really is different to what we're used to.' she said.

One by one the others tried the bow, and all of them struggled to some degree or another. Predictably, Deena and Deana's light builds gave them the most difficulty, but they too persevered, and after a month everyone had achieved the same level of skill that they had with the normal bow.

'I can't wait for spring, to try it on horseback!' said Berthilda, grinning like a loon.

Grimketil and his men arrived first at Tamworth, laughing and joking with the populace.

'Hello Winston old friend!' he called out to the inn keeper. 'I hope you've placed a bet on me winning!'

'Oh course my Lord!' Winston shouted back. 'How could I do otherwise for such a reliable customer?'

'Right answer!' laughed Grimketil.

The crowd tittered at the badinage but the inn keeper's wife knew the truth of the matter. How could Winston have said otherwise when the thegn's bar tab stood at over two shillings? Vile as he was, the man had to be humoured, at least until he'd paid his bill! Then her attention was stolen away by the nasty, smug expression on Cuthbert's face, bringing up the rear on a handsome grey, and she had to remind herself that he was supposedly a priest.

Thomas and his coterie arrived an hour later, along with Hengist, Kelsey, half the village, and a number of carts. The sheer novelty of ten young women dressed as men, brought out the whole of Tamworth to see them, a point well noted by Grimketil.

'Ha! Foolish people, stirred by nothing more than the perverse!' he spat.

'It's a larger crowd than that which greeted us my Lord.' observed Sigwulf with his usual lack of intelligence and tact.

Grimketil's eyes flicked heavenward in a silent beseech to the Almighty.

'All the more reason to relish the brat's head being separated from his shoulders!' he snarled, looking around the room in distaste.

The Queen had made the accommodation arrangements, and her deep distrust of Grimketil was on open display.

'But we can't ask him to stay in the guest accommodation!' Offa had argued. He's always stayed in the hall before now. He'll be greatly offended!'

The Queen had been firm however.

'He can be offended all he likes. He'll still be nowhere near as offended as I am by his raid on our son's village! I won't have him or his men in the hall, except for the feast. Wulfstan and his people will have a night free from interference. I insist!' she said.

Which was how Grimketil found himself highly miffed, in second rate quarters.

Thomas on the other hand, was on familiar ground. The coterie set themselves up in the same room that Thomas had used during his recovery, and much to the royal servants' dismay, his villagers took over the room next door. It was a bit crowded, but they made it homely enough.

Wulfstan took advantage of his not being needed for a moment, to seek out the Queen, and found her in the main hall, consulting with Ravena over the evening's arrangements.

'The Prince's villagers seem to be making themselves at home in the royal apartments.' said Ravena sourly.

The Queen nodded slowly. 'It does rather lower the tone somewhat, but I trust Grimketil so little, I wouldn't put it past him to slaughter a few of them before the night is out. So I've agreed with Wulfstan that we can make an exception, just this once.'

'Your Majesty knows best.' said Ravena, her face blank of expression.

For the merest moment, a smile flickered across Cynethryth's lips before she was all business again.

'That alcove in the middle of the west wall, where we normally set up one of the beer barrels, we have to leave free for the Prince.'

'Why Your Majesty?'

'Because he has some special gift for the King, and he needs a spot in the hall to put it.'

'It will get beer spilt on it.' observed Ravena. 'The men are used to the barrel being there.'

'Oh I don't know. Would you spill beer on the King's present, in his presence?' asked the Queen.

'Perhaps not Your Majesty.' Ravena conceded.

Wulfstan laughed heartily. Clearly Ravena hadn't been completely cured of her reservations about him just yet.

Just then Thomas arrived with half a dozen of the villagers, all carrying bits of equipment.

'Hello mother!' he cried. 'How lovely to see you again! I've missed you!'

She opened her arms to his, and they embraced happily.

"Hello Ravena.' he said, once they'd finished. 'I've missed that sparkling smile of yours as well.'

Ravena, whose face had radiated a perfect nonchalance throughout, simply inclined her head and said. 'Thank you Your Highness. You are most kind.'

Thomas grinned broadly. 'Not at all, not at all. Where can I put my surprise mother?'

Cynethryth pointed to the alcove. 'Will that be alright?'

'Perfect!' he said. 'Bring it all over here lads.'

'We'll leave you to it then. Come Ravena, we need to see that the King's beer has arrived.' said the Queen.

For the next hour and a half, Thomas worked tirelessly with his team to set up his creation. When it was done, he stepped back and looked at it with great pleasure.

'It looks even better than it did at the manor. It deserves a mighty home, and here it's got one.'

'It's magnificent!' said Fulton.

'Well you should know! You built bits of it!' smiled Thomas. 'I can't wait to see their faces this evening.'

Then very carefully, he covered it with a cloth, and left it under the watchful eyes of one of the King's guards.

The guests began filtering into the hall for the feast an hour before sunset. Thomas joined the top table, whose occupants were in exactly the same places as the last time he'd been there. The coterie were positioned with their backs to the west wall, between the end of the royal table and the alcove containing the present. Grimketil and his men occupied the table against the east wall, and the remaining parts of the hall was filled by the rest of the court. Servants flitted to and fro delivering drinks to the guests, and cooks tended the various meats roasting above the huge central fire.

Once Offa was sure that everyone had arrived, he stood up and called for silence.

'My friends, it is good to see you all here! Tomorrow we hope to witness a great spectacle, as my son tries to win his bet, and Grimketil tries to keep his head!' he boomed.

A wave of laughter washed around the room. Even the coterie joined in, despite knowing that the betting was firmly against them.

'Before we start however, Wulfstan tells me that he has made me a gift, to remember him by.' continued Offa.

There was more laughter, but a bit stilted in some places, as it seemed to imply that the King too believed the fight was a foregone conclusion.

Thomas led the King and Queen across to the alcove, and took a corner of the cover sheet in his hand.

'In fact Your Majesty, you may find it a timely reminder indeed!' he said, and whipped away the cloth to reveal a breathtaking sight.

It was a staggeringly beautiful clock, just over three feet high and two feet wide, rectangular in section with a wrought iron frame visible up the edges. Its front surface was a beautifully polished slice of walnut, with a long rectangle of deep red glass running almost completely from top to bottom. Set into the red glass was a series of white glass numbers, running from zero at the bottom, to twenty four at the top. A vertical slot in the walnut to the right of the red glass allowed a silver pointer to slide up and down, which at this moment was almost pointing at the number eighteen.

'It counts off twenty four equal length hours each day, so it's actually better than your sundial, whose hours change a little as the days lengthen and shorten throughout the year. It works throughout the night, as long as you keep the room above freezing, and it works when it's cloudy, making it particularly useful in Mercia!' said Thomas.

At that very moment the pointer moved up a little to point directly at eighteen, and a little silver bird on the top of the device started to flap its wings up and down. Just beneath it, two pipes sounded the call of the very first cuckoo clock since the time of the ancient Greeks.

Offa gasped in amazement.

'Astonishing! But how does it work?' he asked.

Thomas briefly showed him the internals. Some of it, such as the gearing to drive the little bird, and the bellows that created its song, were beyond him, but he grasped the concept of the water buckets. It was very similar to the setup Thomas had used in his earlier work to measure the length of a second.

'It's accurate to within a few seconds a day Your Majesty. All that needs to be done is for a servant to refill the top reservoir once every twelve hours, and it will run for as long as you want it to. You can change the time if you need to, by adding or removing water from the bottom reservoir.

Offa looked at it in awe.

"Where did you find it, and how much did it cost?' he asked.

'I found it inside my own head Your Majesty, and it cost just the time and materials my people and I needed to make it.' replied Thomas.

'Inside your own head?' asked the King, perplexed.

Thomas managed a small smile. 'As we discussed a year ago in this very hall, when you were so vexed with me, I said that as a child I played, and as I played I watched, and as I watched I learned, and as I learned I thought. Thanks to your bet and your money, I have now been able to actually do, and turn my thoughts into reality, like this.'

Lost in thought, Offa nodded his head in silence, and fingered a white backed glass tube running up the front right edge, attached to the walnut just in from the iron frame.

'That Your Majesty, is another device. It measures how warm it is. Watch.'

Thomas retrieved a bowl of cool water from the coterie's table, and rested it gently against the mercury filled glass bulb at the bottom. As the King leant in to watch, the mercury gradually sank lower down the scale.

'If it hits zero, then you can expect water to start turning to ice soon after, and if you took it off the clock and stuck it in hot water over a fire, it will reach one hundred just as the water starts to boil.'

'Amazing!' breathed the King.

'There's one last thing Your Majesty. You may be wondering about the pretty little flask on the top?' continued Thomas, pointing to a beautiful teardrop shaped flask about a foot high, with a spout coming out and up from the bottom.

Inside the flask was some water, stained dark with oak bark liquor, but there was something strange about it.

'Look at that!' gasped the astonished King. 'The levels are different between the flask and the spout, even though they are connected!'

Thomas tried to explain.

'Swing your hand through the air please Your Majesty.'

Offa did as he he'd been asked.

'You can feel the air, yes? So even though we can't see it, we can feel it. When the wind blows strong in a storm, we feel it all too well! So it has substance, yes?'

Offa nodded, his face a picture of concentration.

'So it must have weight too? Pick up a knife and it rests in your hand. Tip your hand and it falls to the ground, just as you do when you dismount from a horse, as does beer when spilled from a horn. Everything falls to the ground, so air must too.'

Offa nodded his agreement with this strange logic, so Thomas continued.

'I had my glassmaker create a glass jug, similar to this one, and left it sitting there with water part way up it, just like this in fact. I noticed over the next few days that the levels changed, and I managed to work it out. What seems to happen is when the spout goes up and the flask goes down, the weather is more likely to get worse. When the spout goes down and the flask goes up, the weather tends to get better. It must be something to do with the air changing with the weather, but I don't yet know why. All I know is that it works!'

In fact of course, he knew perfectly well, but it didn't seem the right time or place to be going into a complete explanation of fluctuating air pressures and their meteorological consequences.

'So I can predict the weather with this?" whispered Offa.

Thomas shook his head.

'Not reliably I'm afraid Your Majesty. If the change is small, or it happens slowly, then it indicates that it's more likely to go one way or the other, but it's not a guarantee. However, if you get a big change, really quickly, then it's almost certainly going to happen.

Offa turned his head to look at him, disbelief written all over his face.

'And you... you learned all this by... just watching? And you worked out how to make this entire thing... because you played?'

'And watched, and learned, and thought, and tried things out, Your Majesty.' Thomas nodded.

The entire hall was so silent, they actually did hear a pin dropping from a serving woman's hair onto a silver serving spoon.

Offa straightened himself up and shook his shoulders.

'Marwig tells me that you have cut the death rate in your village to almost zero.' he said.

'That's true Your Majesty.'

'And that you have a new farming system, which will treble production?'

'Starting next year Your Majesty. I can do many things, but I can't speed up Mother Nature.' Thomas smiled.

'Marwig also tells me that you and your women successfully defended the manor against an armed night attack by a band of outlaws?'

Thomas nodded.

'Then you have won every aspect of your bet with me but one. I am sorry Wulfstan. I have never been so wrong about anyone in my life, and I apologise. I should never have doubted you.'

Thomas shrugged.

'If you hadn't, then perhaps none of this would have come to pass.' he said, indicating the clock. 'Apologies gratefully accepted Your Majesty.'

Offa shook his head sadly.

'Well, whoever wins tomorrow, the King will certainly lose. I shall either lose a son I never knew I had, or I shall lose one of my finest warriors.'

Then, recollecting that everyone was watching him, he led Thomas back to the royal table, his arm firmly around his shoulders.

'Well done my son.' he said. 'And thank you. It's a fabulous gift.'

'I have another for you, all ready to assemble.' said Thomas. 'So you can take one with you on your travels, or gift it to someone. Or perhaps you'd like to sell it to recoup the money I've cost you this year! I've got three of my own to sell, so I won't be a drain on the royal coffers anymore.' he grinned.

Offa shot him a look. He knew the diplomatic effects that a gift of one of these clocks would have, and they would be all the greater if he himself was the only source.

'How much are you thinking of asking?' he enquired.

'Two hundred pounds of silver each.'

Offa never batted an eye. If he had a monopoly in their supply, they'd be worth several times that amount, but all he said was.

'I'll take all three.'

'Thank you, Your Majesty.' said Thomas. I'll have them delivered within the month.'

'You'd best make those arrangements tonight Your Highness!' called Grimketil, triggering a wave of laughter from his table. He'd been as impressed as anyone else in the hall, but he knew the value of morale, and wanted to prick the Prince's bubble of happiness.

Rowena glared at him from across the room and was about to say something in return when Freawaru leaned in, and whispered a suggestion into her ear. A ghost of a smile played across Rowena's lips as she nodded, then the two women silently collected the rest of the coterie, and led them in procession from the room towards the kitchens.

'Oh dear.' said Grimketil loudly. 'I am so sorry Your Highness. I didn't mean to frighten your warriors away!'

The gaiety levels in his half of the hall stepped up another couple of notches, but Thomas just smiled indulgently.

'Women's business I suspect. I'm sure they'll be back in their own time.' he said mildly, before addressing his conversation towards his little sisters.

Rowena led the coterie past the kitchen ranges, and into the buttery and the King's beer barrels.

'Now, you all know what to do?' she asked.

Before they could reply, a young voice rose from below.

'I don't!'

'Gundy!' said Berthilda. 'Whatever are you doing here?'

The little girl grinned. 'I was just counting things, trying to understand how this place works. It's big!'

'Yes... you would be, wouldn't you.' laughed Melody.

'So what are you doing then?' asked Gundy.

'We're going to give Grimketil and his men a present. We're going to give them some beer. Very special beer.'

Gundy's face creased into a frown.

'Why? They're horrible! He tried to steal me!'

Rowena knelt down and explained what they were going to do. At first Gundy's mouth opened wide in astonishment, then almost split with the widest naughty girl grin the world had ever seen.

'Oh good! Can I make one for Cuthbert? He's at that table too!'

Rowena looked uncertain, but another voice made up her mind for her.

'I think that's an excellent idea young lady.' said the Queen.

'Your Majesty!' gasped Rowena.

Cynethryth stood there smiling warmly, a drinking horn in each hand.

'I've come to get the King some more of his special beer.' she explained.

'Your Majesty, we-' Rowena started to explain, but the Queen put up her hand to stop her.

'I know exactly what you're doing.' she said, causing their faces to pale. 'And I heartily approve!'

She burst out laughing. 'I know all about it girls. Let's get on with it, and I'll lead us back out into the hall in case Grimketil tries to suggest you're poisoning him.'

Each member of the coterie filled their horn until half an inch from the top, then followed the Queen back towards the hall. They halted in the corridor, where everyone but the Queen, squatted down for a few moments, one hand in the straw on the floor, the other holding their horn.

'I can't!' whispered Deana to her sister. 'I haven't got enough!'

'Oh give it here then.' hissed her sister. 'I've got plenty for both of us.'

Then she had another thought. 'They can never tell the difference between us anyway!' which set the whole coterie off into giggles.

The Queen waited until everyone had regained their composure, before leading them, horns brimmed, into the hall and across to Grimketil's table.

'Heads up.' Wulfstan whispered into Thomas's ear.

Thomas thought he could tell by Wulfstan's insane giggling what was happening, but it wasn't until the coterie came to a halt, that the penny really dropped.

'What? All of them? Even Gundy?' he gasped.

Wulfstan's insane cackling gave him his answer, and keeping his face straight over the next few minutes was one of the hardest things Thomas had ever had to do in his entire life.

'Lord Grimketil.' said the Queen. 'Your opponents wish to honour you with a final gift before tomorrow, as a token of their respect.'

The coterie lined up on the opposite side of the table to the diners, each bowing respectfully as she passed across her horn.

'Lord Grimketil.' said Rowena. 'One last drink for the road, your favourite I think.'

An astonished Grimketil glanced at the Queen.

'It's perfectly alright Grimketil. I supervised them myself. They're not poisoned!'

He nodded uncertainly, took Rowena's horn, and sipped carefully. It was almost exactly the same as he'd had that night a year ago. It was like nothing else, and he wondered how on earth she did it.

'You can have one too priest!' said Gundy.

Cuthbert's eyes widened in alarm, and his body retreated just a touch from this strange intense child.

'She's gone to a lot of trouble for you Cuthbert.' said the Queen. 'It would be poor manners to refuse.'

Much against his better judgement, Cuthbert accepted the gift with a cursory nod of thanks, but Gundy stayed where she was, looking at him.

'Aren't you going to try it? It's from the King's special barrels you know.' she said sweetly.

Trapped, Cuthbert took a sip, and then aware that the Queen was watching him too, plucked up his courage and swallowed a large mouthful.

'Very nice.' he said. 'Thank you miss.'

The Queen nodded her approval, and the women returned to their seats. Gundy walked back out to the kitchen, where her naughty girl grin returned in full force.

'Hah! That'll teach you, you nasty, nasty man!' she whispered to herself.

Then she returned to her observations, revelling in the new knowledge that grown up women could be naughty sometimes too!

Grimketil sipped his drink slowly, and decided it was as good a time as any to stack the deck in his own favour.

'Your Majesty, may I ask a question about our battle tomorrow?' he asked loudly.

The hall fell back to a hush as everyone waited to see what he was about to do.

'I take it that there is no archery allowed, given this is a test of manliness? It would hardly be much of a test if we stood on either side of the field and threw sticks at each other. I'm certain this is the case, but I just thought I'd ask.'

Offa nodded instantly.

'Of course there's no archery!'

Thomas raised his hand.

'Excuse me Your Majesty, but there were never any discussions about weaponry when we agreed our bet. The bet was just about who would win, not how it would be fought. My warriors have been practising with the bow all year. It is hardly fair to change the game at the last minute, and take away one of our most powerful weapons.'

'You see!' hissed a very angry Wulfstan in his ear. 'I told you at the time the King would do this!'

Offa looked at him sadly.

'Wulfstan… my son… it should have been clear to you, that bows would not be allowed. There is no honour in a bow. I am sorry that you misunderstood, but on this point Grimketil is quite right.'

To a woman, the coterie was staring at Thomas, wanting to know how he was going to get them out of Grimketil's trap.

'Well Your Majesty, I don't think it is as straight forward as that. Grimketil is aware I think, of just how good my warriors are with the bow, and he's simply scared of what they'll do to him if you let them have them.' he replied.

Grimketil sat up straight, his face angry.

'Your Majesty! I am not frightened! It is simply a matter of what is honourable and what is not!'

Thomas opened out his hands, as a priest might introduce a sermon to his flock.

'Well then, if it's honour we're talking about, and Grimketil is allowed to stipulate one form of arm to be removed from the equation, surely I should be entitled to request the removal of another? To restore the balance? To make the bet fair, so that people cannot say the bet was won because the King changed the rules?'

Offa was deeply affronted and opened his mouth to remonstrate, but was beaten by the Queen.

'The Prince raises a good point Your Majesty. He is not suggesting that you are cheating by this decision. He is simply telling you what others may accuse you of, perhaps even those who write the history of our land.' she said glancing at the Archbishop, who couldn't stop his cheeks blushing in an unwilling acknowledgement that this might indeed be the case.

Offa glared at him.

'Quite.' he said. 'What are you suggesting Wulfstan?'

Thomas steepled his hands and looked at them as if deep in thought.

'Well Your Majesty, bountiful as your coffers have been throughout the year, I didn't feel I could justify the expense of chain mail for everyone. I know Grimketil's men all have chain mail shirts, and it's a significant advantage. On the other hand, a man only wears it if he doubts his own ability with sword and shield, so if we ban mail too, that might even the playing field, enhance Grimketil's honour, and remove any possible stain on your own history. What do you think?'

Watching from further down the room, Marwig nodded his head in appreciation. 'This young man has diplomatic skill as well as all his other talents.' he thought to himself.

Offa saw the nod and misinterpreted it.

'Marwig? You agree with my son on this matter?'

Marwig put on his most studious face.

'I cannot fault the reasoning in any way whatsoever Your Majesty.' he said, neatly avoiding taking sides.

'Grimketil? Any objections?' asked the King, skewering him with a look that said "You'd better not have!"

Outplayed, Grimketil grudgingly acknowledged his assent.

'I suppose so Your Majesty.' then looking around at his suddenly a lot less cheerful men added. 'I really don't think they would have been needed anyway, so my men shall not wear mail tomorrow.'

'Then that's settled!' said Thomas happily. 'You don't mind Grimketil, if I allow my party to at least demonstrate their prowess with the bow before the battle? I promise they won't hurt you!'

Grimketil tossed his head.

'You can demonstrate whatever you want as far as I'm concerned. It will make no difference to the outcome.'

'Prayer will make a difference My Lord.' said Cuthbert oilily. 'I shall be out there on the field of battle to make sure that God is on your side.'

Thomas had just managed to overhear the stage whispered remark and gave thanks for his youthful ears.

'Cuthbert? Surely that would count as trying to bring another weapon into play, in theory the biggest possible weapon of all?' he asked.

The Archbishop interjected.

'It's perfectly reasonable. We pray for the King and his country every day. Why shouldn't Cuthbert pray for his lord?'

Thomas looked him straight in the eye.

'If Cuthbert engages in verbal prayer at any point in tomorrow's battle, I shall consider him to be acting as one of Grimketil's soldiers and he becomes a valid target.'

'Are you threatening a priest?' demanded the head of the Church.

'No.' said Thomas calmly. 'It's not a threat. It's a promise.'

'Your Majesty!' Jaenberht pleaded to the King. 'I beg of you, talk sense to your son! You can now see for yourself the kind of unreasonable behaviours he inflicted upon poor Cuthbert at his manor. He must not offer violence to the Church!'

Thomas laughed.

'I heard about Cuthbert's claims. The King's officials have been interviewing my people today about exactly that, getting all their versions of events, including that of Fulton, the man Cuthbert conned into being his beast of burden, before abandoning him without even a meal when they reached Canterbury. They know the truth.'

'They are lying!' cried Cuthbert.

Thomas give him his warmest smile.

'My dear Cuthbert, you don't even know what they said! You instantly assume that everyone will be against you, all of the time… but of course there's a reason why you do that.'

'What reason?' asked Cuthbert, falling into the trap.

'That you know you're a thoroughly nasty person, empty of love, empty even of kindness, and that nobody would ever support your fantasies for any reason except fear. And of course, it's too difficult for them to keep up with your own lies because they change all the time! They know they'd get caught out as you changed your story to suit events. Much easier for them just to tell the truth.'

Cuthbert sat white with shock at being spoken to like that in the royal hall, with everyone of consequence present to hear it.

The Archbishop started to expound again.

'Archbishop Jaenberht,' Thomas said, cutting him off, 'please don't start down the path of saying the clergy never tell lies. I understand you've already lost that argument. Cuthbert made a very specific threat, to personally intercede with the almighty to change the result of tomorrow's little game. That means he will be taking an active role as one of Grimketil's warriors, increasing his number beyond mine. If Cuthbert does that, I will take him out to rebalance the numbers, and that is an end to the matter.'

'Your soul will be damned for it if you do!' shouted the Archbishop, goaded beyond endurance.

'Then it is your duty as head cleric, to see that the situation doesn't arise. Wouldn't you say? Or are you going to suggest that you personally could offer up verbal prayers on my side to offset Cuthbert? If you do that, yourself you understand, then I'll leave Cuthbert alone because things will be balanced again. Your call. You don't need to decide now. Your choice will be perfectly clear on the field of battle. Now, would you mind passing the salt?'

For once in his life, Archbishop Jaenberht was completely lost for words, and being sat at the King's own table, and right next to this infuriating brat, he couldn't even leave! Wordlessly he handed over the salt bowl as requested.

'Thank you so much.' said Thomas cheerfully. Then he decided to kick things up a level. If Grimketil wanted mind games, he could have them.

'Incidentally Grimketil,' he said, 'I see your sidekicks Ward and Radley aren't with you. What's the story there?'

Grimketil looked up from his food, not entirely unsurprised by Thomas's question and had his story straight.

'They took themselves off on an expedition and never returned. I am led to believe that they died of the bloody flux.' he said smoothly.

'Dysentery? Ooh, nasty!'

Thomas paused for a moment, before continuing.

'I imagine you miss their companionship at moments like these.'

Grimketil shot a sour, sideways glance at Sigwulf.

'Actually I do.' he said.

'Then I am delighted to be able to help you.' said Thomas, and clapped his hands together.

Sighard and Fulton appeared, each carrying a wooden tray with a wicker basket over it. They came in from the top left corner of the room and passed in front of the royal table, generating a series of gasps and dropped jaws as the diners saw through a window in the basketry, what lay within. Then the two men walked over to Grimketil, placed the trays on the table in front of him and removed the baskets.

Grimketil recoiled in horror at the perfectly preserved heads of Ward and Radley.

'I've had them as my guests since they made their appearance at my manor one moonlit night, together with an armed outlaw band, and tried to rob the place. Altogether they killed three of Marwig's men, and four of my villagers. The only saving grace is that they haven't needed much food and drink since then. Anyway, I'm awfully glad to be able to return them to your care, and before you say it, of course, you're most welcome!' said Thomas nonchalantly between mouthfuls.

Grimketil simply stared at the remains of his two men, face frozen in horror.

Thomas looked concerned. 'They are yours, aren't they? We were all pretty sure they were yours, especially the one we think is Ward. He recognised Berthilda and told her that you'd promised to give her to him as a wife. Anyway, we've managed to keep their faces well preserved so we could check.'

Offa offered his own opinion.

'They're Ward and Radley alright. I recognise them myself. What were they doing at Wulfstan's village Grimketil?'

'I, I, I do not know Your Majesty. I wasn't even aware of them leaving. It was their own initiative.' stammered Grimketil, frying in the King's gaze.

'They were killing Marwig's men, trying to steal my horses, and did actually manage to kidnap two children, including the little girl who gave Cuthbert her beer.' said Thomas. 'Then they were hunted down and killed, by one of my team.'

'By one of yours?' said Sigwulf weakly.

'By one of my ladies, yes.' replied Thomas who paused before twisting the knife. 'Just the one. Why? Did you think it had been someone else?'

'We assumed-' Sigwulf managed before Grimketil's elbow whacked him in the ribs.

Thomas looked at them both, one eyebrow theatrically arched in question.

Offa's face darkened.

'So you did know after all.' he said softly. 'Not the bloody flux then? This does not reflect well upon you Grimketil, not well at all!'

'I swear to Your Majesty that I didn't know they'd gone!' pleaded Grimketil desperately.

'Oh well,' said Thomas, with unbearably good cheer. 'At least the Archbishop here can give them the last rites!'

19 THE CLASH OF ARMS

The following morning dawned bright and still, perfect weather for a sporting event, which is how most of the audience viewed the coming spectacle.

Offa and the rest of the royals were ensconced on a raised viewing platform, to ensure they could see everything that went on, while most of the rest of the populace stood around the edge of the field.

The "playing area" itself was roughly a hundred yards wide, and three hundred long, oriented east west.

Just before noon, Grimketil walked out onto the field of battle led by Cuthbert, who was saying a range of prayers very specifically asking for the Almighty's assistance on behalf of his lord.

A few minutes later a cheer went up, indicating the appearance of the Prince's party. And what an appearance it was!

Wulfstan rode at the head of the procession, Obsidian gleaming in the sun, but it was what the Prince was wearing that stunned everyone. On his feet were beautiful leather boots, then elegant, close fitting blue trousers. His upper body was clad in a stunning tunic, the largely blue, light weight fabric billowing loosely around him, with bright yellow slashes on the sides of the body, and on the arms. His new sword hung at his left side, along with the buckler, and on his head sat a conical helmet of polished steel.

The coterie followed, Rowena and Berthilda, Freawaru and Storm, Deena and Deana, Melody and Scarlett, then Topaz and Jade bringing up the rear. All ten were dressed identically to the Prince.

Behind them came Hengist and Kelsey, the rest of their weapons in a cart driven by Fulton, then the Gundy family, and the rest of the villagers. Every one of them was beautifully dressed in close fitting, colourful clothes, mother of pearl buttons sparkling in the sun. The audience had never seen anything like it. Not even the King and Queen looked this good!

Thomas led the coterie up to the royal pavilion, followed by the Gundy family and the villagers, while Hengist, Kelsey and Fulton went off to the far end of the field.

Lynette walked out to the front of the villagers, bowed to the King and Queen, then turned to face her people, baton held high in her right hand. The coterie walked their horses around the back of the villagers and took up their own places, all eyes on Lynette.

A couple of gentle waves of her baton and the familiar strains of Jerusalem floated out across the stillness into Thomas's ears as he floated above, relishing every glorious note, the harmonies of a multi-part choir sending him into raptures.

He and Wulfstan had found themselves swapping places earlier that morning as everyone was getting dressed.

'That's good!' Thomas had said. 'You're much happier with this fighting business than I am!' which had made Melody ask Wulfstan what was so funny.

Now Wulfstan sat astride his horse in front of the King and Queen, listening to the glorious music. He was the man of the moment, and knew it. This must be what the King felt most of the time.

In front of him, Jaenberht was listening in astonishment. Used to the incessant droning of monks, the rich, soaring harmonies of the hymn lit up parts of his brain he never knew existed.

Beside him, the King and Queen were equally entranced, but nothing like as much as the princesses who looked on open mouthed at their amazing brother.

Marwig glanced sideways, and noted the one person on the royal pavilion not really appreciating things. Ecgfrith, the heir to the throne, was clearly weighing things up. The clock had been a shock for him the previous night, then Wulfstan's sudden wealth thanks to Offa buying the additional clocks, and now all the clothes and the music. Perhaps the future wasn't so assured as he'd thought it was?

The song came finally to an end, and the whole place lit up with applause. It was a full three minutes before it died down enough for the villagers to make their way to their allocated space, on another platform to the left of the royal party. Wulfstan had insisted they had a good vantage point.

'Didn't we do well mother?' asked Grimhild, a huge grin on her face.

'Yes darling. We all did very well indeed. And you remember what you are to do now? Do you have everything you need?' asked Lynette.

'Yes mother.' said the little girl happily, heading for the top of the platform where she'd get the best view.

Wulfstan led the coterie off to the far end of the field, where the three men were waiting with the bows and quivers.

'Line abreast formation everyone.' he ordered.

The coterie spread out on either side of him, Berthilda, Freawaru, Storm, Deena and Deana to his left, Melody, Rowena, Topaz, Jade and Scarlett to his right.

'Forward into canter!' he cried, and all eleven horses moved easily into trot, and then to canter.

Grimketil and his men stood in a line, shoulder to shoulder in the middle of the field, right in front of the royal family. They would fight the way they had always fought, on foot.

'Close up the shield wall! The Prince might say it's a demonstration but let's take no chances!' commanded Grimketil.

His men raised their shields, interlocking them so the shield on the left overlapped the one on its right. Grimketil in the centre, had placed Sigwulf on the far right of the line, partly to keep away his careless chatter, partly because he was such a good blade.

'Forward gallop! Bear left! Ready bows right!' shouted Wulfstan as they closed to within a hundred yards.

The riders urged their mounts to top speed, and keeping the line straight, aimed the horses slightly to the left, bringing their bows across to the right of their horses' necks to aim at the cluster of men ahead of them.

'Hold position!' screamed Grimketil as the ground shook under his men's feet.

As the distance between the two groups narrowed to within twenty yards, Wulfstan let them off the leash.

'Shooting pattern three!' he cried.

All eleven bows launched their arrows. In the following twelve seconds the riders turned right into a nose to tail line cutting across the front of Grimketil's position, released another volley to their left, then turned ninety degrees to the right again so they were once more riding in parallel with each other, but away from their foes, and shot a Parthian volley over the rear of their mounts as they galloped away.

In less than twenty seconds, thirty three arrows had found their marks. Every one of Grimketil's shields had a line of three arrows running from the shield boss to the top of the shield.

'It's a good thing for Grimketil that you agreed to having no bows Your Majesty.' said Marwig over the King's shoulder. 'The battle would already be over!'

The King nodded, never taking his eyes off the riders as they returned to their cart. "Just imagine what they could do in a proper battle!' he replied.

'This is a proper battle dear, if you'll remember.' said his Queen a little stiffly.

The coterie collected a spear each and returned to their in line formation. Wulfstan brought them up to the gallop in the same way as before and charged at his foe. The time for demonstrations was over!

Grimketil was appalled. Civilised men of honour simply didn't fight from horseback! Horses were for travelling and looking good! He hadn't anticipated this at all.

The horses were less than twenty yards away when he heard Wulfstan's command to fire, and eleven spears flew out from behind the horses' heads.

Grimketil's men had no choice but to catch them on their shields. The speed of the horses added to the strength of the throws, caused the barbed spear heads to smash deep into the wooden shields, and the soft iron necks of the angon spears to bend and droop.

'Argh!' cursed Rowley, the man on Grimketil's right. 'It's gone through my arm!'

Everyone else simply threw away their shields, which was what the angon was all about. Its barbs made it very difficult to pull out of a shield, and even if the victim managed to do it, the fact that it bent on impact meant they couldn't throw it back.

Grimketil looked down the field anxiously to try and see what Wulfstan would do next. If they came again with more angons, he had no defence.

'What are they up to now?' asked Offa, to nobody in particular.

'I can't see Your Majesty. I was expecting them to come again with more spears, because they certainly have them in that cart, but they appear to be trying something new.' said Marwig, who had the best eyes on the platform.

This time the horses lined up just nine across, Deana and Scarlett falling back and slightly in from the two ends to hide behind Deena and Jade respectively.

'Smoothly up to gallop! Attack pattern seven!' cried Wulfstan.

'Attack pattern seven?' asked Sigwulf. 'What's that?'

'How the devil should I know?' muttered an exasperated Grimketil. 'In line, spear butts down, points up and front!' Grimketil himself felt just a little lucky that he had at least partial protection from Rowley's unwieldy shield.

The horses by now were at full chat again, rushing towards them, yet there were no spears in sight. Then, at just ten yards distance the line split, five horses to the left, four to the right rushing past the startled men, just out of spear range. The men immediately began to turn to face the new potential threat from behind them, not seeing the remaining two horses until it was too late.

Deana and Scarlett also rushed down either side of Grimketil's band, the braided rope tied between their two horses flying along behind them. It caught the men behind the knees, hitting them hard before the thinner cord that connected it to the horses' saddles snapped. Every one of Grimketil's men was brought to the ground, heads and shoulders taking a pounding, but Rowley worst of all. It had been the rope catching under his shield that had snapped the cord, completely breaking his arm, but leaving it still pinned to his shield by the angon.

He was chalk white and deep in shock as Grimketil urged him back to his feet.

'Come on old friend.' he urged. 'It's fight or die remember?'

He cajoled the rest of them back into some sort of line, but their morale was in tatters. Another mounted assault would finish some of them, he was sure. To his dismay, he could see them riding slowly down the field towards him. What fiendish plan did they have now?

Suddenly a powerful voice lifted itself up in prayer. It was Cuthbert, standing halfway between his lord and his king, and making another impassioned plea for the Almighty to intervene. Grimketil's men took heart, and stood up straighter, ready for whatever came.

'Melody?' said Wulfstan quietly. 'You're on!'

Melody gave him a pinched smile and urged Embers up to a gentle canter, riding out a little ahead of the others.

'He wouldn't dare!' growled the Archbishop as he watched the riders gather pace. Melody looked to be charging straight at Grimketil, bow part drawn and aimed right at him.

'You ordered no bows!' he snapped at the King. 'Not content with offending God, your son is treating his own father with contempt!'

Before Offa could reply, Melody flicked her horse to the right towards Cuthbert, while the rest of the coterie charged on towards Grimketil.

'Stand your ground!' Grimketil yelled as another flight of angons flew towards them.

There was the awful sound of metal slicing through flesh, and screams as four of the spears struck home, plus another from Cuthbert. He'd been praying loudly, eyes firmly shut, counting on Wulfstan being too frightened of the Archbishop's wrath to strike him.

Melody had shot her special arrow, the one the Prince had ordered made the previous night. It struck Cuthbert in the left cheek, just as he was shouting out the word "God", his mouth wide open. The broadhead sliced clean through the thin membrane of flesh, passed between his teeth to skewer his tongue, before exiting through his right cheek, and still it wasn't done.

Thomas had ordered a special sleeve with forwards facing barbs to be mounted on the arrow immediately behind the broadhead, held in place with a fine thread. As the broadhead punched through Cuthbert's cheek, the sleeve barbs slammed into the outside of his face. The impact broke the restraining thread, allowing the sleeve to slip down the arrow's shaft until it came to rest against a tiny iron nail jammed into the side of the arrow.

The barbs at either end made it impossible for Cuthbert to pull the arrow from his mouth, and he staggered from the field, blood pouring down his chin, his inarticulate screams cascading over his skewered tongue.

Offa laughed.

'Well at least she didn't actually kill him!' he said to Jaenberht. 'And Wulfstan didn't use a bow against Grimketil's legitimate players, so you have no complaint. Wulfstan told you he wouldn't stand for that, and he didn't!'

The Archbishop stared at his priest, impotent rage coursing through him. Someone would pay for this day's work, they really would pay, starting with Offa's reputation in the history books!

Grimketil assessed the damage. Three more of his men had received injuries to their left arms trying to deflect the spears. Encouraging them as best he could, he had them reform the line.

Eleven of Wulfstan's villagers walked out of their viewing area, and spread out in a circle twenty yards out from Grimketil. Wulfstan brought his riders up to a gentle canter, and rode them line astern around the men three times before coming to a halt, one horse per villager.

The coterie dismounted and drew their swords, but made no move towards Grimketil, who had formed a much smaller circle of his own.

'Well? Come on then oh mighty warrior!' called Wulfstan. 'We're on foot now.'

Grimketil made no move, and kept his men in their defence.

'You're a very hard man to please Grimketil!' Wulfstan shouted. 'First no bows, then you were shocked by the horses, and now you won't fight at all! I just don't know what to do with you! Okay girls! Close in. If they won't come to us, we'll have to go to them. Pattern nine!'

Grimketil watched them approach. He was puzzled by their delicate swords, and the little shields they carried, but he wasn't worried. His men were more than a match face to face on foot, even injured as they were.

'Let them get to within ten feet, then charge out and get them.' he said softly. 'They'll be expecting a command, so go on your own initiative, so they'll get no warning.'

The women moved steadily in, keeping a careful eye on their opponents, and always noting where their friends were. On and on they came until Rowley leapt at Deana.

He was a strong man, frustrated, and in great pain from his arm, but he was still able to swing his shield around, angon or no angon. It caught Deana off balance, and the follow up blow of his sword knocked her to the ground. She rolled quickly to her left, onto her back so she could defend herself but for a seriously injured man he moved unbelievably quickly. He hurled a blow down at her, so violent that it knocked her own blade out of the way, and smashed hard, into her chest.

'Noooooo!' screamed Deena, but by then she had her own problems. Her opponent had strapped up his own wounded arm with a strip of cloth torn from his tunic, but more importantly, he was fighting mad.

'Right girly, time to join your little friend!' he cursed, and launched his attack.

Deena deflected the blow with her buckler, and struck at his face. It was so quick, and the blade so slender that he didn't see it coming to slice away a piece of his left cheek.

By the time he was in a position to retaliate, she'd danced away, and had her buckler out in front, hiding her own sword. He came at her more respectfully this time, with a straight thrust towards her chest, which she caught between sword and buckler, pushing him down, and giving herself the time to bounce away again.

His next strike was high from the left, a brutal attempt to slice off her head, but again she deflected it with ease, and this time he'd left himself open. In less than a second her blade was in his chest, his aorta severed. Before he hit the ground, she'd already turned away to help her sister.

Melody and Wulfstan were fighting side by side, having had the bad luck to pick Sigwulf and his friend Kenton, both fine blades. They'd managed to stave off four powerful attacks already, when the men managed to manoeuvre their lighter opponents around so they were back to back. Wulfstan and Melody's evasions from a coordinated strike saw them bump into each other and lose their balance, allowing Kenton to bring his blade down in a ferocious blow onto the top of Melody's head.

It made hardly a dent in her steel helmet, but she went down without a sound. Wulfstan heard the blow and knew instantly what must have happened, but he was busy deflecting a blow himself.

Sigwulf grinned. 'Time's up little boy!'

Storm and Freawaru were having a much easier time of it. The fact they were far stronger than they looked, had fooled their opponents, and patronising attacks saw both men dead in just a few seconds.

Jade and Topaz were initially an even match for their two, neither side able to penetrate the other's defences.

'Pretty little sword madam.' said Topaz's fellow.

'Why thank you.' she replied. 'I had it specially made you know.'

'I don't doubt it!' he laughed. 'I'm looking forward to hanging it on my wall once I've killed you.'

The laugh caught in his throat as Topaz trapped his sword between her buckler and the ground, and thrust her blade right through his chest at the same moment that Jade's opponent's blade slammed hard into hers, jolting her backwards.

Rowena had chosen Grimketil himself, Berthilda the man to his left, and Scarlett the one to his right.

'Watch her Huntley.' cautioned Grimketil to Berthilda's opponent. 'These two are a bit special. Don't underestimate them.'

Huntley ignored him, and struck so fast it would have killed whoever it hit, but Berthilda was faster. She stepped to the right, deflected the blow with her buckler, and thrust her own sword straight through his eye and into the brain. She allowed his falling body to pull itself clear of her blade, which she wiped clean on his trousers.

'Need a hand Rowena?' she asked casually.

'No thanks.' came the reply, as Rowena easily deflected Grimketil's feint. 'I'm quite happy dancing on my own for a while.'

'Then if you don't mind, I'll help Scarlett finish off hers.'

'Well, it's pretty even so far.' observed Marwig. 'Fascinating swords aren't they?'

'You must have known about those Marwig.' accused the Queen. 'Why did you not warn me?'

'Because he made me give him my word that I would tell no one, so that they would be a surprise to Grimketil. He is a wise boy, your youngest son.'

She looked at him over her shoulder.

'I thought I could trust you Marwig! You have let me down.'

'With respect ma'am, I believe I rendered you more service by keeping my mouth shut on this occasion, than I would have by telling you. If Grimketil had gotten wind of the new blades in any way, say from the servants overhearing something, then he could either have worked on a counter, or tried to have them banned as he did the bows.'

She continued her stare, and then nodded.

'Perhaps you are right. After all, you usually are!'

'Your confidence has blossomed into arrogance Rowena. It won't be good for your eternal soul, which of course is all you'll have left in a moment or two.' smirked Grimketil, flinging a blow at her right hip.

Rowena caught it effortlessly on her blade, and swung her buckler into his face. He managed to avoid most of the impact by twisting his head away, but it cost him a precious second of recovery time and the point of Rowena's blade caught him square in the chest.

Grimketil staggered back a step under the force of the blow, but to Rowena's surprise, her sword bent instead of sliding between his ribs. She glimpsed a flash of silvery rings through the rent in his tunic.

'You're wearing mail!' she gasped. 'But you gave the King your word!'

Grimketil laughed. 'What I actually said, was that my men would not wear mail. I never mentioned myself!'

'Fine! It will give me more time to play before I kill you.' said Rowena between her clenched teeth.

Rowley's blade made an incredibly loud clang as it hit Deana's chest, tearing away her pretty tunic to reveal shiny metal underneath.

She smiled at him and bounced to her feet, as he looked at her in disbelief.

'What's the matter soldier? Never seen inside a girl's tunic before?'

He was still staring at her when Deena's blade came through the front of his chest.

'Thank you sister!' said Deana.

'My pleasure! It's a good thing for you that plate armour worked as well as the Prince said it would!'

Jade was grateful for it as well, as she too lost her beautiful top.

'You're not supposed to be wearing armour!' complained the man. 'Your Prince made the agreement!'

'It's not a mail shirt silly!' she giggled. 'This is one solid chest I've got here! Unlike yours.' she observed as Topaz's blade cut a massive hole in the man's torso.

'I'm fine sis.' Jade faux scolded. 'There's no point in splashing about more blood than is absolutely necessary!'

'Pity about your top.' observed Topaz. 'I suppose the Prince might give you another. I wonder how the others are getting on?'

'Jump right!' commanded Thomas, from his position above and to the side.

Wulfstan responded instantly, just in time to avoid a wicked downwards slash from Melody's vanquisher.

'You must have eyes in the back of your head boy!' sniggered Sigwulf. 'I'm going to hit you so hard your front ones will end up there too!'

'Roll left!' screamed Thomas, who could see the other man preparing to strike once more.

Tucking his arms well in, Wulfstan dropped to the ground and rolled as a blade swung savagely above him where his waist had been. He completed his roll and as his sword arm came out from under him he thrust it straight up into the man's groin, to the hilt.

The impaled man gave a scream and jumped away, inadvertently making the wound far worse, as Wulfstan's blade sliced easily through his belly. Blood sprayed powerfully from his femoral artery, and his severed large intestines cascaded through the gaping hole.

Wulfstan bounced to his feet and looked at the filth from the man's bowels that coated his blade.

'Oh dear. That's not going to be nice to clean!'

Sigwulf looked disbelieving at his friend writhing on the ground in his death agonies. Then as he brought his blade back into play against the Prince, he became aware of the fact that he and Grimketil were the only ones left alive, Scarlett having just finished off her man.

Topaz, Jade, Freawaru and Storm surrounded him, their blades flickering wickedly in the sun, the odd drop of blood sliding off them into the grass. He turned constantly, making regular feints to keep them at bay.

'You have no business on the field of war! This is the world of men!' he screamed with his usual lack of tact and intelligence.

'Fair enough.' said Freawaru. 'As soon as we've finished, I promise we'll leave it to you.'

Sigwulf scowled and sent a tired thrust towards her face. She sidestepped it easily, caught the blade on her buckler and stepped in quickly for a thrust of her own. The blade cut through his Adam's apple and all the way back to his vertebrae. His eyes opened wide in surprise before rolling back in his head as he fell to the ground, blood fountaining out from the severed artery.

'Well done Freawaru.' said Wulfstan. 'Nice work. Just Grimketil to go I think. Is Melody-'

Topaz and Jade were kneeling down, looking at their fallen friend. There wasn't a mark on her. She just lay there, completely still. Topaz carefully rested the back of her sword blade on Melody's upper lip, and sighed in relief when she saw a soft mist form on the steel.

'She's alive at least. She's still breathing. Very lightly, but she's breathing.'

Thomas told Wulfstan how to put her in the recovery position, and went off to see how Rowena was getting along.

'What on earth are they doing now?' asked the King.

'They appear to be lining up behind the one fighting Grimketil.' said Marwig.

'I can see that for myself man!' said the exasperated Offa. 'What I meant was, why on earth don't they just surround him and finish him off?'

Grimketil was equally perplexed, as he exchanged sword taps with Rowena. Apart from Topaz, Jade and Wulfstan who were attending to Melody, the rest of the coterie had lined up behind Rowena and were chatting excitedly amongst themselves, paying him almost no heed.

'You're all mine Grimketil. They'll only get involved if I make a mess of things.' Rowena explained.

Grimketil nodded his understanding, and struck low towards her knee, but he was tiring now, and she deflected it easily with her buckler before launching an attack of her own with a thrust to the face. Too slow to be able to defend with his sword, he ducked his head out of the way and stepped to his right. Rowena's blade landed on his left shoulder, slashing away his tunic to reveal the mail shirt in all its glory.

'Grimketil's wearing mail!' gasped the King. 'The man gave me his word!'

The Queen glared at him. 'I've been trying to tell you for years the man couldn't be trusted! Now perhaps you'll believe me!'

'Very pretty.' said Rowena, admiring the shimmering rings. 'The King doesn't look too pleased though.'

Grimketil glanced towards the royal pavilion, and the look on Offa's face did not bode well.

'Trouble tonight for you then!' she laughed. 'On the other hand, Hengist is really looking forward to this evening. More than any other evening in his life perhaps. Do you want to know why?'

Grimketil's brows furrowed.

'Why?' he asked.

'Because he and Wulfwynn are finally going to be together at last. They're going to get married as soon as you're dead and gone.'

His face twisted in fury, and he aimed another cut to the right side of her head.

'I'm not gone just yet!' he snarled.

Rowena parried, then slid her sword down his blade towards the hilt. The basket of her own sword protected her hand, but Grimketil's quillons did nothing against such an attack. The edge of her blade easily severed the tendons on the back of his hand and his sword tumbled to the grass.

He looked at it in disbelief, before raising his face to look at her.

'Yes you are!' she said, slashing her sword across his throat, severing his neck from one side to the other as far back as his spine. His lips parted slightly, the light faded from his eyes and he fell.

'I've never before seen that literally happen.' observed Marwig.

'What do you mean?' asked the Queen.

'A man falling on his sword.' smiled Marwig.

20 THE AFTERMATH

Happy that Melody was being taken care of, Wulfstan collected his fighters, and led them up to the foot of the royal pavilion, where they all bowed to the King.

'I believe I have won the bet Your Majesty.' said Wulfstan.

'And handily at that!' replied the King, who'd stood up to greet them. 'A stunning display, absolutely stunning.'

'Well done most beloved son.' said the Queen, coming down to kiss him on the cheek.

'Yes. Well done little brother.' offered Ecgfrith, his face curiously lacking in warmth.

Wulfstan smiled warmly enough for both of them. 'Thank you big brother.'

Then he saw Grimhild hovering shyly off to his right with her family. He beckoned her over.

'Father, I'd like you to meet Grimhild. She has a very special present for you.'

"Really?' asked the King, looking at the slip of a girl walking timorously towards them, a roll of velum in her hand.

When she reached them, she mutely offered it up to Wulfstan, but he smiled and said. 'No, I think you should give it to him yourself. You made it. You've earned the right.'

Her face filled with awe, the little girl held out the roll to Offa.

'Thank you.' he said, still perplexed.

'Open it father.' said Wulfstan, resting his hands gently on Grimhild's shoulders and giving them a comforting squeeze.

The King untied the ribbon, and unfurled the vellum. It was completely filled with writing. He looked up at Wulfstan, perplexed, as he was unable to read.

'Perhaps the Archbishop would be good enough to read it to you?' suggested Wulfstan.

Jaenberht, still smarting from Cuthbert's arrow, took it from the King and started to read. It was an account of the fight they'd all just watched. The King turned back to Wulfstan, stunned.

'But how is this possible?' he demanded.

Wulfstan pointed at Grimhild.

'Grimhild wrote it, live, as the battle played out. I placed her up on the highest corner so she'd have the best view, and she wrote it all down as it happened.'

'But she's just a child! And no cleric! And a girl come to that!' expostulated the Archbishop.

'Well spotted Archbishop! Correct on all three points.' agreed Wulfstan, then addressed the King once more.

'I've opened up a school father, teaching children, and some adults, how to read, how to write, how to count, and sing, and many other things. When my students are ready, they will open schools of their own, and you will have access to your own scribes and counters throughout the Kingdom.'

'He already has that!' Jaenberht interrupted with some heat. 'The Church does all that for him already!'

'So it does.' bowed Wulfstan. 'But I know how busy you all are with the important religious affairs of the Church. It doesn't seem fair to take their efforts away to the mundane and prosaic matters of the real world. And of course, there are times when the interests of the Church and the interests of the Crown are not aligned, and they are vexed with each other. It would be no bad thing for the King to know he has control over his own accounts... his own laws as they are written down... and of course, his own history, in such... trying times.'

The light dawned in Offa's eyes at just what Wulfstan was offering him. He looked down at Grimhild again.

'And this young woman is your first?'

Wulfstan nodded.

'Along with the other members of her family, and of course all of my fine warriors here too.'

The King stepped forward and put his arms around Wulfstan. 'That my boy, may end up being the finest gift of all. Thank you! Although,' he said, knocking his knuckles against Thomas's breastplate, still hidden underneath his tunic, 'we have yet more to discuss I think!'

Then he stepped back and announced to the crowd.

'Let the celebrations commence!'

A huge cheer went up, and most of the crowd moved slowly off to get the party started. Tamworth would celebrate till dawn, and there was a lot of day to go before night fell to start with!

Offa laid a mighty hand on his son's shoulder.

'Is there anything I can do to make amends for misjudging you so badly?' he asked softly. 'Anything at all?'

Wulfstan looked up into his eyes and said. 'I would like to ask for just one thing father.'

Ecgfrith watched him carefully, his eyes narrowing as he anticipated the demand he feared to hear.

Wulfstan beckoned to Hengist, who was out at the far left of Wulfstan's villagers, hand in hand with Wulfwynn.

'I would like you to restore Hengist to his rightful place, and let him and Wulfwynn marry as soon as possible. Tonight, if we can make it happen. They have been kept apart for too long.'

Offa looked at him in disbelief.

'That's it?'

Wulfstan nodded.

'That's all father.'

Offa shook his head and beckoned Hengist to come to him.

'My son has consistently told me since the… incident… that you were not at fault. He has stood by you, and you have stood by him. He could have asked for anything at all and I would have given it to him, and all he asks for is for you to be restored. If you can install that kind of loyalty in my son, then you must indeed be a fine man. I restore you to your title and estates.'

Then he smiled.

'I'll even give you a pound of silver as a wedding present!'

Hengist bowed.

'Thank you Your Majesty!'

The King and Queen then led the royal party off towards the palace, where their own feast was waiting. The Archbishop didn't look at Wulfstan as he walked past, but Marwig gave him a huge wink. Then

Wulfstan spotted a familiar face in the small group of spectators who hadn't rushed off to the beer and food.

'Ethelwulf! Where have you been?'

His childhood friend ran up and embraced him heartily.

'Where have you been?' repeated Wulfstan. 'I missed you!'

Ethelwulf looked embarrassed.

'Have you any idea just how difficult it's been to get anywhere near you and your people?' I tried and tried, but the guards wouldn't let me in!'

'Well, you're here now, and you're coming to the feast with us.' Wulfstan insisted.

There was a gentle pull at his sleeve.

'What's going to happen to us now?' asked a very worried Gundy, tears welling up in her eyes. 'I mean you've won and everything. Does that mean you're going away now?'

Wulfstan looked around at the anxious faces of the rest of her family, and the other villagers. He held up his hand.

'Everyone please relax. Hengist has his manor back, but that doesn't mean everything we've been doing comes to an end. We'll have to work some things out, but everything's going to be just fine for you all. I promise! We're going to finish what we've started.'

'And us Your Highness? What have you decided is to happen to each of us?' asked Rowena.

Wulfstan gave her his warmest smile.

'Well, you have your freedom as of this minute, so each of you can decide to do whatever you want. When the King gives me the silver for those clocks, you'll each have a pound of it, which will set you up for life.'

He looked around the coterie. Their heads were nodding, but there were no smiles, so he continued.

'Of course, I would rather that none of you left me at all… If you were still slaves, I wouldn't ever part with any one of you. You are all dear to my heart, and I love you deeply. But I no longer own you, so you have the freedom to leave, and I'll give my blessing to anyone who does.'

'So…' said Freawaru. 'We can stay if we want to? That's an option too?'

'Absolutely!' said Wulfstan.

Suddenly there were smiles all round, and much patting each other on the back. Rowena laughed.

'Then I don't think you'll ever be rid of us!'

'Hurrah!' shouted Oscar.

'Hurrah!' shouted the rest of the village.

'And a big hurrah from me too!' cried Wulfstan. 'Come on everyone, let's celebrate!'

Meanwhile, in Wulfstan's room, Thomas was keeping an anxious vigil over Melody as she lay in bed. Her breathing was, if anything, a little shallower than before, and he was worried that she wasn't going to recover. But there was something else. The golden glow was brighter than ever.

Slowly, cautiously, a woman's head pushed out from Melody's body, and looked around. Whoever it was, it wasn't Melody, because it looked nothing like her.

Suddenly she saw him, her eyes widened in alarm, and she began to retreat back into the body.

'It's alright.' said Thomas gently. 'You're perfectly safe. I'm the Prince's man. My name's Thomas. What's yours?'

*** To be continued ***

ABOUT THE AUTHOR

K.T. Findlay lives on a small farm where he dovetails his writing with fighting the blackberry, and convincing the quadbike that killing its rider isn't a core part of its job description.

ALSO BY K.T. FINDLAY

A Thoughtful Woman

AUTHOR WEBSITE

www.ktfindlay.com

Made in the USA
Monee, IL
30 May 2021